THE UNINVITED GUEST

RUBY SPEECHLEY

Boldwood

First published in Great Britain in 2025 by Boldwood Books Ltd.

Copyright © Ruby Speechley, 2025

Cover Design by 12 Orchards Ltd.

Cover Images: Shutterstock

The moral right of Ruby Speechley to be identified as the author of this work has been asserted in accordance with the Copyright, Designs and Patents Act 1988.

Every effort has been made to obtain the necessary permissions with reference to copyright material, both illustrative and quoted. We apologise for any omissions in this respect and will be pleased to make the appropriate acknowledgements in any future edition.

A CIP catalogue record for this book is available from the British Library.

Paperback ISBN 978-1-83751-409-0

Large Print ISBN 978-1-83751-408-3

Hardback ISBN 978-1-83751-407-6

Ebook ISBN 978-1-83751-410-6

Kindle ISBN 978-1-83751-411-3

Audio CD ISBN 978-1-83751-402-1

MP3 CD ISBN 978-1-83751-403-8

Digital audio download ISBN 978-1-83751-405-2

This book is printed on certified sustainable paper. Boldwood Books is dedicated to putting sustainability at the heart of our business. For more information please visit https://www.boldwoodbooks.com/about-us/sustainability/

Boldwood Books Ltd, 23 Bowerdean Street, London, SW6 3TN

www.boldwoodbooks.com

For Becky, with love

PROLOGUE

Look at you.

So full of yourself.

Who do you think you are in your flouncy wedding dress, swinging it this way and that as you try it on in the shop?

I see you.

You think you look like a princess with all those petticoats and sequins, satin swishing about.

You think he loves you? You're delusional.

He loves me.

I know he does.

You'd better watch out because I'm coming for him.

Don't get in my way or you're going to regret it.

'Right, are we ready to go?' I lift Freya up from her highchair and give her a big kiss on her soft plump cheek. 'I'd much rather stay here with you,' I whisper in her ear, hugging her tight.

'Let's go get this hen party started.' Danielle points to the word 'Hen' in pink sequins on her white T-shirt then swings her arms, showbiz style, and points at mine, which says 'Bride to Be'. 'And don't let me forget to pick Sarah up on the way,' she laughs, grabbing her car keys from the coffee table.

'As if,' I say, turning to my parents and handing Freya to my mum. She twists her little body and tries to turn back to me, arms outstretched.

'Could you put her down for a nap around two, but don't let her sleep too long?' I say to Mum.

'I know darling, please don't fret. We managed all right with you, and you're perfectly fine.' Mum bounces Freya up and down on her hip. 'We're going to go to the park, aren't we?' Mum says and Freya smiles.

'We can play on the swings, and I'll hold your hand as you

slide down the big slide. We might even buy an ice cream.' Dad holds her tiny hand and her eyes widen.

'I've put all-day sun lotion on her, but make sure she wears a hat please.'

'I will.' Mum tucks Freya's arm down when she tries to reach out for me again. 'It's all right Pumpkin, Mummy will be back soon.' But Freya shuts her eyes, pushes out her bottom lip and starts grizzling.

'She's still so little and I've not stopped worrying about every little thing. Please call if you're not sure of something.'

Freya's coming up to two and a half and I've been back at work part time for the last eighteen months. I'm passionate about my trust officer role in a children's charity, but I felt so guilty going back to work. Freya took a while to settle at nursery for half days, but now she loves it. She's only stayed with Mum and Dad a couple of times before and it didn't go as well as I thought it would. I'm hoping this time will be easier.

Freya leans forward and reaches out to me again, tears swimming in her eyes. I unfurl her hot fists and kiss her palms. Why didn't I insist on going out to dinner instead of going away for a whole weekend? The anxiety in my stomach twists tight. I've agreed to play daft hen-party games and wear pink and white T-shirts instead of spending time with my daughter. It's not really me.

'We will, I promise. We've got Danielle's number too. Nothing is going to go wrong.' Mum squeezes my arm and she and Danielle nod at each other.

'Thank you. Sorry for being so... nervy, it's just that it'll be the longest I've left her with anyone.'

'It will be fine.' Mum hugs me. I put my arms round them and listen to Freya's gentle breathing.

'Jamie should have had his stag do on a different night, then he could have looked after her this weekend, and I could have been there for her on a different weekend so he could go out.' I can feel my blood pressure rising. I need to calm down.

'Stop fretting, Megan. Go and enjoy yourself,' Dad says, pushing a stray hair off my face, his fingertips skimming my cheek. I nod. I need to trust that their parenting skills are up to scratch even though they're not as young and agile as they were. It doesn't mean they're not capable. And I hate even thinking it. But Mum's hearing is worse and Dad being seven years older is really starting to show. He has a full head of white hair and takes various supplements for his stiff joints. Having older parents has rarely concerned me, but their recent health problems have made me have to face it. What if Dad's back goes again when he picks Freya up? He was laid out on the floor barely able to move all day last time. And when Freya gets moving, even I have to be quick to catch up with her.

'We're going to have a great time,' Danielle says, her brows furrowed, probably wondering if we're ever going to get out of there. She does understand my concerns though. She hears it all the time in her job as a primary school teacher. She's brilliant with children.

'I know, I promise I'll try to, okay?' I don't want to spoil the weekend for everyone, despite my moaning and hesitation. I'm not comfortable being the centre of attention but it will be lovely getting everyone together. I need to stop stressing and enjoy myself.

Danielle and my parents follow me out to the hall. I check my hair in the mirror above the console table. It's a messy attempt at a sexy updo, secured with a big clip, but I'm pleased with my new highlights. I take my oversized sunglasses off the top of my head and admire Danielle's shoulder-length chestnut hair. I wish mine was as effortless to look after as hers. It's so shiny and always looks good.

Still, there are bigger things to worry about with the wedding in less than a week. *My* wedding. I smile to myself. I can't believe I'm finally marrying Jamie in only five days' time. I'm looking forward to becoming Mrs Jamie Ward. We've become parents together and now this is the cherry on the cake. I let out a contented sigh and beam at everyone.

'I'm so happy for you.' Danielle leans in for a hug.

'When did I become such a cliché?' I laugh. But I can't help it, Jamie is the love of my life. I'd never met anyone like him before. We connected straight away. 'Clicked', as Mum calls it. When you know, you know, she told me. It was the way he looked up at me when he came in the pub that night to join his friends for a drink and sat at the table next to mine. The whole room around him seemed to fall away and it was just the two of us gazing at each other. I'd heard about moments like that and never really believed they were possible, but when it happened to me, it was like being caught in a special moment when the universe paused just for us. Dad calls it love at first sight. He said that was how he felt when he first saw Mum. She still goes into a soft-focus smile when he says that.

The sun is shining for us on this early morning June day as Dad opens the front door. He lets out a tiny gasp and shuts it again, turning to me, his face pale. He swallows hard, his Adam's apple bobbing up and down. It's sweet that he doesn't want to let me go.

'It's okay, Dad.' I wrap my arms around his slender depend-able frame and hug him tight.

'Just have the best time.' Mum reaches for my face, cupping it in her smooth hand-cream-fragranced hand.

'I will, I promise. I'll send photos. Only appropriate ones of course.' I let go of Dad and give Mum the biggest hug and kiss her on both cheeks.

'I'll let you out the back; bad luck to go out the front, isn't it?' Dad says, nodding towards the kitchen, trying to usher us down the hall.

'What? Don't give me all that superstition nonsense, Christopher,' Mum tuts and reaches for the door despite him shaking his head, eyes widening. She ignores it and almost pushes him aside. Danielle and I can't help but giggle behind our hands.

The front door flies open in one sweep of Mum's arm, and our giggles evaporate as we all stare out at the lawn. Someone has erected a stand of deep scarlet flowers in the shape of letters spelling:

RIP MEGAN

'What the actual...?' A shiver runs through me. I grip Dad's arm. It's the sort of floral display I've only seen in a hearse, propped up against a coffin.

'Who would do something like this?' Mum shrieks, keeping Freya's face turned away.

Danielle presses her hand to her throat. Both her and Mum are looking at me and each other, covering their mouths, unable to hide their pained expressions.

I run down the path and out of the gate, look left and right, hoping to see even the smallest trace of whoever dared to leave this here. But there's no one in sight.

My heart is pounding into my throat. I'm frozen to the spot trying to work out who could have done this. It can't be a passing dislike, but a deep-seated hatred. To go to so much trouble and expense. The message they've sent is loud and clear.

Someone wishes I was dead.

2

After we've reported the crime to the police, Dad loads our luggage into the boot of Danielle's VW Convertible. He's moved the flowers into the garage in case the police want to examine them for fingerprints, although we're guessing the person who left them was wearing gloves.

Danielle and I climb into her car and as she starts the engine, I wave goodbye to Freya and my parents. My hands are shaking. Am I doing the right thing leaving my daughter after such a blatant threat? My first thought was to cancel the hen weekend, but my parents and Danielle think I should go ahead, not be scared off because that's probably what the perpetrator wants. The roof is down, and music is already pumping out of the speakers, so I don't hear what they say, but I read their lips: *Good luck*. Mum helps Freya wave goodbye to me.

The roads are relatively clear for a Saturday morning, considering we've left later than we planned. I lean my head back on the seat, trying to think who might hold a grudge against me. The warm gentle breeze carries sweet floral aromas around us, but right now all I can think of are freshly cut funeral flowers.

We stop at Sarah's house about a mile away. She comes bounding out of her flat as soon as we pull up. Her bottle blonde pixie cut is shining bright in the sunshine. She's dressed casually in a pair of dungarees, vest top and flip flops to match her friendly and laid-back personality. It's the sort of outfit she wears when she volunteers in the farm shop café at weekends, a hundred yards up the road. During the week she's a corporate event planner and along with the other hens, has helped Danielle organise this weekend.

'How are you both?' she squeals, leaning in to give me a peck on the cheek. A fresh citrus smell wafts from her skin. She chucks her holdall into the back seat and climbs in next to it.

'Good mostly,' I say, then when she sees my frown, I tell her about the flowers on the lawn.

'That's so creepy. Do you think someone's following you?' She looks around as Danielle starts the car.

'I hope not; I hadn't thought of that,' I say, alarmed.

They have been planning my hen weekend for weeks. I've gone on about nothing else on my social media platforms, in private groups and publicly, which means whoever did put those flowers there could be in any area of my life. Or maybe it's someone I don't know at all, looking in, jealous of everything and everyone I have in my life. I know how blessed I am, not everyone is as lucky as me, but it's not always been that way.

'I can't think of anyone I've upset enough to do something as cruel as this.'

'Maybe it's someone who doesn't think you deserve your happy ever after,' Sarah says.

'But why? Is it because I'm marrying Jamie, or doesn't it matter who the groom is?' To my knowledge I've not done anything to hurt anyone, at least not deliberately. It could be some small thing I'm not aware of, because no one is perfect.

'Try not to think about it now. We're going to have an amazing weekend. I can't wait,' Sarah says.

I wish I knew everything they've got planned for me, but some of it is top secret. All of it will be fun, I'm sure. I wasn't bothered what it was before, but now this has happened I feel jittery, unsettled. I don't want to mention it because they've both gone to so much trouble, but right now I'd be happy to go home and snuggle up on the sofa with Jamie and our little Freya.

But that can't happen. I'd let too many people down. After all, this is the official countdown to our big day. Also, a part of me doesn't want to shrink away from a vicious threat from a nasty person. All I can do is control what *I* do. And I intend to enjoy myself.

The weekend will no doubt be over in a flash, so my plan is not to get too drunk, try to enjoy it and remember as much as I can so I can cherish the memories. Between us, we've come up with rules about what can and can't be posted on social media. Everyone who's said they're definitely coming has been sent the Dos and Don'ts list. Danielle wanted people to sign an agreement, but I think that would have been a step too far. I trust my friends, and I don't expect to get so drunk that I don't remember what I'm doing or who's photographing me. And anyway, I only intend to have one hen night in my lifetime, so I need to make the most of my last hours as a singleton.

'Are you sure we haven't forgotten anything?' Sarah asks Danielle.

Everything that could possibly go wrong suddenly crashes across my mind. What if no one else turns up? Or the cottage we've hired is a dump and nothing like the glamorous pad in the photos? We've never used this catering company before, what if we all go down with food poisoning?

'I don't think we have,' Danielle says firmly, not taking her eyes off the road. 'One of us can always pop back to my house if we need to. It's not that far.'

Danielle is my chief bridesmaid and is taking it so seriously, working on her speech, making notes on her phone when she remembers something we did together back in school or college. She's been in my life since nursery school and I love that our mums are still friends. Sarah is the one who's organised the games, with Lauren's help. The venue, meal and club for this evening have been Danielle's responsibility.

'I'm glad we didn't decide to go abroad,' I tell them.

'Me too,' says Danielle, 'imagine all the mosquitoes.'

'And the randy barmen.' Sarah pulls a face of disgust, and we all laugh.

It was one of the options we considered, but because of the cost of living going up so sharply, it didn't seem fair to expect everyone to pay out for flights on top of everything else. I told Danielle and Sarah I'd be happy with a quiet meal at my favourite Indian restaurant, but they wouldn't hear of it. Wanted me to have a 'proper' send off on my journey into married life.

'So who do *you* think sent me those flowers?' I ask both of them, not really wanting to talk about it, but if either of them has any thoughts about who it might be, I need to hear it because I can't get it out of my mind.

'I've been wracking my brains, and I honestly don't know,' Danielle says, turning to look at Sarah who also shakes her head and adds, 'Everyone likes you. You've not upset anyone, so it doesn't make any sense.'

I trust them both so if they don't have a clue, how am I meant to?

'I hate to say it, but do you think it's safe for you to go out on your own in the run up to the wedding?' Sarah asks. 'I mean it's a... death threat, isn't it?'

'Do you really think this person means to harm you?' Danielle glances across at me.

'I don't know.' I shudder.

Someone out there has it in for me.

3

The house we've booked for the weekend is only a forty-minute drive away from my parents' house in the lush Peak District, and only a short taxi drive to Manchester, where we'll be heading this evening. It couldn't be more idyllically located for a hen party. We'll be able to make as much noise as we like, and no one will hear us. I shut my eyes and inhale the aromatic summer breeze sweeping over my face and try not to think of Freya crying for me.

When we arrive, Danielle is the first to jump out. She rushes up the drive to the huge wooden double-fronted door. Sarah and I get out and stand behind her as she knocks lightly. Moments later the door swings open to Emma holding a magnum of Bollinger champagne in her arms. Her new ombre hair is pink and purple at the ends.

'I love it,' I shout at her over the hens whooping their greetings at me and cheering at the tops of their voices. I thought we'd be the first ones here and I'd have a chance to settle in, make a couple of calls, but being late has put everything out of kilter.

We step inside and Danielle takes the glass flutes from Emma who then pours our drinks. Danielle hands me the one decorated with 'Bride' in gold letters and when everyone has a glass, she shouts cheers. I go round hugging each of my guests, clinking glasses – a few friends I've not seen for a while, a couple of girls I went to school with and a few colleagues from my current job. I met Emma most recently at my local running club. She's quickly become a good friend, someone to confide in away from my regular friends.

I spot Lauren from secondary school lurking at the back. She smiles and holds my gaze. I smile back. Her hair is highlighted like mine. She's never been a big hugger. We used to be best friends but after I got together with Jamie, we lost touch. I invited her thinking it was a good opportunity to put our differences aside and rekindle our friendship, but I need to find out if I can trust her again.

She was with me when I met Jamie, claimed to have spotted him at the same time as me and hates that I had the balls to make the first move. I didn't realise at the time that she was sitting next to me hoping he'd speak to her. She has this traditional idea that men should always make the first move. But I got up and just started chatting to him. We hit it off straight away. Danielle told me much later that Lauren had been upset and jealous when she heard we were in a relationship, and although she's never said that to me directly, she's made little digs every now and again. As far as I know, she's not found her soulmate yet, but I'm sure she will one day. Now Jamie and I are getting married, I hope we can put all that behind us and move on. Unless I've got it completely wrong and Lauren sees this weekend as her chance to get me back.

'Sorry we're so late. Something... unexpected came up. I hope you've all had breakfast,' I say, deciding it's best not to tell them about the flowers on the lawn straight away, otherwise it's going to overshadow the rest of the weekend. And I don't want to give oxygen to whoever has done this to me.

'We've all eaten, thanks,' Emma says, looking round at the others who nod their agreement.

'The pancakes were delicious,' Bonnie from work says, rubbing her stomach, her soft brown ringlets jiggling at the same time.

Danielle booked a catering company for half a day – breakfast and lunch, and a restaurant for this evening.

'Hope everything's okay?' Emma frowns, leaning towards me.

'Yeah, it's fine.' I smile and brighten my expression. It must be clear on my face that something is on my mind.

'Let's show you around,' Emma says and catches Danielle's eye before leading the way.

We start in the lounge, which is a huge space decorated in white with a pink neon slogan in script writing hanging from the wall, saying 'One Loyal Friend is Worth More Than a Thousand Fake Ones'. I remember liking it from the video tour online. Two cream sofas face each other around a white marble fireplace. Shimmering pink, blue and silver balloons are everywhere, and a couple of them are in the shape of champagne bottles and joined wedding rings.

'And this is the gorgeous patio and pool area,' Sarah says. In front of the bi-fold patio doors are huge sparkling diamanté letters spelling 'HEN NIGHT' in glistening white lights. It's an immaculate ultra-modern pad with four double rooms and a master suite for me, plus four eco-pods sleeping two in each, in the third-of-an-acre garden. Twelve hens in total and one bride to be.

Danielle continues the tour through to the kitchen-breakfast room, closely followed by the hens. Two chefs are on the other side of the kitchen preparing breakfast for the three of us. One is chopping pineapples, mangos, passionfruit and strawberries, and the other is cooking fluffy pancakes.

I trail my fingertips across the white sparkly granite of the vast island. I love that Danielle takes the time to explain to everyone the schedule for the weekend.

'We'll be having all our meals in here,' she tells everyone, 'except when we eat at the Italian restaurant I've booked for tonight.' She moves swiftly into the next room which overlooks the garden. 'As you can see, this room is set up as a beauty spa, and there's a jacuzzi through that door behind you, Megan.' I open the door to a blue-and-white tiled room with a round pool at the centre.

Danielle continues, 'So we've got four beauty therapists coming in shortly to kick off our pampering sessions. There'll be face masks, manicures and pedicures. We'll play some games, have a light lunch, then we have four hairdressers arriving later to do our hair before we hit the town. I've booked a VIP booth in an exclusive nightclub, which we'll head to after the meal. Then it'll be back here for a nightcap and bed.'

'It all sounds perfect, thank you Danielle,' I say and all the hens echo their thanks too.

'We need to check out by 10 a.m. tomorrow morning, but you're welcome to leave your luggage in the hall if you want to go off and do some exploring around the Peaks before heading home,' Danielle adds.

'After the three of us have eaten, we'll play our first ice-breaker game,' Sarah says, 'in the meantime, go and claim your rooms if you haven't already. Obviously the master bedroom with the en suite is reserved for Megan.'

'And don't forget hen night golden rule number one, Megan. No phoning the groom.' Danielle holds out a velvet-lined bag, and I reluctantly drop my mobile into it. 'And rule number two goes for everyone else, no mobiles on the night out. What happens on the hen night, stays on the hen night. So, I'll be taking them away later.'

As everyone heads up the stairs, I spot one woman hanging back, trying not to be seen. Her hair is so dark it's almost black and her eyes are a startling green. I immediately wonder if they're contact lenses. Whether they are or not, I don't recognise her. She could be from Jamie's family, although I'm not aware he invited anyone. I quietly observe her as she glides upstairs somewhat reluctantly, as if she's found herself here by accident but decided she may as well stay.

Whoever she is, I need to find out.

4

'Hello, I don't think we've met?' I hold out my hand to the girl with the green eyes. She's the first one down, ready to play the ice-breaker game. She smiles at me confidently and shakes half my hand with surprisingly cold fingers.

'I'm Beth. I'm from Australia. A cousin on Jamie's side... obviously.' Her accent isn't all that strong. She opens her palms out to me and bats her eyelashes.

'Lovely to meet you. It's good of you to come.' I summon up my friendliest smile, and try to remember if Jamie mentioned a cousin called Beth. I did say he could invite any of the women in his family, not really expecting him to. He's not talked much about his family, except that his mum died, and he lost touch with an aunt, uncle and cousins who moved abroad, but I couldn't remember where. He said he was upset they didn't contact him after his mum's death, so he didn't stay in touch with any of them.

God, I really need to cheer up. This is my party after all. But I'm tempted to call Jamie right now in front of her and ask him why he didn't tell me she was coming.

'Our parents fell out a while back, so I'm here on a peace mission,' Beth says.

'Any family of Jamie's is very welcome,' I say, pasting on a smile.

Danielle stares at her blankly. She clearly knew nothing about this woman gate-crashing. Lauren on the other hand looks smug. I hope it's not a mistake letting her be involved in my hen weekend. Could she be holding a grudge against me?

I sigh inwardly but can't shift this dead weight in my chest, remembering what happened this morning. The feeling that someone hates me so much to do *that* sends a chill right through me.

I follow Danielle and Sarah to the kitchen and pick at my breakfast while they both wolf theirs down. I've lost my appetite. This is exactly what the person wants – to ruin my hen weekend – but I can't let them.

Once everyone is sat out on the terrace under the sun umbrellas, Danielle introduces Beth to everyone. Sarah asks one of the catering staff to bring out a tray of glasses and open a bottle of champagne, then she does the honours pouring it and Danielle helps her hand out the drinks.

'Please raise your glasses to our gorgeous friend, Megan,' Danielle says. 'May you enjoy your last few days as Miss Lewis. Happy hen night!' Everyone raises their glasses and cheers loudly, repeating, 'Happy hen night, Megan.'

'Soon to be Mrs Ward,' Lauren adds and clinks her glass with mine. 'Speech, speech!' she shouts and a couple of others echo her call for me to say something.

I stand up. 'Thank you all so much for coming. I hope you enjoy this weekend as much as I know I will.' I gaze around at them and wish there was more joy in my heart. I feel so flat, as though this is just an ordinary get-together. I should feel excited and lifted by this gathering of trusted friends from all chapters of my life, but I can't help looking at them differently, trying to detect the tiniest hint of malice amongst their smiling faces. I don't want to believe it's any of them here today, but the perpetrator has made me suspicious of the very friends I love the most.

'Are we all ready to play the ice-breaker game?' Danielle picks up a stack of index cards and pencils. She passes them to Sarah who hands one of each out to everyone.

'The game is called, *Two Truths and a Lie*. All you have to do is introduce yourself then tell everyone two truths about yourself and one lie and we have to guess which is the lie. To give you an idea, it's best to keep your truths simple but surprising and say all three confidently and play it cool so it's harder for us to guess.' There are a few groans and half laughs but soon everyone has quietened down and is writing.

After a couple of minutes, Danielle asks if everyone is ready.

'Shall I go first?' Lauren says. Danielle and I nod.

'Okay, I'm Lauren, an old secondary school friend of Megan's.' She grins. 'So here are mine. When I was a child, I wanted to be a librarian. I'm terrified of rats, and I can't swim.' Her smile widens and Bonnie, one of the girls I work with calls out, 'I think the last two are truths and the first one is the lie.'

Lauren shakes her head. Someone else guesses that the lie is that she can't swim.

'No, the lie is that I'm terrified of rats. In fact, I love rats and I have two pet rats at home, called Ant and Dec.' Everyone groans and laughs.

'They are actually lovely creatures, very misunderstood,' Lauren tells us. Danielle and I raise our eyebrows; I'm not sure I'll ever be convinced of that.

'How about you next,' I say to Danielle.

'Okay. I'm Danielle, a bestie of the bride to be. We've known each other since nursery school. I'm chief hen party organiser so feel free to come to me if there's anything I can help you with over the weekend. So, my two truths and a lie in no particular order of course are, I still like to build things with Lego, I don't like chocolate and, I'm a rollercoaster junkie.'

Everyone looks at each other in surprise. I know the answer so keep quiet.

'Is the lie that you don't like chocolate?' Tilly, one of my friends from work, asks.

'Drat, did I make that too easy?' Danielle says, then adds, 'Actually you're wrong.' She flashes her eyes and points her finger at Tilly.

'What?' someone else shouts. 'You really *don't* like chocolate?' Danielle shakes her head.

'Are you even human?' Beth asks and everyone laughs.

'It must be the Lego one then,' Emma says.

'Yes!' Danielle claps. 'I hate Lego with a passion.' Her face screws up as she says it.

'But you really love roller coasters?' Emma asks.

'Yep, the more terrifying the better,' she says.

'Wow, I didn't know that. Hats off to you. I don't like going on any rides, they make me feel sick.'

'Your turn,' Danielle says to me.

'Okay, well I'm Megan, the bride to be. Obviously.' I wave my jazz hands in the air. 'If you don't know that, what are you even doing here?' I laugh and all the girls join in.

'Okay, so I have a heart tattoo at the top of my leg.' I glance around at a few raised eyebrows and a couple of people scribbling notes on their pieces of paper. 'I can speak three languages, and I shaved one of my eyebrows off when I was seven.'

'Oh my God, I have no clue,' says Samantha, who I know from years ago at college. 'Which languages do you speak?'

'French, Spanish and English.'

'Hmmm.' She rubs her chin. 'I remember you learning Spanish.'

Sarah goes round topping up all our glasses with champagne.

A couple of girls nearest me peer closer at my eyebrows then whisper and giggle to each other and write something down.

'I'd say the tattoo is a complete lie,' Beth says from the far side of the room. Her long tanned legs are crossed at the ankles.

I shake my head.

'Is the shaved eyebrow the lie?' Emma asks.

'Yes.' I touch my eyebrows.

'I'd never have put you down as being inked,' Beth says, pulling her top up to reveal a medium-sized skull tattoo on her midriff.

'Oh. Well. Mine's just a tiny thing, nothing as daring as yours,' I say.

Tilly, Samantha and Bonnie go after me, then Danielle asks who wants to go next.

'I'll go.' Beth stands up and drags her chair forwards. She plants it right opposite me and crosses her legs.

'Great, go ahead,' Danielle says.

I lift my drink and swallow a mouthful of bubbles, my eyes shifting to meet Danielle's. I'd love to know what she's thinking of this new girl.

'Hello, how ya going? My name's Beth. Thanks for letting me barge in at the last minute. I'm Jamie's cousin from Oz, so at least he's got *someone* representing his family at the church! He doesn't really have many left on the British side. He told me if I came along to the hen party, I'd be made to feel welcome, and he wasn't wrong.' She pouts and blinks slowly as she scans around all the guests' faces, who seem utterly enthralled by her. There doesn't appear to be a scrap of make-up on her pretty face, but she doesn't need it, her lightly tanned skin is smooth and perfect. She uncrosses her legs and links her hands elegantly around her knee. A slinky collection of brightly coloured bangles make a soft clinking sound on her wrist every time she moves.

'I've never played this game before, so here goes, my truths and a lie. First up, I wear coloured contact lenses.' She pauses, letting us all take in her green eyes. 'Next up, I learnt to read when I was just three years old. And last of all, I'm a drummer in an indie band.'

There are a few muted gasps, then everyone falls silent, scribbling answers on their pieces of paper. This one's too easy. She's wearing coloured contact lenses without a doubt, so the lie must be one of the other two, but I'll wait for the others to have a guess. No one has eyes that green.

'I think the lie is being able to read at three years old.' Sarah scrunches up her nose and raises her palms in the air like this guess is a no-brainer. 'Unless you were a child genius.' She chuckles.

No one else speaks. Maybe they're too scared to get it wrong. To me, it seems the most likely one to be a lie.

'Anyone else want to have a guess before Beth reveals the truth?' I ask.

'Is the lie that you're a drummer in a band?' Lauren sounds unsure, but at least she's having a go.

Beth crosses her arms and grins at me, like she's suddenly got the measure of us.

'Please put us out of our misery,' I say.

'And the lie is...' She drumrolls with her hands on the wicker side table. '...that I wear coloured contact lenses.' She says it in such a blasé way, that I do a double take.

'What? Your eyes can't be that green,' I blurt out, then immediately feel my face flush with heat at my outburst.

'Well sorry, but they are,' she says, pouting again and blinking slowly just so I can look at her shiny emerald eyes. Her lashes also seem too thick and dark to be natural. God, what is wrong with me. Why am I being so catty? I suppose I'm still hacked off with what happened this morning. It's like I don't trust anyone.

'More importantly, you were reading at the age of three? Tell us how that's even possible?' Emma's eyes widen.

Beth combs her hand through her hair and lets it fall back naturally. 'I have something called hyperlexia.'

All her sentences end in that rising inflection Aussies have, like it's a question when it's not.

'What's that?' Lauren scrunches her nose.

'It's an ability to read far above what's expected at the child's age. Comes from an intense fascination with letters or numbers.'

'You must have a really high IQ,' Danielle says, moving her chair closer, looking at her intently.

'So you play in a band as well?' Bonnie asks. And gradually everyone seems to gravitate towards Beth, wanting to know more about her, hanging on her every word.

Mesmerised.

And I can't help feeling a little put out.

5

After a dip in the pool and a pamper session with the small army of nail techs and facialists, the chef lays out a light lunch just inside the patio of different salads, fruit, cold meats and seafood. The sun is high in the sky and at its hottest. I spray another layer of factor 30 sun lotion onto my shoulders which are fast turning from lightly flushed to lobster red and more than uncomfortable. I pass the bottle to Beth, who's planted herself next to me, but she passes it straight to Emma and continues talking to her about touring with the band. She exudes confidence. Maybe if I looked more like her, I'd be that confident too. Her skin is a perfect even golden brown, not a hint of strap lines or over-exposure on one inch of it. I'd never get away with wearing her hot-pink bikini. I move to a shaded spot and throw on a kaftan in a lame effort to stop myself becoming so sunburnt that I can't get dressed later.

The caterers let me know the food is ready. One of them brings out a newly opened bottle of chilled champagne on a tray full of glasses and a fresh jug of ice-cold lemon water. Sarah pours the bubbles and hands the flutes round.

Considering Beth hadn't known anyone before she arrived,

she's been quick to make new friends and has a huddle of them around her by the side of the pool. As soon as I moved away, they pushed a group of sun loungers close together. I wave at them to come and eat but I'm met with laughter and whispering behind cupped hands, which makes me think of a spiteful clique of girls at high school. I wish I'd insisted on cutting down the numbers to five or six, but Sarah and Danielle thought it would be more fun to have a bigger group.

'Do you want me to say something to her?' Danielle offers, pushing a fork of salad leaves into her mouth. She sits next to me, her plate piled high with cold roasted vegetable pasta and chicken Caesar salad.

'No, leave them, it's fine. I don't want to make a thing of it. It's good that Beth has joined in and made friends so easily. I'd rather that than her be someone who sits in the corner not joining in.' I'd like to get to know her too. I'm tempted to ask Danielle for my phone back. Ask Jamie about her. Why not mention his cousin was coming? Perhaps it slipped his mind. Seems unlikely she would jump on a plane from Australia at the last minute. 'Did you know anything about Beth coming?'

Danielle shakes her head.

After lunch, Danielle gathers everyone into the living room, I suspect partly in an effort to break up the little group around the pool.

'As the bride to be, we've each bought you a personal present that we hope will make you smile, Megan. Something to send you on your journey into married life that will remind you of your friends. The brief we gave everyone was not to spend more than thirty pounds, and it should be something memorable, thoughtful and/or amusing.'

'Do you want to start with mine?' Lauren says, holding up a silver gift bag with a glittery sash across it.

'Thank you.' We hug and I take it from her. The top is stuffed with matching silver tissue paper which I pull out. Inside is a clear box decorated with hearts. I frown, not sure at first what it is. Then I catch a glimpse of the metal chain and start laughing.

'Show us then.' Danielle can hardly contain her excitement. I hold up the box and open it. Inside is a pair of fur-lined hand-cuffs which are met with giggles and shrieks of laughter from the girls. I continue opening everyone's presents, many of them adult toys or items of lingerie, which, while amusing, all feel a bit dated and cliched.

'Just two left now, mine and Beth's,' Danielle says. She indicates to Beth to pass me her present first.

'I didn't know about the gift giving, but I'd brought something for you anyway. I hope you like it,' she says and hands me a beautifully wrapped package tied with ribbon. It's the size and shape of a hardback book but not as thick. I carefully untie the ribbon and rip off the shiny gold paper. Inside, I unwrap several layers of tissue paper and take out an oak frame with a soft carved scalloped edge. I've opened it upside down, so I carefully turn it over and it's a family photo with Jamie at the centre. There are five people sitting beside him on a plush sofa, and he's captured in the middle of them all laughing. Jamie is much younger, maybe in his teens and so handsome with his clear blue eyes and cropped fair hair.

'It's beautiful. Is this Jamie's family?'

'His mum is on the left, not long before she died, then there's my mum and dad and me. My parents were in London for a week when this was taken, then Jamie and his mum came over to Australia to visit our side of the family, long before they fell out.'

'You said earlier you're here on a peace mission. Can I ask what it was about?'

'Jamie's never said?'

'No.'

'I shouldn't really say then. Ask him.' She shrugs as if it's nothing, but Jamie speaks so fondly of his mum, I can't imagine something like that not affecting him. He's had such a struggle with depression and drinking since he left the army and had a breakdown. I don't want to provoke an episode by bringing up any bad blood.

'Mum gave me a box of old papers to look through when she was having a clear out after Dad died. I found this one in there, so thought I'd put it in a nice frame for you. It's a lovely photo of Jamie, isn't it? I thought you'd like it. He'd not long come out of the army then.'

'It's beautiful and really thoughtful of you, thank you.' I look at it again, closer this time. Jamie's hair is so short, he looks like a skinhead. He's wearing a smart pair of trousers, and a crisp white open neck shirt. The young woman sitting next to him is in a pale green shift dress, leaning into him, her mouth open, mid-laugh. That's her, Beth. Her hair is fairer, mid-brown. She looks so young, like a sister. I don't like to ask her age.

It's good of her to have made the effort to be here, but odd that he didn't think to mention it to me, because as far as I'm aware, no one called Beth has been invited to the wedding.

6

Danielle stands up and claps her hands. 'Right, let's go outside and play another game then we'll start getting ready for our big night out.' Everyone looks up at her, dutifully nodding and carrying their drinks out to the patio, where they make themselves comfortable on the sun loungers. I sit on one under the shade of a parasol.

'First up, who'd like to play, Would She Rather?' Sarah asks, and a few people call out in agreement.

'No. Truth or Dare,' Lauren shouts louder and half my guests shout, 'Yes,' and clap and chant the word over and over.

'Okay, we could do one game now and one later, what do you think, Megan? Which one first?' Danielle asks.

'Would She Rather.' Although I'm not keen on either game as it's all bound to be centred around me. On the other hand, I don't mind giving my guests a laugh.

'Great. We'll play Truth or Dare later.' Danielle nods to Sarah, who hands out printed sheets with 'Megan's Hen Party' printed at the top in curly pink writing. There's a list of options down the middle and a tick box either side.

'Everyone ready?' Sarah asks as she stands up. 'I'm going to call out each question and you tick one of the options, whichever one you think Megan would rather do or have. Got it?' Sarah hands out a pen and mini clipboard to each person.

'What about Megan?' Lauren asks.

'Megan is going to fill in her answers too and we'll call them out at the end. Okay, here's an easy one to start with. Question one. Would she rather, have a glass of prosecco or a glass of red wine?' Sarah looks around as everyone's heads go down to tick one of the boxes. 'Question two, would she rather have a beach holiday or a hiking holiday?' There are a few puzzled looks, including from Beth, who's probably going to struggle to answer any of these as she doesn't know me.

'Question three, would she rather have a long relaxing bath or a hot steamy shower?'

The question is met with a few wolf whistles and giggles. Lauren nudges Beth and they snigger like ten-year-olds.

'Question four, would she rather fall over in public or say the wrong thing?'

Someone groans and a few of them tut and hold their fingers to their lips.

'Question five, would she rather give up her phone for a week or give up sex?'

Everyone laughs and my face heats up. I sip my champagne, hoping it will cool me down.

'Question six, would she rather keep the lights on or turn the lights off?'

Lauren exaggerates a wink, and everyone laughs loudly, then they shush and elbow each other. Anyone listening in a neighbouring garden would think we're all silly teenagers.

'Question seven, would she rather sunbathe with her top on or top off?'

Lauren glances around the room grinning. I glare at her.

'And number eight, last question. If she found a dead body, would she rather go to the police or keep her mouth shut?'

A few gasps are followed by everyone chatting loudly. Sarah claps her hands to get their attention.

'Right, can we have hands up when I call out each option, then Megan, you tell us which one you'd rather.'

I nod, my mouth clamped shut. No prizes for guessing who came up with these questions. Trust Lauren to try to embarrass me. I smile at her to show I don't care. But I do. I invited her to be one of my bridesmaids as an olive branch, thinking she'd changed. I thought if she helped organise a couple of the games, she wouldn't feel left out and was more likely to behave herself. I'm beginning to wonder if I made a terrible mistake.

'Right then, question one, prosecco or red wine.' Sarah counts the hands. Only one hand goes up for red wine and that's Beth, who doesn't know I hate it.

'Prosecco every time,' I tell her, and everyone laughs and claps.

'Beach holiday or hiking holiday?' Sarah asks.

'Definitely beach.' I nod.

'Only two people got that wrong. Next, long relaxing bath, or a hot steamy shower?'

Lauren pinches her nose and shimmies up and down.

'No contest, a relaxing bath.' I smile at Beth as she gets that wrong too.

'Me too, every Sunday night after a big roast dinner,' Lauren says.

'I thought you'd prefer a steamy shower.' Beth winks and Lauren giggles. It makes me wonder what Lauren has told her about me.

'Next one. Fall over in public or say the wrong thing?'

The vote for this one is half and half.

'I'd rather fall over in public although I probably say the wrong thing more often.' I laugh and they all join in. 'What would *you* all rather do?' I ask them.

'I'm always falling over,' says Lauren, 'and I hate saying the wrong thing... not!' She shrieks with laughter and to my surprise Beth and a few others laugh too.

'I say the wrong thing all the time without meaning to,' Sarah adds, passing Danielle the list while she opens a new bottle of champagne.

'Question five. Would Megan rather give up her phone for a week, or sex?' Danielle pouts as if pre-empting the answer. I think she's had too much to drink already.

Everyone shouts 'sex' at the same time and laughs hysterically. I roll my eyes but can't help laughing too.

'My phone is definitely more addictive. Danielle has locked it away so I can't contact Jamie, or my family and I have to admit, I'm lost without it.'

'That is so sad,' Beth says and after a dramatic pause, 'but it's definitely my problem too.'

'And me,' Emma says, and a few others nod.

'Question six. Lights on or lights off?'

Three people shout, *lights off*.

'Lights on.' I grin.

'Question seven. Top on at the beach or topless?'

Most of them shout topless and I nod, fluttering my eyelashes. It sparks a discussion about who would and who definitely would not take their top off when sunbathing.

'Last question. If Megan found a dead body, would she rather go to the police or keep her mouth shut?' Danielle asks and presses her lips together while she considers the hands shooting up. 'Almost everyone thinks you'd go to the police.'

'Of course I would.' I flash my eyes at them and sit up in the lounger.

'I'm actually surprised at you,' Lauren says to me, raising one eyebrow. 'I wouldn't have had you down as a squealer.'

'Wouldn't most people tell the police? I'd want them to catch the perpetrator.' I frown at her.

'I agree,' Danielle says.

'I think I'd be too scared to speak up,' Tilly says and several of the others nod.

'Who wants another drink?' Sarah brings over the bottle of champagne.

'I'm not sure I can manage another drink yet,' I say, then add in a lower voice, 'I wish I could check everything's okay with my parents.'

She nods and touches my arm.

'I think you should let Megan have her phone back, at least to check her messages, make sure her daughter's okay,' Sarah says to Danielle. She knows what was left on the lawn this morning, so understands I need to make sure nothing else has happened. I thought Danielle would have realised that too.

'Okay, okay,' Danielle says. She grabs her handbag from the kitchen and brings it out. Lauren conducts all the girls to chant, *phone, phone, phone*, while Danielle rummages around in her bag for it. She ends up tipping the contents out onto the table. A whole mix of items clatter onto the glass, including a set of keys, a notebook, sanitary products, pens, tablets and a mini packet of tissues.

But no phone.

'Where is it?' I ask, a knot rising in my chest.

'I've no idea. I put it here, I promise you.' Danielle shakes her head, staring down at the contents.

'Well, it's not there now, is it?' Lauren says, her wide eyes landing on each person, one by one. She's met with shrugs and shakes of the head.

'Which one of you has taken it?' Danielle asks.

'Come on, joke's over. Whoever took it, please tell me where my mobile is,' I say.

'Look, I'm going to leave my handbag by the front door so you can put it back without owning up.' Danielle holds her bag up so everyone can see it.

'Maybe *you* put it somewhere else and just can't remember?' Beth smiles broadly and side-eyes Lauren, then lies back on her sun lounger. It's possible she's right but for a stranger she's quite forward in speaking her mind.

'That is entirely possible, but if it is a prank, I'm just not in the mood.' I sigh and look at her and Lauren smirking. My stomach sinks. Lauren's never grown out of trying to get one over on me and make fun of me in front of people. Like the time she sent a sex toy to Jamie, making out it was from me. She's never forgiven me for going out with him. Her snide comments about me muscling in on him and breaking 'the sister code' just got too much and we stopped contacting each other. I thought we'd have got past all that by now, but I'm beginning to wonder if she's changed at all.

'What's wrong, has something else happened?' Emma scans our faces, waiting for one of us to tell her. 'You... you don't seem yourself today.' She moves closer to me and lays her hand on my arm.

I glance at Danielle and Sarah, and they nod their encouragement, so I explain about the funeral flowers on my parents' front lawn and how I need to check in with them, make sure they and Freya are okay and nothing else has happened.

'My God. That's awful,' Emma says, echoing what everyone else is saying.

'Who would do that?' Bonnie asks.

'Someone you didn't invite to the wedding perhaps?' Lauren suggests.

'Possibly, but who would be that upset?' I shake my head, still confused about what I've done to warrant such a malicious act.

'Could it be someone who's holding a grudge?' Emma asks.

'I don't know what about, but whoever it is, it's really unnerved me.'

'You've told the police though, right?' Lauren says.

'Yes, we reported it online straight away. They're supposed to call back. I gave my parents' phone number so I didn't have to deal with it here, and it happened on their property anyway. I'm hoping the police will speak to the neighbours, see if they saw a car or anyone hanging around outside the house. My parents have kept the flowers so the police can examine them too.'

'That's so shocking though. It can't be a coincidence that it happened today, can it?' Emma asks, and sips from her glass.

'Everything about it feels deliberate to me. The timing, the location. So I'm sorry I'm not my usual jolly self. I will cheer up, I promise. I won't let whoever did this ruin our weekend.' I stand up. 'Can we lighten the mood now? The hairdressers will be here any second, so I suggest we go upstairs and continue getting ready.'

'Good idea, I'll put on the playlist Sarah's kindly put together for us. It'll come through the speakers in every room.' Danielle gently touches my shoulder. I turn to her and we hug. I'm more grateful than ever for her support.

We all follow Danielle and Sarah up the grand double-width staircase. On the mid-landing, half of us turn towards the left wing and half to the right. It seems indulgent for me to have the master room to myself, so I've invited the guests in the glamping pods to grab their outfits and come up here.

Sarah and I link arms at the top of the stairs and chat over how we're going to do our make-up as we head down the corridor towards my bedroom.

I push open the door and draw in a sharp breath.

Sarah screams.

The sight of a bright red splatter of blood on the bed is horrific. The others come running, gasping and shrieking, huddling at the doorway around Sarah, who's in shock. I step into the room. A familiar chemical smell of nail lacquer punches me, but we didn't have our nails done up here.

'What's happened?' Danielle asks, the last to arrive. I tentatively touch a wet patch of red with my index finger. It's too gloopy to be blood. I examine it up close and smell my fingertip. 'It's all right everyone, it's not blood, although it really looked like it at first glance.' I hold a hand to my chest. The beautiful white crocheted bed cover is ruined.

'Are you okay?' Danielle asks, coming towards me with Sarah.

'Look. It's a match.' I hold my freshly manicured nails next to the crimson splashes. 'It's mostly dry as well. Must have been done a little while ago.'

'But *who* would do this?' Danielle asks.

Sarah shakes her head. 'Could have been any one of us.' We all look around at each other's blank faces. If it is one of us, they have a good poker face.

'Or it could be one of the nail techs. Did they come up here?'

'I don't think so, unless one of them needed to use the bathroom. Seems unlikely any of them would do this, but it's too much of a mess to be a simple accident.'

All the hens splay their fingers out in front of them. All freshly painted nails in the same crimson colour I requested, each with a soft pink and white French manicure on their ring finger, complete with a tiny pearl stuck in the middle of the nail.

'I'll get onto the head nail tech woman and ask some questions,' Danielle says. 'Let me take some photos. They'll have to pay for the damage if it was one of them, although I doubt if anyone will own up.' She pulls her phone out of her back pocket and takes a few different shots.

'We don't know for certain if it was one of them,' I say quietly, surreptitiously checking everyone's expressions, but no one is giving anything away. No one looks guilty.

'Come on,' Sarah says, guiding me out of the room by the elbow. I glance behind me as we leave and see a couple of the girls carefully pick up the corners of the crocheted cover and the plain white one underneath, and neatly fold them over. It's kind of them to remove all traces of the mess for me, so I don't have to see it again. Except the stark red and white image is imprinted on my mind like I've witnessed a crime scene, and it's not going to be easy to shift.

In Sarah's room, she pours me a glass of water and sits with me.

'Are you sure you're feeling okay?' she asks.

'I wish I could ring Jamie. He'd know what to say to calm me down.' I'm supposed to be enjoying myself, but I can't help thinking that someone is out to hurt me, or at least ruin my hen night.

'Do you want to use my phone?' Sarah whispers, as though someone else is in the room.

'Thanks, but I don't want Danielle telling you off. Maybe you could text him for me instead, ask him to ring my parents and check up on Freya?'

'Yeah, of course.' She taps in the message on her phone and presses send.

'I'll make sure we find your phone, I promise,' Sarah says. 'And I'm sure someone just had an accident with a bottle of nail varnish and is too embarrassed to own up.'

'Probably.' I shrug.

The doorbell rings and several pairs of footsteps run down to answer it. The hairdressers have arrived going by the chatter, and they're on their way upstairs. Sarah follows me back into my bedroom. There's a fresh cover on the bed and apart from a tiny spot of red on the carpet, no one would ever know what had happened here.

My hairdresser Abby comes in with three of her assistants and I'm grateful to see her smiling face. She's been my mum's hairdresser for twenty years and now she's mine too. She's taken aback at my teary eyes and opens her arms. I walk into their warm hold.

'You okay, my darling?' she says into my hair.

I nod and pull back.

'Really?' She tips my chin up as though I'm a child who's been hurt and won't say who did it. 'Do you want me to call your mum? She told me what happened this morning.'

Abby was there to protect me from all sorts of bullies when I was growing up. Her hairdresser shop was always a safe place for me to dive into whenever I was in town and one of the bitchy girls came after me. She'd make me a cup of tea and let me have a doughnut and make sure I had a copy of *Smash Hits* magazine to read. I once asked one of those girls when we bumped into each other in the cinema toilets, why they picked on me. She was alone and so was I. She answered me straight: *You've got the looks, but you ruin it with your retro-grunge get-up.* Her top lip curled as she waved her hand up and down at my baggy jumper and scruffy jeans, then tutted as she left.

These days I try harder to fit in with all the latest fashions. I did some modelling for a catalogue company when I left school. I learnt how to dress for my petite size and shape, what clothes suited me, how to hold myself so I didn't slouch. There were girls far prettier than me, but one photographer said I had an easy-going personality and the ethereal looks of the girl next door.

'Come and sit in front of the mirror.' Abby pats the back of the chair, with a warm smile to match her bouncy auburn hair. Behind me she instructs her assistants to start blow-drying Tilly, Emma and Bonnie's hair while the others wait on my bed or on the chaise longue against the far wall. The music from the tiny speakers dotted around the room becomes louder as ABBA's 'The Name of the Game', starts playing.

I smile at Abby in the mirror. I'm desperate to tell her about the nail varnish on the bed cover, see what she thinks of it, but how can I in front of the other girls without sounding like I'm accusing one of them? Could a friend really have done this to me? I'd like to ask them one by one where they were in the last half hour or so. Two or three left the living room, but which ones and how long were they gone for? I wasn't paying that much attention I was so busy concentrating on the answers to the stupid game. Is this linked to the funeral flowers left for me this morning? Is it Lauren's idea of a prank? If it is, it's not funny at all. My gut is telling me it could be more sinister, like this person is genuinely trying to scare me. But why?

Who knows how far they're prepared to go.

8

Abby sprays heat protection product on my hair as we chat away about the wedding arrangements and how my mum insists we have little boxes of favours and hand-written name cards for everyone coming to the sit-down meal. I'd have been happy for Jamie and me to jet off to a beach and get married in the presence of a couple of locals. But my wedding day is a family event, Mum keeps reminding me. I think she's been looking forward to it from the moment I was born. I'm excited and scared about getting married in equal measure. Abby is already booked to do my hair and Mum's on the morning of the wedding.

'Do you want a cappuccino?' Lauren pops her head around the door.

'Please, if you're making one.' I picture the sophisticated coffee machine in the kitchen and wonder if she knows how to use it. She brings in my half-drunk glass of champagne and puts it on the dressing table in front of me. I'd forgotten I left it downstairs.

'Apparently Beth is a trained barista. Result huh? She's offering to make whatever fancy coffees we like.'

'In that case, cappuccino with chocolate sprinkles please. Do you want anything, Abby?'

'No, I'm fine for now thanks, love. Had a cuppa before I set off.'

I finish my champagne in two glugs and the bubbles give me a satisfying light-headedness. Lauren takes my glass and goes back downstairs.

'I bet you're looking forward to your honeymoon,' Abby says. She's an expert at keeping the conversation going to distract me from the tedium of doing my hair. She's nearly always upbeat and sitting in her chair can be a dose of therapy, like a quick reset before I continue with my life.

'*So* much, I can't wait to lie on a beach in Guadeloupe,' I say and shut my eyes with a smile. 'Just the thought of the warm sand, gently swaying palm trees and sparkly blue water is enough to calm me.' I let out a breath and feel my muscles relax. 'Jamie could really do with a break. He's been so stressed about the wedding, which is why we've tried to keep it as simple as possible.'

'That's good. I think smaller weddings are much nicer, more intimate. Some of the weddings I go to are so outrageously huge and lavish it's a wonder the bride and groom remember all their guests' names!'

I laugh. Abby always manages to see the funny side of life.

'Is Jamie still having therapy?' She pauses and tilts her head at me in the mirror.

'Yeah, it's really helped him control his anxiety, along with the medication of course.'

We wouldn't have been able to do any of this without it. I don't mention the effects of the tablets, such as constant tiredness and lack of libido, because overall they do a good job of lifting his mood. But he's drinking more again and has angry outbursts when he's had too many. One step at a time. Instead, I picture walking along the beach with him, ankle-deep in clear water, hand in hand. Going to the Caribbean was my idea, so we could be as far away from everything as possible. I didn't mind paying for it; my parents are paying for the wedding. Dad is traditional in that sense, insisting they foot the bill, even when Jamie offered to contribute. It was good of him, as I know he can't really afford the wedding they've had in mind for me since I was little. I insisted we pared back on everything so he wouldn't feel overwhelmed by it all. It would have been unfair for him to have to pay.

It took him a while to get back on his feet after leaving the army. It was a shock to everyone when he left, apparently, but he confided in me about it not long after we got together, how he was being bullied so badly he'd considered taking his own life. Fortunately, he was able to leave because he was still so young, but went straight into a completely different environment with no job, nowhere to live and having to make decisions for himself. He was so used to being told what to do. I hadn't realised that many ex-service personnel leave the army with no transferrable skills and need to find a trade to retrain in. Jamie chose to become an electrician and he's doing well now after those first few rocky years on civvy street.

'Here we are,' Lauren says, putting the cappuccino on the dressing table in front of me.

I take a sip and the froth is so creamy, I blow the steam off and take a larger mouthful.

'Please tell Beth, this is seriously good.'

Lauren nods like she already knows.

'A few of us were just wondering if you'd be up for one more game before we go out?' She twists her hands together like she does when she's excited and I suspect she's got some awful surprise prepared for me, but I don't want to spoil their fun, so I'm not even going to ask what it is.

'Sure,' I say casually, trying not to show my inner terror.

'Great!' She claps her hands.

'By the way, any sign of my phone yet?'

'No.' She says it in an unnaturally high voice which instantly makes me certain she's the one who's taken it and hidden it on purpose. 'You shouldn't need it.' She frowns at me. 'You know you're not allowed to call the groom, don't you?'

'Yes, I know.' I roll my eyes. Lauren goes back downstairs.

The three hairdressers finish blow-drying Bonnie, Emma and Tilly's hair.

'These are all done. Don't they look great?' Abby says. She stands behind them facing the mirror.

'You all look gorgeous,' I say.

'Why don't you all go down for coffees and we'll finish the last few blow-dries in the kitchen? Let's give the bride to be a bit of breathing space, shall we?'

The hens nod and go downstairs, followed by the three other hairdressers. Abby shuts the bedroom door quietly.

'Thank you,' I sigh.

'It can all get a bit overwhelming, can't it?' Abby rests her hand on my shoulder and looks me in the eye in the mirror.

I nod, swallowing the sudden lump in my throat.

'Please can I borrow your phone to call Jamie?' I whisper, holding my hands together hoping she'll take pity on me.

'You know the rules...' she says, imitating Danielle's sing-song teacher's voice. She grabs her handbag from the bed and digs around in it. 'Lucky for you, I'm a big believer that rules are there to be broken.' She holds her phone up and waggles it at me.

I take it from her like it's a priceless bar of gold.

'You're a lifesaver, thank you.'

9

'Hey Jamie,' I whisper. His mobile is the only number I can remember off by heart apart from my own. The signal isn't great, but hopefully I'll stay connected as long as I don't move around too much. I ask straight away if he received Sarah's text and checked up on Freya. He confirms he spoke to Mum and Freya is absolutely fine.

'So how's it going? I thought you were forbidden from ringing me.' He chuckles.

'I am,' I giggle. 'I needed to hear your voice, so I'm calling from Abby's phone.'

'I miss you too. So what have you been up to?'

'Pampering, party games, food, drink and now I'm having my hair done ready for when we head into town. How about you? Are you at your stag do already?'

'Yeah, a few of us had lunch together at the steak house and now we're going to the comedy club.'

'Have you been drinking already?' The question slips out before I can stop myself.

'Only a couple of small ones. We'll probably finish off at the pub.'

He means whiskies. And I know it'll have been at least double that. But tonight, I have to let it go. It's the one night he should be allowed to drink as much as he likes, but I can't help worrying he'll overdo it and then anything could happen. For other people a few whiskies would be their limit, but for Jamie, it barely touches the sides. I understand it's his coping mechanism for anxiety, but it doesn't make it any easier to cope with.

'Wish I could see you. Is there any way we can secretly meet up?' I can't help wanting to check up on him, but I've asked his best man Joe to keep a close eye. He knows about Jamie's history of depression and the reason why he quit the army so young.

'Wouldn't be fair on everyone else though, would it?'

'I know. Are you going to that pub near the nightclub?'

'I expect so. Look, enjoy yourself with your friends and I'll stick with mine. We've got a whole lifetime of being together,' he says.

'You're right. I can't wait though. I love you.' I send kisses down the line and wish he was here so he could wrap me in his warm strong arms. But my smile drops when the image of the funeral flowers on the lawn crosses my mind. I want to tell him, but he'll insist on going straight to the police to find out if they've got any leads yet, and it will ruin his stag party and my hen night too. No, it can wait. We deserve an evening off to relax and have a bit of fun. I'll tell him about it tomorrow when we get home. I want him to enjoy his evening without a care in the world, if that's possible when we have a two-and-a-half-year-old toddler staying with my parents.

'Hey, everyone gave me some lovely presents.' The last word slurs at the end and my eyelids are starting to feel strangely heavy.

'You sound like you've had a bit to drink already and you're checking up on me!' He laughs. The sudden rise and lack of control in his voice makes it even more obvious he's had more than two drinks. Why can't he ever be straight with me?

'I've only had a few.' I reach for my coffee and take a mouthful. I blink a few times. I do suddenly feel quite drunk. 'By the way, you didn't tell me your cousin Beth was coming. It was so embarrassing not knowing who she was.' My words slur a little more and I can't help but giggle. I wait for Jamie to apologise for not telling me about Beth, but he doesn't answer. 'Anyway, she gave me such a thoughtful gift – it's a framed family photo of you with your mum. She's in it too, with her parents.' I frown, thinking now how odd it is her giving me a photo of someone else's family. I try not to laugh at the strangeness of it. I really have had too many drinks. But it is kind of funny. I mean, the only person I know in the photo is Jamie. I suppose it's really meant to be a present for him.

'You didn't say you had family in Australia or why you'd fallen out with your mum before she died.'

'No,' he says. 'And I don't remember that photo.' He sounds so serious and manages to swerve my question.

'Beth said you were about nineteen.'

He's quiet for a few seconds. I wait for him to speak. 'What else did Beth say?'

Is he annoyed with me? I hope he's not going to go into one of his silent moods.

'She said her mum gave it to her. Thought it would make a lovely gift for us. It's in a hand-carved wooden frame. You look so handsome and smart. She said you were the youngest in your regiment, even though you'd just left the army. Thought I'd like to have it because you were so young. It makes me wish I'd known you then.' I try to cover up the slurred words, but it's difficult. I don't normally get drunk this quickly.

The silence on the phone is palpable.

'Can you hear me? I'm sorry, I've drunk way too much, too quickly and it's suddenly caught up with me.' I wonder if the line has broken up his end or if he's getting annoyed listening to me.

'She seems nice though. Feisty and outspoken but fitting in quite well so far. In fact, she's already hit it off with the girls.'

Jamie still doesn't answer.

'Are you there?' His silence is scaring me. It's never a good sign. 'Okay, I don't think you can you hear me very well, so I'd better go before I get caught.' I chuckle, glancing at Abby listening at the door for anyone coming, expecting Danielle to march in at any moment.

'I didn't invite Beth. She invited herself,' he says at last.

'Oh, she said she'd be made to feel welcome?' I hate catching him out in a fib, but it's not a big deal. 'Anyway, if that's the case she probably wondered why she wasn't invited, especially as you don't have anyone else from your family coming. So I don't mind, honestly.'

Before Jamie can respond, Danielle storms into the room and snatches Abby's mobile from my hand.

10

'You know the rules,' Danielle trills, taking great glee in pressing the button to end the call.

'Spoilsport. It was an important call. I had to speak to Jamie make sure he was okay, and to see if he called Mum to check on Freya,' I groan at her.

Danielle shakes her head, cheeks flushed in her small triumph. Abby reluctantly holds her hand out to take her phone back and drops it in her handbag.

'Right. Come down for cocktails when you're done. And no more sneaky phone calls to the groom.' Danielle waves her finger at me like I'm five years old then marches out of the room, a self-satisfied grin on her face.

'Sorry about that, I'm getting you into trouble too,' I say. Abby tells me not to worry. She finishes curling my hair and sets it with hairspray. I drink back the rest of my coffee, wondering if it's the caffeine that's accelerated the effects of the alcohol on me. I close my eyes, but my head keeps spinning. In the mirror I eye up the bed behind me and wish I could sleep it off, but it would flatten my hair and all Abby's hard work.

After Abby's gone, I shut my eyes for a few minutes. I open them to the sound of a light knocking on the door. Without waiting for an answer, Lauren opens the door and pokes her head round.

'How are you feeling? Are you coming down?' she asks, a big grin on her face. 'We're about to play another game.'

I nod, my eyes still heavy and scratchy. She goes back downstairs. What is she up to? I'll have to drink water for a while to sober up or I'm going to be wrecked before the evening has started.

I drag myself into the en-suite bathroom and gasp out loud. Written on the mirror in red lipstick are the words:

I'M GOING TO KILL YOU

I run out of my room onto the landing.

'Danielle, Sarah, come up here please!' The distress in my tone brings them running to the bottom of the stairs. I gaze open-mouthed at their faces looking up at me, my brain frantically trying to work out who did this.

Lauren is the first one up the stairs, taking two at a time as she often does, closely followed by Danielle and Sarah. They follow me into the bathroom and gasp when they see the threat scrawled on the mirror.

'Who would do this?' Sarah says and puts her arm around me while Danielle takes a photo to show the police.

'Nice try, Megan.' Lauren grins at me.

'What do you mean?' I scowl at her.

'You were here alone so could easily have done this yourself.'

'Why would I? And ruin my favourite lipstick as well? I don't think so.'

'I'm just saying, you were the only one up here.'

Danielle shakes her head. 'That's ridiculous, Lauren. Lots of the girls have been in Megan's room. Any one of them could have done it. Just wait for us downstairs, please.'

Lauren shrugs and leaves the room.

'Shouldn't we tell the police?' Sarah says.

'Not right now, or we'll never get out of here. We could send the photos to the police who are dealing with the funeral flowers,' I tell them.

'But one of your guests *here* must have done this,' Danielle says.

'Maybe it's someone's stupid idea of a joke.' I sigh.

'Nothing about this is funny, Megan. Especially after the flowers this morning,' Danielle says.

'Let's leave it for now, *please*,' I implore them. 'And there's no need to mention it to the others yet either.'

'I expect Lauren has already done that.' Sarah rolls her eyes.

They clean the lipstick off the mirror for me and go downstairs while I finish getting ready. Once I'm dressed and I've retouched my make-up, I head for the stairs to join the others. I can hear the buzz of excitement on the patio as soon as I reach the living room. Everyone claps and cheers when I step outside. I inwardly sigh with relief that Lauren doesn't appear to have told anyone about the writing on the mirror, but I'm still wary, wondering who would dare to write such a threatening message.

All the hens are wearing their party dresses, and everyone has beautifully styled hair and make-up, ready to hit the town. I insisted Danielle ditch the tacky hen party accessories such as matching short bridal veils, T-shirts and feather boas, for more subtle choices, such as our nails being painted the same bright red, and a corsage around the wrist made of faux white pearls and a soft pink rose. The finishing touch is everyone wearing an elegant tiara. Mine says 'BRIDE TO BE' in subtle diamanté letters on the crown.

'We thought we'd give you a taste of your Caribbean honeymoon.' Lauren points to a tray of pink rum punch cocktails in flamingo glasses on the kitchen counter and a zero-alcohol alternative, which looks just as good so I pick one up and take a sip of the ice-cold drink. It'll give me a chance to slow down my alcohol intake. There's a spicy kick on my tongue as I swallow it, so I take another bigger mouthful.

The sun is sizzling hot and seems to have intensified as the day has gone on. We may as well be in Ibiza going by the scene in front of me – strappy brightly coloured dresses, glamorous sunglasses, faux tanned legs, and high-heeled peep-toe sandals. I sit next to Beth on the garden sofa. I feel I ought to keep a closer eye on her after what Jamie said, if he is telling the truth. At least she's made the effort to be here. Invited or not, she's part of his family. It would be rude to turn her away, and anyway, I'd like to get to know her better.

'I say we skip the game and order the taxis now.' I tip the last of my drink into my mouth and reach for another as a waitress carries the tray around. 'I need some food to soak up all this alcohol.' I pretend to tip off the end of the sofa as if I'm already completely drunk. I do feel like I've had too many. As everyone laughs, I feel a hand press on my side, gently pushing me to straighten up. Beth's eyebrows rise at me moving so close to her, but an understanding smile plays on her lips.

'Oh no you don't. Come on. One more game. You promised,' Danielle says in her best child-entertainer voice, trying to make me feel bad while at the same time rousing the group to back her. Sure enough, several voices shout, *Come on, Megan,* and, *One more game.*

Beth leans towards me an inch, head down. 'Wouldn't go

against this lot if I were you,' she says under her breath so only I can hear her. She's smiling at me with that steely confidence she has, and I can't help but smile back. There's something about her that's so alluring. I'm tempted to ask her why she's come if Jamie didn't ask her, but it seems too mean, and I don't want to embarrass her. I'm genuinely curious about her. As she's bold enough to turn up uninvited, she can stay. Maybe she *thought* he did ask her. I mean, what sort of person comes to a party they weren't invited to? Someone who's supremely confident, I'd say.

I didn't invite Beth. She invited herself. Jamie's words keep swirling in my head. Which one of them is telling the truth? Maybe he meant he didn't invite her to the wedding, hence the hen party too. That would explain why her name isn't on the guest list. But *why* wouldn't he want her there? Perhaps she's got a track record of being a party animal, causing trouble, getting too drunk, telling rude jokes. But it's unlikely he'd be bothered by any of that. I think she sounds *fun*.

'Right, everyone has to sit in a circle,' Danielle says, pointing at who should shift their chairs. 'We're going to play Truth or Dare. Over to Lauren who's put this game together for us.'

'I will make a note of what everyone chooses, so there's no cheating.' Lauren holds up a list of our names and has already written a T next to Danielle's name and a D next to her name. 'Once you've chosen, if you refuse to answer the question or do the dare, you will have to complete a forfeit.' Lauren and Danielle can hardly contain their excitement at this and lots of discussion follows as to what forfeits there might be.

Lauren makes a note of everyone's preferences. More people opt for truth questions rather than dares.

'Right. Are we all ready? As the bride to be, Megan, you can go last,' Danielle says. 'Sarah, you're first and as you've opted for truth, here it is: What's your biggest fear?'

'That's easy. It's waking up in the night covered in spiders,' Sarah says and shudders. Noises of disgust erupt from everyone. I brush down my arms at the thought of spiders crawling over my skin.

'I think that's set a rather chilling tone for the game,' Lauren announces, shuddering too. 'Emma, you've also opted for a truth, so here's your question. What's your worst habit?'

Emma presses her index finger to her lip as she thinks. 'Paul tells me it's leaving my nail clippings in a neat pile by the side of the sink.'

'Ew, I think I'm going to vomit.' Beth lurches forwards, pretending to retch. She catches my eye and smiles at me.

'I don't think it's that bad. He's got far worse habits, but I won't disgust you with them.' She laughs.

'Oh, go on,' Bonnie says leaning forward, eyes shining.

'Yeah, just tell us one,' Samantha calls, elbowing Bonnie and they grin at each other.

'Alright, well, he collects the fluff from his tummy button and keeps it in a jar.' Emma pauses and cups her hand to her mouth. 'And worse than that, he's been collecting it since he was seven years old.' She lets out a long groan.

'What the hell?' Lauren shouts and Beth opens her mouth and dry retches. I shake my head at the way they seem to bounce off each other like they're a double act.

'Okay, okay, shall we move on? Lauren, you're next. You've chosen a truth as well. Are you ready for this?' Danielle says.

Lauren's eyes widen. She finishes her drink.

'How many people have you slept with? Note: *people* not *men*.'

'Can you even remember?' Bonnie laughs and Lauren shakes her head as she laughs too.

'Um.' Lauren silently counts on her fingers.

'Don't forget that fireman you met at my party,' Bonnie shouts, 'or that waiter in the Italian restaurant.'

'My best guess is fifty-two,' Lauren says at last.

'It's probably double that,' someone whispers at the back.

'I heard that!' Lauren laughs.

'You're next, Beth,' Danielle says, 'you've opted for a dare.' Beth closes her eyes and selects a question randomly from the pack. Her lips twitch but she doesn't quite smile. She hands it to Lauren who reads it out.

'Hopefully you've chatted enough to everyone to be able to do this one. Ready? Please reveal a secret about someone here but don't tell us their name.'

'Hmmm.' Beth taps her chin, fixing her eyes on every person one by one. No one looks comfortable. She won't know anyone's secrets, so I don't know what they're worried about. I've not spoken to her at length yet, so she can't know much about me, except what Jamie's told her I suppose.

'Okay, so this one excludes Megan.'

I nod, grateful to be left out.

'The secret I have about someone here, is that they've slept with the groom to be.'

A gasp ripples through all the hens. Beth scans around the uncomfortable faces before her. Emma sits on her hands and like Beth, looks directly at Lauren.

'What?' I spit the word out and try to decide if that's guilt on Lauren's face because Emma and Beth are glaring at her like they know something. Maybe Lauren is trying to wind me up having this question included. I try not to show the shock I feel in my expression which will give away how fast my heart is pounding. *Causing trouble where there is none*, comes to mind, something my mum used to say about a spiteful girl at my primary school. But it can't be Beth's fault, she hardly knows me. Lauren must have put her up to this somehow. What if it's true and someone here has slept with Jamie? Lauren's made it clear she wanted him. She wouldn't have slept with him to get revenge, would she? No, of course not. She loves a prank, but she'd never stoop that low. But it does feel like Lauren is pulling Beth's strings to get at me.

A knot of anxiety sits in my chest that I try to swallow down. I don't want anyone to think I'm bothered by what she's said, but I'm struggling to maintain a cheery demeanour. It doesn't help that I feel sleepy; my head is so fuzzy. It must be the alcohol still. I tell myself I don't need to worry; Jamie has always been faithful to me. He cares about me too much to do anything to hurt me. Yet as I scrutinise each face around the room, I feel completely unsettled by Beth's words.

Could one of my friends have betrayed me?

11

'Let's all assume that it's false and Beth's skewed idea of a joke because we don't want to start a hen fight, do we?' Danielle says in a firm voice but with a twinkle of amusement in her eye as she holds up a hand to silence Lauren who tries to protest by interrupting.

'Exactly. I'm guessing it's not true anyway,' Sarah says and Emma nods in agreement. No one else says anything, they all look stunned.

'Right, shall I go next?' Danielle cuts in.

'Good idea,' I say. 'So you've opted for a dare. Let's have a look. How about this one: run outside and belt out the ballad, "The Power of Love" by Jennifer Rush at full volume. We're already outside, so that's perfect. You can sing that. It's one of your favourite songs.'

Danielle looks up to the sky and groans but with a big smile across her face. If anyone can hold a tune, she can. 'Okay, I can do this,' she says and stands up, clearing her throat. She starts singing about the whispers in the morning, holding her palms to her chest, exaggerating the drama of the words as she works up to the lines about her being your lady and you being her man. It doesn't take long for Sarah to open YouTube on her tablet so we can all sing along, standing up doing the same head and arm flicks as Jennifer does in the original video, while imagining we're commanding an audience with our sultry good looks, big hair and shoulder pads.

When the video finishes, we all collapse about laughing at each other and the tension between us dissolves.

'God, I love that song sooo much,' I say, showing everyone the goosebumps on my arms, grateful for the temporary distraction. 'Can I let you all in on a little secret?' My eyes are heavy, still full of tears from the emotion of the lyrics. Danielle hands me a tissue and touches my arm to check I'm okay. They all nod. 'We're going to be walking down the aisle to this song. Isn't that wonderful?'

They all hug me in one big group and just like that, we're weeping together, thinking of our loved ones. Except Lauren and Beth. Lauren is standing a few paces away, lighting a cigarette. It's the first time I've seen her smoke since she arrived. Last time we saw each other, she'd given up. I wave my hand to invite them to join us, especially Beth. I feel bad that we all know each other, and she doesn't know anyone. Lauren takes a drag then balances her cigarette on the end of the brick barbeque and they both come over.

'Look at us, we're soft as anything while the boys are probably busy watching a bunch of strippers right now,' Lauren says, bringing us up short with her usual bluntness.

'I bloody hope not,' I say, and break up the group hug. 'As far as I've been told, they've had a meal, are going to a comedy club then a few drinks at a pub.'

'Doesn't mean there won't be *afters*,' Emma says, elongating the last word and winking at us like she's in a seventies sitcom.

'We could always go and spy on them,' Danielle says.

'No, it's okay. I trust Jamie,' I say firmly.

'Trust is so fragile though, don't you think?' Lauren says with a gleeful glint in her eye. 'It only takes one little crack...'

'All right, thank you Lauren,' Danielle snaps, then she frowns at me so Lauren can't see her face. It takes a lot for her to get annoyed, but Lauren is constantly interrupting the flow.

'Right, who wants a top up?' Sarah says, going round with another tray of cocktails.

'Yes, I'll have another mocktail, thank you.' I take a glass. I thought my head would have cleared by now, but it's still fuzzy.

'Now it's your turn, Megan.' Danielle shakes the bowl of questions. 'You've opted for a truth rather than a dare, so put your hand in and pick a question.'

I stand up and reach into the shallow dish of folded pieces of white paper. There are hardly any left, but I rummage my hand around in a circle a couple of times, feeling the edges of folded paper until my fingers take hold of one. I lift it out and Lauren exaggerates drumming her fingers on the side of the table as I unfold it. Reading the words, I purse my lips and draw air in through my nose, then quickly fold it up again, hoping no one notices. I swallow hard. The video Ryan emailed me fills my mind.

'I don't like that one, I want to choose another one,' I say quickly when I notice Emma has spotted me. I go to drop it back in with the intention of picking another piece of paper before anyone can object, but Danielle playfully slaps my hand away.

'I don't think so. Bride to be or not, we *all* play by the rules.'

'What?' I squint at her. My eyes feel so hot and uncomfortable I could rest my head on the back of the chair and fall asleep. 'But surely you can bend the rules for me; it is *my* party.'

'No. Sorry.' Danielle folds her arms and grins with pleasure at upholding the game rules. Lauren pulls the dish out of her hands and moves it to another table, well out of my reach.

'Well, I'm not answering that.' I drop the piece of paper on the ground.

'If you don't answer the question, you have to pay a forfeit,' Danielle says.

'I can't believe it! This game is so fixed. You lot are meant to be my friends. How have I managed to pick just about the worst possible question?'

'Of course we're your friends, but they are the rules of the game, and we have to stick to them or it's not fair,' Danielle says, and Lauren echoes her words, with a few of the others chiming in. Of course, they say it with smiles on their faces, as though this is all a bit of fun, but the truth is they don't mind humiliating me just a little bit.

'If you really were you'd let me off,' I say sulkily. 'Do it this once, please! I'll buy the first round of drinks.'

'You're buying the drinks anyway, aren't you?' Emma laughs.

I've had enough, I'm done with pleading. I still feel tipsy and so sleepy, even after those sweet mocktails, I'm starting to think I'd rather have a lie down than go to a nightclub.

Lauren picks the piece of paper up from the ground and unravels it. 'I'm asking myself, what's so bad about this question?' She waves the strip of tickertape in the air, as though it's a winning ticket in a raffle, then flashes it in front of Beth who holds it still to read it.

'This should be an easy one.' Lauren nods thoughtfully. 'It only needs a straight-forward answer, Megan.'

Beth taps Emma on the shoulder, and she shows the question to her too.

'Oh... right.' Emma pulls a heavy frown. 'But rules are rules, Megan. It wouldn't be fair to let you off.'

'You're my friends,' I plead again, palms together. Sweat is collecting on the back of my neck.

'Lauren's right though, what's the problem? This is an easy answer for you,' Emma says.

Sarah, then Tilly, followed by a few of the others, ask what it says. I clench my teeth at Lauren's meddling. Typical of her, stirring this up and now everyone is jumping in. I wish she'd kept her big mouth shut. No one else seemed that bothered until she made a big thing of it. Danielle won't like to be seen as being unfair, especially in front of someone we hardly know, so she probably feels obliged to stick rigidly to the rules.

'Okay, calm down everyone.' Danielle holds up her palms.

But it's not Danielle who manages to finally silence everyone, it's Lauren standing up, announcing she's going to read my truth question out loud. She clears her throat and glances at me as she reads it.

'Have you ever been unfaithful to your fiancé?'

12

A hush fills the room. Lauren reads it again, slowly and clearly, doing nothing to hide her glee at being the one to deliver the killer question.

A few people openly gasp, covering their mouths to hide their shock mixed with what looks like a tinge of delight shining in their eyes at such a delicious question. If everyone was sober, they might be more sympathetic, be able to see that it's not amusing at all for me, despite this being a game. Maybe if less alcohol had been consumed, they'd realise what an unacceptable thing this is to ask a bride to be, amusing as it may be to them. It's way too personal. Whatever answer I give, they probably won't believe me anyway, so I'm tempted to tell a lie.

'I've told you, I'm not going to answer that question.' I feel a rush of heat rise from my neck up into my face. 'I can't believe you put this in there, Danielle.'

Her face flushes too as she hurriedly skims through the notes on her clipboard. 'I don't remember that being one of the questions. It was Lauren who organised the game, not me. But as I said, you have to answer it to be fair to the other players, and we have to stick to the rules...'

'Fuck the rules,' I shout and tip the rest of the tiny, folded squares onto the ground.

Danielle's face crumples and she looks as if she's on the verge of tears.

I immediately regret behaving like a child. Lauren ducks into the house without saying anything.

'I'm so sorry, I didn't mean to take it out on you.' I reach for her arm, but she pulls away from me, shooting me a venomous stare.

'Why can't you just play by the rules for once in your life?' Danielle yells at me in a gravelly voice. She immediately looks as stunned as I must do that these words came out of her mouth. She's never spoken back at me like that before. Her face remains frozen in shock, unsure of what I'm going to say or do next.

I stare back at her, unable to respond to her accusation.

'She doesn't need to answer though, does she,' Lauren pipes up as she comes back outside, breaking the deadlock.

At last Lauren is saying something sensible and supportive. She goes over and sits with Beth, where most of the girls have gravitated, bunched together around her chair.

'I'm running this game, thank you Lauren. And *I* think she does need to answer.' Danielle's voice is high and indignant. Her eyes are creased and fixed on me.

Lauren leans forward. Her face morphs from bright and friendly to frowning and serious. 'What I mean is, if you think about it, she's already answered the question.'

We all look at her blankly, so she continues.

'Her reaction to it tells us everything we need to know.'

Her words are a slap in my face. There's a quiet intake of

breath by everyone followed by a flurry of whispering as this revelation sinks in.

'You mean you think she *has* been... unfaithful?' Danielle mouths the words, as though saying them out loud will make them unbearably real.

Lauren's eyebrows rise up. 'Don't you think she protests too much to be innocent?'

I shrink into my chair. How dare she? I can hardly keep my eyes open. Why am I feeling so sleepy?

'Who was it, Megan?' Lauren's eyes are so wide they're bulging. Her voice is muffled, as though I'm submerged in water.

My mouth opens but I don't know what to say. My head is swimming. I've drunk far, far too much and now I can't see any way out of this. I've been cornered by a person I wish I hadn't invited. This is supposed to be my special weekend to celebrate my last days as a free and single woman, but I'm being hated and ganged up on; on trial, ridiculed. I can't seem to stop the heat in my face increasing, giving away how much this is getting to me, revealing my guilt.

'The rules say you have to answer the question or pay a forfeit, so perhaps Megan would rather do that?' Lauren nods, reminding everyone, and they murmur their agreement as though they're the jury.

'Okay, okay. You want the honest truth?' My words are slurring again; my head is thick and fuzzy. Has one of them put something in my drink? 'It happened once. And, I deeply regret it.' My voice is up and down, all over the place. Maybe I'm dreaming this, and I've been transported to a *Hunger Games* spin-off show. I half expect a presenter to pop out at any moment holding a microphone to ask me a load of in-depth questions about what happened and why I did it.

'I don't believe that for a minute. She's saying what you lot want to hear for a bit of gossip,' Danielle says, half laughing.

'Danielle's right, you're the last person who'd cheat.' Bonnie laughs.

'Nice try though.' Sarah winks.

'I am telling the truth.'

'What?' Danielle glares at me like I've just confessed to a murder.

I look up and Lauren's phone camera is pointing at me. 'What the hell are you doing?' I growl as I stride forward and tear it from her hands. The video is rolling, now pointing at my shoes. I press the delete button.

'Nothing, I was just...' Lauren says, stepping back from me, hands up as though I'm about to attack her.

Without another thought, I hurl her phone into the swimming pool and run into the house.

'What is going on with you today?' Danielle yells after me.

I make it to the toilet in time to be sick. When I come out of the bathroom wiping my mouth, I'm surprised to see Beth there ready with a glass of ice-cold water.

'Are you okay?' she asks in a kind voice, low enough for the others not to hear.

'I feel a bit better now, thanks.' I sip the water.

'You poor thing. They really ganged up on you.'

I dab my mouth with the tissue in my hand.

'Danielle can be a right bossy bitch, can't she?' she whispers close to my ear.

I look at her sideways and raise an eyebrow. I appreciate her attempt to make me smile, but I can't get my friends' horrified faces out of my head. They looked so disappointed in me.

She presses something into my hand. 'Take your phone and

check on your daughter, or whatever you need to do.' She nods at the bathroom. 'I won't say anything to the others.'

'How did you get this?' I look down at it, hardly believing she got this for me.

'I saw where Danielle hid it. Pretending someone took it from her bag.' She winks. 'Now hurry or we'll both be for the chop.'

'Thank you so much,' I whisper, gazing into her green eyes. I could hug her so hard right now.

I go back into the bathroom and shut the door.

Standing by the sink, I hold my mobile up to my face, unlocking the screen, then swipe through to cancel airplane mode. A WhatsApp message flashes up, but there's no name. It's from a number I don't recognise. I click it and frown open-mouthed at the words in capital letters.

PAY £5K INTO THIS BANK ACCOUNT TODAY
OR YOUR WEDDING WILL BE TRASHED

13

I draw in a breath at this stomach punch. Who is this from? They can't be serious, can they? That's so much money and who would want to ruin my wedding?

It's not like the emails I've been getting from Ryan. This isn't his style. He doesn't hide behind anonymous threats. He always makes it blatantly clear they're from him and how much he wants me to pay.

I could just pay it to stop whoever it is from ruining the wedding, but what if they want more? My inheritance came through from Aunty Jean a few months ago. Five thousand pounds would barely make a dent in the amount she left me, but I don't see why I should give in to some scumbag. I need to work out who sent this.

I text Mum to check everything is okay with Freya even though Jamie contacted her earlier, because I still feel shaken at what happened this morning. Thankfully she replies straight away saying she's fine. She's been playing in her pop-up princess tent in the garden and now she's in bed. Then I text Jamie checking he's okay. I wait a few seconds but there's no reply.

I unlock the bathroom door and hand my phone back to Beth.

'Thank you. I'm going upstairs to clean myself up,' I tell her.

Beth nods. 'I'll put this back.'

'I really appreciate you doing this for me.' I'm grateful she could see how important it was for me to check on Freya.

I go up to my en-suite bathroom and brush my teeth. I'm reapplying my lipstick when there's a light tapping on the bedroom door.

'Who is it?' I call. The door opens a few inches and Beth looks round.

'I thought you might like a peppermint tea. My mum always says it settles the stomach.' She's holding two mugs so I invite her in.

'Thank you, that's really thoughtful of you,' I say, breathing in the fresh aroma.

She puts them on the coffee table next to the chaise longue at the far end of the room. 'How are you feeling?'

I shake my head, lips pursed tight, but it doesn't stop a rogue tear spilling from my eye. 'I can't believe what just happened out there.' I cup my face in my hands.

Beth quietly shuts the door then comes over and envelops me in a warm hug.

My head is pounding and my eyes sting with tears.

'They're your friends; I'm sure they don't think badly of you,' she whispers.

'I don't know if I can do this.'

'What do you mean?' she says gently and pulls back a little, trying to look me in the eye, but I keep my face turned away.

'This.' I break away from her and open my hands out in front of me. 'Make out everything's all right, that I deserve to be Jamie's wife.'

'Sorry Megan, but I don't understand.' She hesitates, then adds, 'Did you really cheat on him?'

I nod. 'There, Lauren can do her worst now.' I flick my hand in the air.

'She told me how you two met and—'

'How she hoped he'd ask *her* out?' I interrupt, annoyed that Lauren has told yet another person how I apparently stole Jamie from right under her nose.

'Yeah, basically. She said you made the first move. Approached him even though she saw him first and you knew she had her sights on him. Thinks you threw yourself at him, so he didn't have a chance to speak to her.'

'Really? Jesus. That is so unfair.' I laugh bitterly at Lauren's childishness. 'We saw him at the same time; we both commented on how gorgeous he was. She never said anything to me about her hoping he'd ask her out. I didn't realise it was a competition.' I sit on the sofa and Beth sits next to me, nodding sagely, as though she doesn't want to fuel this argument further.

I fold my arms over my chest. 'Jamie has a perfectly good mind of his own, so I think he'd have told me to sling my hook if he hadn't been interested in me.'

'I'm sure you're right and honestly, I'd have been forward like you.' She switches into a conspiratorial whisper. 'More fool her for waiting, I say. I mean, why expect the bloke to do the asking? Spoiler alert: we're capable of making our own decisions.'

'My point exactly, but Lauren's very... traditional. Thinks it makes a woman look cheap if she makes the first move.'

'You say traditional, I say old-school. That is so old-fashioned. I mean who thinks like that any more, except maybe our grandmothers? Even our mothers forged ahead in the fight for equality. I guess some poor souls still want to wait to be asked.

My view is why would you give men all the power? And look what happened, Lauren missed out.'

'Thank you. I'm glad someone understands my point of view. I don't know why she has to keep going on about it. Jamie said she's not his type anyway. Lauren is so out of order bringing this up time after time. It's like she's holding a vendetta against me. No wonder we fell out.' I pick up my mug and drink a mouthful of refreshing tea.

'She does seem to have it in for you. It's a little bit creepy.'

I stare at her, not knowing what to say. Why didn't I realise how much resentment Lauren was still holding against me? 'I invited her to be one of my bridesmaids in good faith, thinking we could leave all this in the past, but she can't seem to do that.'

'What actually happened with this other guy, if you don't mind me asking?' Beth curls her hands around her mug. 'Was it someone you know?' Her eyes scan over my face.

I dip my head and wonder how I can avoid answering.

'I mean as far as I can see, you love Jamie and can't wait to marry him, so why be unfaithful?'

I swallow hard. Beth is so direct I'm half terrified of what she'll say next.

'I... made a big mistake, drank too much and hooked up with my ex, Ryan. A one-night stand. I'm deeply ashamed.'

'Well, we've all been there.' Beth sips her tea, eyes fixed on me over the brim, encouraging me to continue.

'We met up one night a few months back. It was Ryan's birthday, he was on his own feeling down, and I felt sorry for him. He said he missed me, couldn't live without me. I tried to console him and... it just kind of happened.'

'Easily done.' Beth shakes her head.

'My ex can be very... magnetic.'

Beth's eyes widen a touch. 'Sounds like you still have some chemistry between you.'

I feel my face heat up. 'I can't lie, our sex life was wild, but a proper relationship is about more than that, isn't it?'

'I guess so, but the bedroom side of things is pretty important too, for the long-term. Men do love a dominant woman. Did you ever wonder if going back to him was a sign that you should still be together?'

'Absolutely not.' I frown at her suggesting such a thing when I'm about to marry her cousin. 'Things between us hadn't felt right for a long while. He couldn't hold down a job for more than a few weeks and he wasn't always nice to me. He'd storm off and leave me if he didn't get his own way. It didn't matter where we were. Once he left me at a bus stop on my own late at night. Just marched off.'

'That is pretty shitty behaviour. How long were you with him?'

'A couple of years on and off. And he's terrible with money, mainly because he hardly ever has any. And he has a jealous streak. Jamie is nothing like that. He's sweet and kind and gentle.' I smile just thinking about how lovely Jamie can be. Most of the time. Except when he's had too much to drink.

'I should have told Jamie what happened straight away, but as you may know, he struggles with his mental health, and I knew he'd take it really badly.' I pause. Beth seems to really get that I didn't mean for this to happen. 'Can I tell you something else in confidence?'

'Of course you can, I'm not going to tell him or anyone else.'

'Thank you, because he'd probably hate me telling anyone this, but he struggles a bit... in bed.'

'What do you mean?' She tips her head to one side.

'Jamie's libido is quite low because of the anti-depressant

medication. Don't get me wrong, he insists he still fancies me, and I do believe him, but it doesn't always *feel* that way.'

'Why's that?'

'He doesn't often ejaculate, says he's not able to, but it makes it feel like he hasn't enjoyed it, no matter what he tells me.'

'That's completely understandable.'

I knew she'd get it. 'Ryan knew exactly how to push my buttons and make me feel desired again. And once he'd started kissing me there was no going back.'

'These things happen in the heat of the moment. I think you did the right thing not telling Jamie. It's not always wise to confess, just to make yourself feel better. You do have to consider how it will affect the other person.'

'But how could I have been so weak and given into temptation? I feel so awful about it.'

'Hey, you need to go easy on yourself.'

'I've been trying to put it behind me, but how can I, now all of my friends know?'

'Your friends aren't going to blab.'

'But you're Jamie's cousin. Aren't *you* going to tell him what I did?' I sip my tea, feeling the steam on my already hot face. I could hardly blame her for wanting to be loyal to her family.

'No, of course not. It's not my secret to tell for a start.'

'I don't want to hurt his feelings or give him any reason to walk away from me. Maybe that's selfish. Do you think he'll still want to be my husband after this?'

'Of course he will. He'll forgive you because he clearly loves you. You can't throw everything away because of one mistake. Christ, if we berated ourselves for every little infidelity, no one would ever get married, would they?'

I let out a deep sigh and rub my palms together. It feels good to talk about it. I've only confided in Emma and she didn't have any solutions.

'Have you thought about telling Jamie the truth? It's probably not wise starting a marriage with a secret as big as this.'

'I know I'll have to tell him at some point, before someone else does, but this would be a huge blow to him. And we have our daughter to think about. We're happy.' I start to cry, and she puts her arm around me. 'I can't believe I did such a stupid thing.'

'And how did you leave it? Does this Ryan know you're getting married?' Beth frowns.

'He does, but now he won't leave it alone. He keeps sending me messages, begging me to go back to him.'

'Shit, Megan. This needs sorting out before your big day.' Her face is creased with concern. She looks genuinely worried for me.

'I know,' I say. 'And now he's blackmailing me.'

14

'Oh, Megan. What's he blackmailing you over?' Beth touches my arm, looking right at me. Tears prick my eyes.

'I didn't realise at the time, but Ryan filmed us having sex that last time. He always talked about filming it just for us to watch, and I always refused. But now I realise he got me drunk and slept with me just to... to get a memento and to exploit me.' I screw my face up at being used like that during such an intimate moment.

'What a bastard thing to do.' Beth puts her arm around my shoulders and pulls me to her.

The shame has been overwhelming at times, especially keeping it from Jamie. This rush of emotion opening up about it, is such a relief.

It's a minute before I recover enough to gently pull away. I'm suddenly embarrassed for telling Beth, letting myself get so upset in front of a woman I hardly know. But she is so easy to talk to. A virtual stranger on the cusp of becoming part of my family. I feel I can trust her. I sense she won't judge me in the same way as some people who know me might.

'What have you done about it up till now?' she asks.

'I told him to leave me alone when he first started sending me messages, but it made him worse. Now he won't stop and he's threatening to show the video to Jamie before the wedding.' I can't mask the desperation in my voice. I've been mulling over what to do for so long.

'That'll be because you replied to him. It showed him you were listening – he knew he had your attention. I'm afraid any response is like oxygen to someone like that.'

'I tried to ignore him, but he wouldn't stop, then he became nasty and sent me a clip of the video, demanding a large amount of money to stop him forwarding it to Jamie.' I press my fingers to my temples.

'Little toe rag. Like he really wants *you* back. Sounds to me as though he knows that's not going to happen, he just wants to make money out of you now to punish you.'

I nod, tears in my eyes.

'I think I can help you.'

'Seriously?'

'Too right. I've dealt with something similar myself not many years back with my ex. I thought I knew him, but he turned into a different person as soon as we got serious. He became abusive and controlling, and I realised I was trapped. Took every ounce of courage for me to fight back and escape.'

'I'm so sorry, that sounds terrifying.'

Beth nods. 'So I'm not afraid to tell this scumbag to back the hell off on your behalf. In fact, I'll enjoy it.' She knocks back her last mouthful of tea.

'Would you really do that for me?' I wipe my nose on a tissue and look her in the eyes. She's exactly the sort of person Ryan would listen to because she won't give him any other choice.

'You bet I will. He sounds like a real piece of work.'

'Thank you. That's so kind of you.' She really seems to understand what I'm going through and genuinely wants to help me. It feels surprisingly safe speaking to her so frankly. She's part of Jamie's family after all.

'What he did to you is cowardly. I know the type.' She nods, sagely.

'Thank you,' I say again, grateful that she came today and took the time to listen to me and offer her help. 'You're staying for the wedding, aren't you?'

'Of course. I wouldn't miss it.'

I've been so close to telling Danielle everything, but I didn't want to burden her with this. And deep down, much as I love her, I think she'd judge me. Besides, she wouldn't have any idea what to do to stop Ryan without potentially making the situation worse. But here's someone who I know has the balls to put him in his place.

There's a loud knock and Danielle opens the door and looks in. She stares at me then Beth and doesn't speak for a second, probably surprised to see us chatting alone together.

'Are you two coming down? The taxi's on its way,' Danielle says.

Beth springs out of her seat. 'I'll let you finish getting ready.'

'Thanks for helping me,' I say.

She smiles at me and follows Danielle downstairs.

Hiding what I did from Jamie has been eating me up. I can't have him finding out my secret. Who knows how he'll react. He could get angry and never speak to me again or he could go into a meltdown and harm himself. Every scenario I think of is not a good one.

I need to stop someone else telling him first.

15

I check myself in the mirror and join the others downstairs. Lauren is hanging back on her own.

'I'm really sorry for kicking off at you, Lauren. I promise I'll buy you a new phone.'

'I just wanted to take a few photos otherwise we'll have nothing to look back on.' She sounds genuinely upset, like she really wanted to capture memories of today for me.

'That's true.' I turn to Danielle who is collecting everyone's mobiles as they go out of the front door. 'Shouldn't at least a couple of us have our phones tonight, for safety if nothing else?'

'I've got mine and Beth has hers. As long as we all stick together, we'll be fine.'

Parked out the front is a bright pink limo. The driver, who looks like an extra from the Dreamboys, is waiting for us in an immaculate white sailor's suit and cap, holding the door open.

'After you,' Danielle says. We all troop out and climb in, and I wonder if there'll be enough room for us all. Lauren has brought an oversized handbag with her, and I really want to tell her to leave it behind, bring something smaller, but there's plenty of room once we're all in. The driver opens a bottle of bubbly and hands it to Danielle to pour into plastic flutes laid out on a tray. I really don't want any more to drink, so I have a half measure.

'Let's all raise a toast to Megan, wishing you a happy hen night!' Danielle says as the limo slowly pulls away.

Everyone clinks their plastic glasses and repeats, 'Happy hen night!'

'Bunch up so I can get a group photo,' Lauren says, kneeling on the carpeted floor. Beth passes her mobile phone to Lauren, and we all squash together and smile, holding our drinks up. I try to look happy, but right now I just want to lie down and nap. I don't know what's wrong with me, although I feel a lot better now I've been sick. I'm not usually such a lightweight with alcohol. I open a bottle of carbonated water and drink that down. It takes the edge off any lingering nausea. All the hens are chatting ten to the dozen and I sit quietly and shut my eyes. I must drift off to sleep briefly because I dream about Jamie running across a field. He's shouting at me to wait, holding Freya in his arms, saying he needs to warn me about something. My head drops to the side, and I jolt awake.

'Are you okay?' Emma touches my wrist. Her face is screwed up with worry. 'You were groaning,' she whispers.

'Oh God, was I?' But she's not looking at me any more; her eyes are fixed to the left, where Beth stands up and conducts all the hens to sing 'Wonderwall'.

'My mum used to play this all the time,' I say, picturing a younger version of Mum and Dad. 'One of my favourite songs when I was little.'

Emma joins in the chorus, and I do too, all of us exaggerating the 'saves me' part.

The thirty-minute journey from the Peaks doesn't seem to take long, and before we know it we're pulling up outside the Italian restaurant in the Northern Quarter of Manchester.

We all troop out onto the pavement and Danielle thanks the driver. We've decided we can book normal taxis back to the holiday cottage later.

Lauren leads the way into the restaurant. We're shown to our table straight away. I'm desperate for my phone. I've not been without it for this long in ages.

I choose a vegetarian lasagne and salad and feel much better once I've eaten. Perhaps I felt off because I was hungry and didn't realise. I still go easy on the wine, mixing it with soda water because I don't want to get drunk again and not be able to remember what I'm doing or know what's going on.

'Happy hen party!' the head water says, carrying a big pink cake towards me. Cliff Richard's cheesy song 'Celebration' comes out of the speakers at full blast. All the hens cheer and whistle as the sparklers fizz on top of the cake. *Megan, Bride to Be* is piped across the top in bold pink icing sugar.

'Speech, speech!' Lauren calls and a few others echo her words and slap the table in unison.

I stand up and thank them all for coming to celebrate, then I cut into the cake and the waitress takes it away to slice into portions. It's the last thing I feel like eating but I make the effort and eat as much as I can. The icing is far too sweet for me and brings back the nausea.

We leave a generous tip and stroll along the pavement arm in arm until we reach the nightclub. It's still relatively early at 8 p.m., but nevertheless we go in and are shown to our double VIP booth which has been specially decorated with a hen party banner and props. So much for us looking sophisticated. There's a neon lit bucket waiting for us with a tall sparkler inside, fizzing next to a bottle of champagne on ice and a bottle of Jägermeister. As we settle in, a waiter brings over a tray of Jägerbombs to start us off. I'm not sure how I'm going to survive the night.

I stick to the sparkling water and join the others on the dance floor. Random people give me the thumbs up and when I look bewildered at their attention, they point to the top of my head, and I remember I'm wearing a tiara with the words 'Bride to Be' on it. I feel like a fake. Why did I think lying to Jamie was a good idea? But what happened was not entirely my fault. I'm worried he won't believe me when I tell him. He won't want to marry me, and if he ends up calling off the wedding, what is the point of my hen do? I pull the tiara off.

'I need to sit down,' I say to whoever might be listening and go back to our booth which is empty. All the other girls are either on the dance floor or standing at the bar. I finish my glass of water and wander off on my own to find the bathroom. It's packed but I don't mind queuing. I like to hear other girls' chatter, about their boyfriends or a man they've seen who they think is a hot dancer. It reminds me of what my life was like before becoming a mum to Freya. My priorities were so different then. How old I feel amongst all these twenty-year-olds.

It's not long before I'm near the front of the line. A woman in a slinky black dress tries to squeeze past me out of the bathroom. I move aside to give her more space but then realise she's looking straight at me with a heavy frown. She looks genuinely worried.

'Are you with that girl with black hair and green eyes?' A cloud of warm whisky breath lands on my face.

'You mean Beth?' I move my head back a touch.

'Is that what she calls herself now?' The woman puts a hand to her mouth and croaks a laugh, shaking her head. Nicotine has left yellow stains on her fingers.

I frown, not sure what to say.

'I'd steer well clear of that one if you value your sanity,' she says in a lyrical accent. And with that she turns her head and strides out of the bathroom, and I'm left wondering what on earth she means.

16

A waiter is arriving with a round of cocktails when I get back to our table.

'I said I didn't want any more alcohol,' I say to Lauren, a bit too briskly.

'I know, I know, which is why we ordered you another mock-tail,' she says, rolling her eyes at the others.

'Thanks, which one is it?'

'A virgin rainbow cocktail. I liked the look of it.'

Everyone laughs. I walked right into their joke. Presumably I'm the least virgin bride ever. She turns away from me.

'Did you see that hot guy who just tried to hit on me,' I hear Lauren say to Samantha. 'He used to be in our year at school.'

'Did he? Where is he then? You didn't turn him down did you?' Samantha says.

'Not exactly. He only bloody called me Megan didn't he.'

'Oh no, you mean...' Samantha says.

'Yeah, funny how people think we look alike but I bet she never gets mistaken for me.'

I pretend I didn't hear. I can't help what people think.

'You might want to cheer up a bit, Megan, you don't want to bring the mood down with your long face. This party is for you after all,' Lauren says to me with a false smile. I wonder where she gets the gall to be so rude to me.

'Thanks for that.' I sit away from her and sip my red, orange and blue layered drink through two straws. It's delicious and soon I'm on a second one and at last I'm beginning to enjoy myself.

'Are you coming?' Emma asks, holding out her hand to me to join her. Sarah, Danielle and the others are on the dance floor again. When I try to stand up, I stagger to one side, almost twisting my ankle, so I sit down again.

'I thought there wasn't any alcohol in those.' I point to the empty glasses.

'We specifically asked for no alcohol, didn't we?' Lauren says to Beth. The tiniest hint of a smile passes her lips, but Beth's face is blank.

'Well, I feel tipsy. In fact, I don't feel well at all.' I press my hand to my chest, suddenly feeling sick at the back of my throat.

'Do you want me to help you to the loo?' Lauren stands up.

'I've just come back from there,' Beth cuts in, 'and they're rammed. How about going outside? Then you can come back in when you feel better without everyone knowing you've thrown up.'

'The fresh air will probably help too,' Lauren adds and Beth nods.

I try to spot Danielle, but I can't see her on the crowded dance floor. I'd be much happier if she was with me. But I don't have time to wait. I lurch forward and Lauren and Beth are immediately on either side of me, each linking an arm through mine, guiding me outside.

I vaguely hear one of them say something to the staff at the front desk. A woman in a polka dot shirt checks our wrist bands and says we can go out and come back in.

As soon as we're outside in the warm evening air, Lauren starts laughing uncontrollably, leading me down the street, but I need to stop, I'm going to throw up. They stand me at an open dustbin and the stench coming off it makes my stomach heave. I'm sick in the bin and down the side. Beth holds my hair back. I don't understand why Lauren is laughing at me.

Beth lets go of my hair and holds my wrists tight.

'What are you doing?' I mumble and spit a long trail of vomit and saliva from my mouth.

Lauren crouches on the pavement and rummages through her bag. She takes out a fluffy pair of handcuffs. The type you can buy from Ann Summers. My stomach turns over. She's planned this. I wonder what else she's brought with her. I shiver. But how has Beth got involved?

'Please don't,' I whimper, begging them to stop, but they're laughing so hard they're leaning into each other.

Between them they pull my arms behind me and handcuff my wrists around a streetlamp so there's absolutely no chance of me getting away. Even though it's a warm evening, I start shivering. My head is pounding but I'm no longer queasy or drunk, I'm fully alert.

A group of men and women pass us, and I shout, 'Help me, please!' But I don't think my voice is as loud as I think it is because they barely turn my way. Lauren and Beth shake their heads, laughing like this is okay because it's just a couple of friends playing a silly joke. The people go from looking vaguely concerned to smiling and they keep walking by. I start to cry. How can Lauren think this is funny? We've been friends for years. I'd never do anything like this to her. Why is Beth letting her lead her on like this? Jamie was the one who was worried he might get a few tricks played on him. Neither of us thought it would happen to me. He'd be as shocked and upset as I am.

'Why are you doing this to me?' I say to Lauren. She shakes her head, the smile mixed with something else; is it spite, some sort of twisted revenge for me being the one who Jamie wanted to go out with, get engaged to and marry? Maybe Beth is one of those people who jumps on board whatever's going on, with any old wild behaviour.

'Please stop, this isn't funny.' I try to sound firm but reasonable and calm. I tell myself I ought to see the funny side of this, but none of it feels remotely amusing. It feels wrong and a breach of trust, abusive even.

'Oh bless, Megan's not enjoying herself. She wants us all to pander to her every whim and this isn't one of them,' Lauren says.

'Please, please stop,' I sob.

'Such a shame. What would Jamie think of you now?' Lauren says, taking a photo of me on Beth's phone.

'No, please don't,' I beg, hearing my own whiny voice which will probably egg her on.

'Oh no, oops, I shouldn't have done that. I've only gone and uploaded it to all my social media.'

'That's not in the rules,' Beth chides her mockingly.

When will the others realise three of us are missing? What if they don't come outside to find us? They could leave me here and no one else would know where I am. I could be here all night. It's going to get cold later. I'll be vulnerable to weirdos and perverts standing here tied up.

The pub where Jamie is having his stag do is just a couple of streets away. If he walked past me now, I'd be so embarrassed in front of him and all his friends. He'd be angry with Beth – he'd tell her this behaviour is out of order.

Lauren reaches into her bag and takes out a can of cola. She opens it and tells Beth to hold her phone up as she steps back from the fizz, which shoots out everywhere. Just when I naively expect Lauren to put the can to her lips and take a sip, she stretches out her arm and pours it all over the top of my head, drenching my hair, arms and chest. I screech a gasp and splutter at the shock of cold liquid over my eyes, nose and mouth, instinctively attempting to save myself but my useless hands are tied behind me. The sticky drink bubbles down my body, through my dress, fizzing like it's acid eating into my skin. I shake and flick my head of sopping hair to stop it stinging my eyes.

Lauren snatches the phone from Beth; both are laughing and joking while they're filming.

What are they going to do to me next?

17

'Now to add the cherry on top, so to speak,' Lauren says to Beth. She digs in the bag again and takes out two small but weighty-looking paper bags of something. It can't be what I think it is, can it?

'Tell me what that is. Please don't do this.'

'Ready on three?' Lauren grins at Beth, completely ignoring me. They nod to each other, acting like they've known each other for years.

'What are you going to do?' I can't keep the panic from my voice. I twist my whole body one way then the other, trying to wriggle free. A group of teenage boys leer at me as they stride past, all bunched together as one, making lewd hand gestures. I can't even cover my face. I can only dip my head in the hope that they won't remember me, but I'm sure one of them held up their phone to film it and another clicked snaps of me. I'll be all over social media by the end of the day and I'll never be able to show my face again. If it goes viral, I'll never live it down. How will Jamie cope with the shame?

'Now!' Lauren shouts, holding the phone up as she and Beth

lunge towards me laughing and whooping. They empty the small bags of white powder all over me creating a big dust cloud. I close my eyes and mouth, trying not to breathe it in, but it goes up my nose and although I try not to inhale it, I cough and splutter. I daren't open my eyes to see exactly what they're doing.

'What the hell is going on here?' Danielle shouts, and I hear footsteps running towards me.

'What have you done to her?' Sarah's voice is loud, even though it's further away, but she is pounding the pavement, approaching from the same direction.

'Spoilsports,' Lauren yells as she runs away in the other direction. I can't tell if Beth has gone with her, then I feel her hot breath on my ear and she whispers, 'Sorry,' then runs away too.

'I'll go after them,' I hear Emma say.

I try to open my eyes, but the flour is dry and weighing heavily on my lids. I desperately want to wipe it away but I'm worried it will go into my eyes. Someone is approaching me and because I can't see who, I stiffen with fear. Whoever it is is unlocking the handcuffs and finally I can wipe my eyes and squint at who has saved me.

'You poor thing. Look what they've done to you; you must be frozen.' Danielle takes both my hands in hers, rubbing the skin, trying to warm them. It's dark now although there's light from the shop windows and streetlamps.

'I want to go home,' I whisper, my lips cracked. I attempt to rub down my arms but the flour and cola have congealed and turned to glue on my dress and skin. I'm frozen and can't stop shivering. My teeth are chattering. I cry again, thinking of Freya at my parents', how upset she'd be if she saw me like this. I'm supposed to stay safe for her; she needs me.

'I'm going to hail a taxi, get Megan back to the cottage,' Danielle tells Sarah.

I'm so grateful I could kiss her.

'I'll go and grab your stuff, tell the others what's happened, that a few of us are leaving,' Sarah says.

'You don't need to come if you don't want to,' I say. 'And tell the others to stay and enjoy themselves.'

'I will do, but I want to come with you. I'm not in the mood to carry on partying after what's happened to you. In fact, I'm bloody furious. No one said anything to me about playing pranks.' Sarah glances at Danielle and she shakes her head.

'I didn't know either.'

'Does someone have a coat I can borrow please?' I ask, barely recognising my own voice it's so small.

'Here, borrow my jacket for now, I'll go and see if Bonnie will lend you her faux fur.' Sarah shoulders off her light cotton cropped bolero. It hardly covers a thing, but at least it's something and I appreciate the offer more than I can possibly express right now.

'How did you unlock the cuffs?' I ask Danielle.

'They weren't actually locked; it's just you couldn't reach them. They must have known that we'd come out looking for you. Just as well, otherwise I'd be calling the police.'

'Have you tried texting Emma to see if she caught up with them?'

A moment later Danielle's phone pings. 'Emma followed them; they've gone in the Drunken Sailor.'

'But that's where Jamie is having his stag.'

18

'Of course.' I tap my forehead. 'Beth would know where her cousin is holding his stag do. I didn't think. Lauren's probably gone to brag to him about what they did to me. Let's get a cab there, I need to stop them.'

'Are you crazy? Leave them; we need to get you home,' Danielle says.

I try to hide my teeth beginning to chatter. I'm soaked to the skin and can't seem to warm up. My hair is flat and wet. I must look a total mess.

'I can't let Lauren ruin Jamie's night too, and who knows what she'll tell him.'

'Then we're coming with you.' Danielle sticks her arm out for a cab.

Sarah comes back out a few minutes later with Bonnie's faux fur and my clutch bag. There's not much in it, a couple of twenties rolled up, and a cherry-coloured lipstick. I've never been so grateful to see her fluffy coat because it's long and warm. I hand Sarah's cotton one back to her and slip Bonnie's coat on and wrap it around myself.

It's not long before a mini cab pulls up. Danielle sits in the front passenger seat, and Sarah and I sit behind her. I'm still shaking all over but don't feel so exposed.

Danielle's phone pings.

'Is that Emma?' I ask. 'Has she spoken to them?'

But Danielle is silent. She tuts but the sound is barely noticeable. She shoves her phone in her bag.

'What is it, what did she say?' I ask.

'It can wait. You've been through enough today, what with the flowers on the lawn this morning and the hateful message on the mirror. I think we should just go back to the cottage.'

'No. We're going to the stag party right now.' I sit forward and catch the driver's eye in the mirror. He gives me one nod. 'Tell me what Emma said. If it's something bad I'd rather know.' But deep down my chest is fluttering about what it might be.

Danielle takes her phone out of her bag again and turns in her seat. She opens her mouth, eyes fixed on the screen, but nothing comes out and she shuts it again. Then she suddenly says, 'It's Lauren. Emma's taken pictures to show you otherwise she thinks you won't believe her.'

'Photos of what?' I frown.

'Lauren. She's all over Jamie.'

'Show me, please!' I say through clenched teeth. Danielle reluctantly turns her phone screen towards me. In the photo, taken from a distance, Lauren's arms are draped around Jamie's shoulders and she's kissing his cheek. He's turned his head to the side to avoid her lips landing on his.

'Of all the people to do this to me, it had to be her, didn't it? No wonder I'd cut her out of my life.' I'm fuming for trusting her.

'She's a nasty piece of work, isn't she?' Sarah says.

Danielle swipes through a few more photos of Lauren with Jamie and his friends at the bar, knocking back tequila shots.

'Why did you invite her? You haven't spoken to her for ages, have you?' Sarah says.

'We'd started chatting on social media and I told her Jamie and I were getting married. She seemed genuinely pleased for us. I honestly thought we'd moved past this, but it seems like she hasn't changed.'

'And what about Beth just turning up uninvited?' Danielle puts her phone away.

'I know, but I couldn't turn her away because she's Jamie's cousin and she's a nice person when you speak to her, although Lauren's been using her to get at me.'

'Lauren's ruined your evening and now they're playing drinking games with the groom to be at *his* stag do. They're meant to be here with you, with us.'

'But hang on, Beth wasn't in any of the photos. Text Emma, ask her where Beth is.'

Danielle taps out the text and hits send.

'When I spoke to Jamie earlier, he said he didn't invite Beth, she invited herself.'

'Oh!' Sarah frowns.

'But I don't know if I entirely believe him, because if she knew where both parties are being held, he must have told her, mustn't he?'

'Who knows.' Danielle crosses her arms. 'What I do know is, Beth can be quite annoying and loud.'

'But only when Lauren encouraged her. I thought she seemed to be getting on well with everyone,' I say.

'Well for what it's worth, I like her, and I agree she gets on with all of us,' Sarah says.

'Although isn't giving the bride a photo of the groom to be with herself in it a bit strange?' Danielle's eyebrows lift.

'I thought so too at first, but it was a nice family photo that

I'm sure Jamie will appreciate more than me,' I say. 'A bit of an odd present maybe, but kind of sweet too.'

'Emma's texted back. She says there's no sign of Beth. Thinks she must have gone back to the club or maybe to find you.'

I nod, not surprised. 'She probably thought Lauren's vendetta against me had gone too far.'

'Here you are,' the taxi driver says, pulling up outside the Drunken Sailor. Danielle pays him and we all climb out.

Sarah catches my arm as I'm about to steam in at full speed. 'Hey, maybe don't go in all guns blazing. See what Lauren's up to first.'

I stand still and pull the coat tightly round me and take a deep breath. 'You're right.'

They follow me to the main door, and I peer through the glass pane. I can't see anyone I recognise, so I slowly push the door open, and we go in.

It's busy with couples of all ages and groups of people at tables or standing around the bar, which stretches right around the corner. There's no sign of Jamie, Lauren or any of his friends. I move through the crowd and towards the far side of the bar where the music is louder. A large group of people are laughing and clapping, standing in a semi-circle. I spot Jamie's best man, Joe, his head towering above most other people's. He moves and through a gap I catch a glimpse of someone in the middle, holding a glass of beer, their other arm in the air, swaying to an Amy Winehouse song, 'You Know I'm No Good'.

'I think that's Jamie,' I exclaim.

'What's going on? Who's he with?' Danielle shouts above the music. She's as short as I am, and neither of us can see much more over the rows of people.

'I can see feathers and sequins. I think it's a dancer,' Sarah says, straining on her tiptoes to see.

My stomach tightens.

'There's Emma.' Sarah points. She's standing with her back to us, clapping along with everyone else. Danielle texts her and she immediately looks round, waves and comes trotting over.

'What are you lot doing here? I thought you were going back to the cottage.' Her eyes are wide from being in the dim light.

'What's going on, and where's Lauren?' I try to move past her, but she holds my arm, stopping me.

'You really won't want to see this, Megan.'

'Why not, what is it?'

Emma glares at Danielle and Sarah as if it's their fault for bringing me here, then she looks me right in the eye. 'You're really not going to like it.'

'Just tell me. What has Lauren done now?'

'Someone has booked Jamie a stripper; well, more of a burlesque dancer.'

'You mean Lauren organised this?'

'We don't know if it was her. Joe thinks it could have been one of the lads.'

'I told Jamie, no lap dancing clubs and no strippers.' I try to swallow the lump in my throat and twist out of her grip.

'Joe swears he didn't know anything about it.'

'Where is Lauren? I'm going to kill her.' As I speak, we're all distracted by several wolf whistles.

'I don't know, I saw her over the other side somewhere. Did Danielle show you the photos? She was all over Jamie.' Emma takes her phone out of her pocket.

'I saw.' I sense her losing her grip on me and take the chance to push past her, deep into the crowd.

I hear Emma and Danielle calling my name, but I'm being jostled around in the sea of people, their surprised faces, the stench of beer breath wafting around me as I elbow my way to the front.

When I get there, I stand stock-still, staring with my mouth open. A woman in a tasselled black-and-red basque and suspenders is dancing erotically to Amy Winehouse in front of Jamie, her back to me. He is completely mesmerised by her as he gyrates his hips, mirroring her moves in a sexy way I've not seen him do before. A bustle of black lace and feathers jiggles as she sways then shimmies her chest forward, showing off her backside and thighs where pencil straight lines run the length of her stockings, emphasising her legs down to a pair of bright red stilettos. On her head a feathered headdress fans outwards from a jewelled mask which covers her whole face except her eyes. She steps one leg up on a chair and unclips her stocking. Slowly she rolls it down her thigh.

'What the hell is going on here?' I shout in a shrill voice. No one seems to hear me, so I step forward and say it again, louder this time. Jamie seems to snap out of a trance when he realises it's me and comes to a staggering halt. The dancer swings round aghast. The crowd gasps as one and then falls silent.

'What are you doing here?' Jamie's words are slurred. He's absolutely bladdered. I'm suddenly aware of how bad *I* look wearing Bonnie's novelty fur coat, my hair covered in Coke and flour, and eyeliner and lipstick smudged across my face.

'I came to see for myself what was going on. Lauren was throwing herself at you and kissing you. Where has she scuttled off to?' I sweep a look around the room. No one makes a sound. 'And now I find you with this.' I indicate to the dancer, who puts her hands on her hips.

'Here she is,' Danielle says, pushing Lauren towards me.

'You're such a killjoy, Megan, it was just a bit of fun,' Lauren says.

'And was it you who booked him this cheap stripper?'

The dancer crosses her arms and comes right up to me, so

close I can smell her sickly perfume. For a couple of seconds, I'm confused.

'Ha! It's actually your worst nightmare,' Lauren jeers.

Without warning I reach up and grab the mask from the dancer's face, scratching her skin with my nails. She shoves me in the chest, and I stagger back but manage to stay on my feet. The crowd lets out another gasp.

'Christ, it's you,' Jamie says and backs away, a mix of fear and disgust on his face. 'Keep her away from me,' he yells.

'Beth? What's going on?' I take a step towards her. She looks completely different in her costume and heavy make-up.

'I'm sorry I wanted to tell you,' Beth says to me.

'Why are you doing this?' I blink at her, trying to take in that this is the same person I was confiding in barely two hours ago.

'I was booked for this job, but I didn't know it was for Jamie at first, I promise you.' She looks me directly in the eye and says quietly, 'He's lied to you.'

'What do you mean? I don't understand.'

'You still don't get it, do you?' Lauren says. 'She isn't his cousin Beth.'

'What?' I frown at Jamie, hoping he might answer, but he has an expression on his face like a truck is about to hit him.

'I'm sorry, it's true. My real name is Brooke.' She's serene and composed as though explaining this is an everyday occurrence.

'So if she's not your cousin, who is she?' I narrow my eyes at Jamie.

'She's my bloody ex-girlfriend,' he shouts, 'and you need to get her out of here right now!'

20

'Your ex?' My legs wobble and Danielle and Sarah catch hold of my arms. The crowd breaks out into frenzied chatter as Brooke pushes through them towards the bar and people gradually start to move away.

'Jamie, is this true?' I'm hoping he'll offer some further explanation because it feels like I don't know him at all right now. With everything else that's gone on tonight, this is hard to stomach. I never thought he'd lie to me about something like this; dancing with a stripper behind my back. The problem is, as soon as the drinks start to flow, he loses the ability to say no.

'Megs, Megs, Megs,' he says, coming forward. Danielle and Sarah move away, and he takes hold of my hands, swaying us from side to side as though proving he dances with everyone, except it feels more like I'm helping to stabilise him.

'Why haven't you mentioned her before?' I ask.

'Because she's someone I was with eons ago. You need to tell her to leave, she's dangerous,' he says under his breath. 'Her being here is a shock to me too. One of those bastards organised this,' he says, jabbing his finger in the direction of his group of mates.

'We talked about what we agreed was acceptable and strippers was on the "no" list for both of us. As for exes...' I shake off his hands and glare at him.

'I honestly thought she was my cousin when you said a girl called Beth was at your hen do. If you met the real Beth, you'd see what a right little scallywag she is. How was I to know it was my ex pretending to be her, playing games with us?'

I don't know what to say.

'Why are you two here in the first place?' Danielle says to Lauren. 'You're supposed to be at Megan's hen night not Jamie's stag party.'

Lauren's face is blank. She looks pale, like she might throw up from drinking too much alcohol. Jamie's friends drag him away by his arms to re-join his party and he pretends to protest as though he can't do anything to stop them.

'Answer the question, Lauren,' Danielle snaps. 'You've ruined Megan's hen night.'

'Why do you always blame me for everything?' Lauren yells at us and storms off.

I swallow hard and slump on a stool at the bar next to Brooke, deflated that she's let me down. I trusted her with my secret. 'Why did you pretend to be Jamie's cousin?'

Not looking at me, she picks up a glass of cola and takes a sip, ice cubes rattling. 'I didn't think you'd let me in if I told you I was his ex.'

My breathing quickens. Danielle and I glare at each other.

'You're right, I wouldn't. But why did you want to gate-crash my hen party? That is not okay.'

'I saw photos of you on Jamie's Instagram and I wanted to know who you were. This seemed like a good way to get close to you, without you finding out who I was.' She bows her head, sips her drink.

'Do you realise how creepy that is?' Danielle pulls a face of disgust.

From the moment Brooke arrived she's been making friends with my friends, finding out things about me, encouraging me to take her into my confidence.

'I can't believe you had the audacity to do that.' I stand, scraping my stool back. 'You've lied to my face, pretended to be part of Jamie's family so I would trust you, and you're not even sorry.'

'I am, honestly, but I wanted to find out what you were like. Get to know the real you.'

'Do you know how weird that sounds? You even lied about tonight. You should have told me you were coming here to perform... this, but you chose not to.' It's taking every ounce of strength I have left not to simply knock her to the floor.

'It's my evening job, and someone booked me,' she says, turning to face me, her thick black eyelashes and gold make-up making her green eyes sparkle even more. 'I'm sorry but I couldn't turn the work down.' She pauses. 'Full disclosure. When I first received the booking, I honestly had no idea it was for Jamie.'

'So who booked you?' Danielle asks.

'They didn't give a real name. It was through my business contact page on social media, so it came through from "Barney Rubble" or some such cartoon character. They paid up front, said when and where, so I didn't question it. I don't need a name, I just turn up and dance,' she says.

I cross my arms. 'So you turned up uninvited to my private party and didn't have the guts to admit that you lied about who you were, and you're an ex-girlfriend! And now this, stripping for my fiancé.'

'I admit when I realised the gig was for Jamie's stag do, I couldn't resist finding out where your hen night was. It wasn't difficult, it's all over your social media. I wondered if I could get in, and the only way I could think of was to say I was Jamie's cousin. I remember him telling me he'd lost touch with his aunt, uncle and cousin Beth after his mum died.'

'But what were you hoping to achieve? I don't understand.' I throw my hands up in disbelief.

'I was curious to know why Jamie had chosen *you* to settle down with.' She gives me a tight smile and I feel like someone's dropped something from a great height onto my head. She knew he was getting married, probably from our Instagram pages. Is it possible Jamie booked her himself? I still find it hard to believe he didn't know it was her, even with a masquerade mask on. Could something still be going on between them?

I clear my throat, holding back a sudden wave of tears threatening to break through. 'Why did you really come?'

A frown crosses her brow as she moves her hand towards mine. 'You needed someone to look out for you,' she says in a gentle voice.

'Leave me alone.' I snatch my hand away and step back. 'I've had enough for one night. You've had your fun at my expense. I'm going back to the cottage for a hot bath.' I head for the door, not waiting for a reply. Danielle and Sarah hurry after me.

21

As soon as we get back to the cottage, I peel Bonnie's fur coat off and Sarah runs upstairs for my dressing gown, then helps me to put it on.

'Are you okay?' she asks. I'm numb, unable to find any words. She gives me a hug.

'Let's warm you up a bit with a cup of tea before I run you a bath,' Danielle says. 'You've had quite a shock.' She takes camomile tea and the glass teapot out of the cupboard.

'I just knew there was something off about her as soon as I met her, but I couldn't work out what it was,' Sarah says.

'She was so convincing,' Danielle says, filling the kettle.

'I thought it was a bit weird that she wasn't on the guest list,' Sarah says, 'but because she said she was Jamie's cousin, I felt I had to let her stay.'

'It's not your fault,' Danielle says.

'I think it's dead creepy that your fiancé's ex turned up at your hen do and lied about it. Do you think they dated for a while? I mean, was it serious?' Sarah asks and Danielle flashes her a stern look.

'I don't know.' I press my hand to my head.

'We need to think what we're going to say to them when they get back. *If* they bother to come back. Lauren went too far with her stupid prank. She didn't tell any of us what she was planning, only Brooke seemed to be in on it.'

'What about Brooke being an erotic dancer?' Sarah says, wide eyed.

'I know, I could hardly believe it when Megan whipped off her mask. She didn't tell us she did *that* for a living.' Danielle pours boiling water into the teapot.

'Or about Jamie's stag do. She's lied to us about everything.' Sarah takes a packet of biscuits out of a cupboard, empties them onto a plate and puts them on the coffee table in the lounge area.

'Do you think Lauren was the one who booked her?' I tighten my dressing gown belt, grateful to be here with two people I know I can trust.

'It's possible Lauren knew about her,' Danielle says.

'Lauren's always been jealous of you and Jamie, but I never thought she'd be spiteful like this,' Sarah says.

'I thought she wanted to be friends again.' If Lauren really does still hold a grudge against me, our friendship has been a sham and I should never have attempted to revive it.

I unlock the patio doors and pull them open a few inches. It's dark and eerily quiet outside now the night is beginning to draw in. The trees cast long shadows across the swimming pool water. It's so still, it could easily be mistaken for a solid surface.

'Here we are.' Danielle brings our mugs of tea over and puts them on the table next to the biscuits. Sarah sits with her legs tucked under her, and starts munching away on a chocolate Hobnob. Danielle leaves the room and comes back moments later with my phone. She hands it to me, head tipped to one side, as if to say sorry for hanging on to it. I thank her. Pressing the button to switch it on, I'm not surprised to see several missed call notifications. Most are from Jamie but a few of them are not. My heart rate spikes. I have to ignore them. The last one from Jamie is only about half an hour ago. There's a text message from him begging for my forgiveness, but also half a dozen from another number. I can't look at them now.

At that moment, my phone lights up to notify me that there's a new message on WhatsApp. Without thinking, I click it open. In capital letters it says:

> PAY £7K INTO THIS BANK ACCOUNT OR
> YOU'D BETTER WATCH YOUR BACK. NOT ALL
> YOUR WEDDING GUESTS ARE YOUR
> FRIENDS.

I purse my lips. This is like the first message I received a few hours ago for five thousand pounds. Perhaps I should have just paid it because the amount has gone up and now they're becoming more threatening. I check back. There's a note in small text saying that disappearing messages have been turned on by the sender and it will disappear twenty-four hours after it was sent. I click for more information and it tells me to tap the bookmark icon, so I can keep this and the last message. But who is sending these? Is the amount going to keep going up? Jamie's the only person who knows about my inheritance. Has he blabbed about it to someone who desperately needs some cash?

'Are you okay?' Sarah frowns, mirroring my own expression.

'Yeah, just a message I wasn't expecting.'

'Why not go and have your bath, try to relax a bit.'

'Danielle's right. Do you want me to run it for you? We'll make your favourite – a bacon sandwich – for when you come down.'

'Thank you both. I think I'd better have a shower instead; my head is still too heavy from all the alcohol I've drunk today and I don't fancy sitting in a bath of all this gunk.'

'That's a good point, although I didn't think you'd had much to drink since we left here,' Sarah says.

'I haven't, but I still feel so rough.'

'That's odd,' Danielle says.

'Did you keep a close eye on your drink at the club?' Sarah asks.

'The only time I wasn't there was when I went to the loo. I can't remember who I asked to guard it for me.'

Danielle tips her head to one side. 'Honestly, after tonight, I wouldn't put it past Lauren to have dropped in a dose of something. She's completely out of control.'

'Just to ruin my night? She's done that already.'

We all hug. I slip my phone into my pocket and take my mug of tea with me upstairs.

As I sit on the end of the bed, everything that's happened today spins through my mind, from the funeral flowers on my parents' lawn to being doused in Coke, floured and tied to a lamppost. It's hard to believe they did that to me. And gate-crashing Jamie's stag do? Surely that's an unwritten rule no woman should break. I trusted Lauren. Has she secretly despised me all this time, simply because Jamie wanted to be with me not her? And as for Beth, Brooke... pretending to be Jamie's cousin. How long were they together? Was it a serious relationship? Everything I thought I knew about her has shifted. I trusted her. Now I'm concerned that she knows about Ryan and the video. Does she plan to tell Jamie? She said she'd keep it to herself and stop Ryan making threats about showing it to Jamie. I should never have put my faith in someone I barely know. But I thought she was family. And now I'm getting these WhatsApp messages. Are they from Ryan as well, threatening to trash our wedding day? What if Brooke set out to ruin my party and humiliate me in front of my friends? Or was that solely down to Lauren? My head hurts. None of it makes sense. Am I such a bad friend to Lauren that she'd gang up with a stranger against me?

I run the shower and after a minute stand under the hot water and let it melt the dried flour off my skin. The grey clumpy mixture swirls around my feet before draining down the plug hole. I use an extra pump of shampoo followed by plenty of conditioner and hope that after this, there's not a trace of it left.

Once I'm dry and dressed in my pyjamas, I truly begin to relax. I eye the bed longingly but daren't get in or lie on top in case I fall asleep. Danielle and Sarah wouldn't blame me I'm sure, but I'd feel bad not going back downstairs to eat the food they've prepared.

I try Jamie's number but it's telling me his phone is switched off and I've no idea why that is or what I should do. I'll have to wait until tomorrow to speak to him.

I'm suddenly compelled to view the messages I received earlier. There's another one from Ryan threatening to send Jamie the video of us in bed together if I don't send him a lump sum of twenty thousand pounds. He's attached a clip to prove it. I click on the link but mute it as soon as the noises start. A few seconds in and I have to look away. I switch it off. I can barely swallow the lump in my throat. I did not give my consent to this. Who else has it been sent to? Who else has seen this?

A scream rises from downstairs, shrill and urgent. I run out of my room onto the landing.

22

'What's happened?' I call out, leaning over the banister to try to see what's going on. There's no answer so I run downstairs.

The thick smell of cooking bacon wafts up to me, stirring my hunger. Bacon sandwiches have been a staple of our hangover toolbox after nights out for as long as I can remember. But right now, I need to find out what's happened, if everyone is okay.

When I reach the kitchen, Danielle and Sarah are standing with their backs to me, faces pressed to the glass of the patio doors.

'He was right there,' Sarah says, stabbing her finger against the floor-to-ceiling toughened pane.

'Who was?' I ask, my breath coming in short bursts.

They both give a start and spin round.

'Jesus, you spooked us,' Danielle says, holding her hand to her chest.

'I saw a man out there, by the pool,' Sarah says. 'He was wearing a black hoodie, joggers and a balaclava. Danielle thinks I'm going mad because he's not there now.'

'No, I don't,' Danielle protests. 'I couldn't see him, that's all.'

'He ran off as soon as the security light came on.'

'We were standing here chatting and I saw a flash of light on the other side of the pool, so I had a look through the window. Then the security light came on and I saw him running away.'

'What was he doing out there?' I cup my hands around my eyes and peer through the glass into the darkness.

'I don't know, just creeping around. I think he must have got out over the wall down the far end,' Sarah says, pulling her long cardigan around herself.

'There's no one out there now. Maybe it was just a chancer who thought he might find a door or window unlocked.' I pat Sarah's arm.

'I heard a noise a bit earlier, but I'm not sure what it was, so it could have been him trying the latch to see if he could get in.' Sarah's hands wrap tighter around her mug of hot chocolate.

'I'll email the owners, see if they can check the CCTV, maybe even notify the police of an intruder. We need to make doubly sure everything is locked up securely tonight.'

Sarah finishes her drink and puts her mug on the counter. I give her a hug.

'And how are you feeling?' Danielle asks me over her shoulder as she opens the oven door and takes the bacon out of the grill.

'Much calmer, thanks,' I say. At least I was until I came down, but I don't say that. It's not their fault my anxiety is sky-high. I purse my lips and quietly blow out a breath.

'Good, mug of hot chocolate for you there.' Sarah points to the end of the counter. 'I think I'm going to hit the sack soon.' She helps Danielle assemble the bacon sandwiches and hands one to me on a plate.

'I've had a text from Emma. She went back to the club to join the others. They'll be on their way back in about an hour,' Danielle says.

'I wonder what Lauren and Brooke are up to,' Sarah says, squirting ketchup in her bacon sandwich.

'I don't want to worry about them now. I think I'd better check round outside before going to bed.' I finish my sandwich, pick up my mug of hot chocolate and unlock the patio door. I step out and the sensor light comes on. There's no sign of anyone, but a couple of chairs have been knocked over. Several strips of paper from the game earlier are scattered on the ground. The ones I tipped out of the bowl. I pick one up and open it. It's the question I chose which I dropped on the ground in disgust. I pick up another, curious as to what I could have picked instead.

That's odd. The same question is written on it, about whether I'd ever cheated on Jamie. Why would there be two the same? I pick up another and unfold it. Again, it reads, *Have you ever been unfaithful to your fiancé?* I pick up one, two, three more. Shit. How is the identical question on all these pieces of paper? I thought I'd picked one from a random selection. Someone has set me up.

My first thought goes to Brooke. Of course it would be her, after she so brazenly gate-crashed this weekend. But then I realise, she wouldn't have known about my secret. But if not her, then who?

'What have you got there?' Sarah asks, standing at the patio door, tentatively looking left then right before stepping out.

'The truth questions I tipped out of the bowl when I got mad about having to give an answer.'

'And don't tell me, you've found one you'd have preferred?' she laughs, checking up and down the garden as she speaks.

I shake my head and her smile drops.

'No, that's what's so strange,' I say. 'All the questions are the same.'

'What do you mean? They can't be, can they?' She tilts her head.

'What's wrong?' Danielle is standing at the patio door.

'Every single one of these pieces of paper has the same stupid question written on it, identical to the one I picked out, so I had no chance of avoiding it. The whole game was fixed. I take it neither of you knew anything about this?' I try not to sound like I'm accusing them, but right now it's hard to know who I can trust.

Danielle steps down onto the patio and stands next to Sarah. Without seeing each other's faces, they both shake their heads solemnly. I feel bad even asking them. My chest won't stop heaving up and down. Someone was out to humiliate me. It's almost as if they already knew what my answer would be.

'We would never do that to you.' Sarah frowns.

'I know. I'm sorry. I had to ask.'

'Lauren's the one who put the whole game together. I left it up to her to find suitable questions, write them down and cut them out. Actually, she wouldn't let anyone help her fold them up,' Danielle says.

'How dare she humiliate me like this. After everything else she's done to me tonight.' Rage flares through me.

'I'm so sorry. If I'd known she was going to do that to you, I'd never have left her to organise it on her own.' Danielle sighs.

'It's not your fault, but this really is it. I cannot take any more crap from her. She had no intention of mending our friendship. I trusted her to be one of my bridesmaids, and this is what she does to me? As far as I can tell, she's only here to do as much damage to me as she can.'

Danielle finishes her drink and puts the mug on the garden table. I tip the strips of paper into her outstretched hand. Sarah helps her set them down in a neat column. Seeing the same words repeated on each one brings it home to me just how much trouble Lauren went to, writing, cutting and neatly folding all these.

'The question is duplicated seven times,' Danielle says in astonishment. 'And somehow Lauren or someone else put them all in the bowl just before your turn.'

'Could she have done this alone?' I ask.

'I doubt it. Anyone could have helped her.' Danielle shrugs.

'Hang on.' Sarah holds up a finger. Danielle and I watch her march into the kitchen, grab a pair of Marigolds from the sink and press her foot on the pedal of the bin. She pulls on the washing up gloves, rolls up her sleeves and digs down, rummaging about, then she pinches something and lifts it out of the rubbish. When she holds it up, we can see straight away what it is – one of the white strips of paper.

'There are more down there, but this is the only one I could reach unsoiled. *What's been your worst argument with the groom to be?*' she reads out loud. 'This one never came up, which proves that someone did switch over the last few questions and replace them with the same question on lots of pieces of paper.'

'My guess is Lauren roped in Brooke to help her. Sold it to her as high jinks for the bride,' I say, and the other two nod.

Sarah drops into a chair. 'Scheming cow. You think you know someone, don't you?'

'She could be the one behind the funeral flowers this morning, and the message in lipstick on your mirror. I didn't think she seemed that upset by either of them. In fact, it was almost like she enjoyed the drama of it all, seeing how badly it affected you,' Danielle says.

'Really? But hang on, could she have known how I'd answer the truth question?'

'She's known Ryan for years don't forget. Their brothers are friends,' Danielle says. 'Seems obvious to me now I'm thinking about it that she could easily have been told or found out about you two. In fact, I'm convinced she already knew what your answer would be.'

'Of course. I forget they know each other. Now it makes sense that she knew all along and just wanted to make me admit it in front of you all. Embarrass me. And for Jamie to find out and break up with me. I bet she's told him about Ryan and that's why he's not answering his phone.'

My heart sinks. How dare Lauren betray me? Her hatred must have been building up for years. Why have I never noticed she was so angry with me?

We all look at each other, not knowing what to say. It's typical Lauren behaviour and we fell for it.

'I can't get my head around this right now. I'm sorry, but I'm going up to bed.' I kiss them both on the cheek. 'I need to sleep on this. It's been quite a day.'

'Yeah, me too,' Sarah says.

'I'll check everything is locked, then come up.' Danielle finishes her drink.

'Better leave a light on in the hallway for the others when they come in,' I say and trudge up the stairs closely followed by Sarah. We go to our separate rooms.

Tiredness hits me as I climb into bed. I shut my eyes, but my mind springs into overdrive, going over all the things that have happened today. Everything that was said to me. I can't turn off the non-stop chatter. At the same time, my ears are alert for any movement in the garden below. Should I get up and shut the big window? What if the intruder comes back and breaks in? But it's so warm tonight, it would be unbearably hot in here. He could get a ladder and climb in while I'm asleep. I could be murdered in my bed.

I stay wide awake, tossing and turning and when I'm finally sinking, eyes closing, a blood-curdling scream fills the night air.

23

The crescendo of the long gut-wrenching scream tears at every fibre of my body. I open my eyes with a jolt. A woman is being raped or stabbed in the garden below. I need to get up, look out of the window, call the police, but I cannot move a muscle. I'm frozen to the spot. I picture a woman splayed out on the grass, a man's hand clamped over her mouth, attacking her with such brute force that she's like a helpless doll beneath him. She's relying on me or someone to have heard her and to do something about it. What if it's one of my friends back from the club? But who? All I know is the three of us are safe inside. Aren't we? Oh God, no. Danielle was the last one downstairs. She said she was going to double-check everything was locked up. What if she saw that man outside again and decided to go out and confront him?

I have to get up.

I have to help her.

What if I've already left it too late? I'm terrified of what I'll witness. But what I'm more frightened of is if I don't do anything. I turn over towards the window. The moonlight is seeping in through the lightweight cream stripe curtains, casting shadows on the walls. I shift to the edge of the bed just as another high-pitched scream rings out. It seems to go on forever, pinning me to the spot once more. My heart is in my mouth as I imagine the victim fighting for her life, and here I am, a coward hiding under sheets.

I clench my teeth and in one swift gymnastic move, I launch myself out of bed to a standing position. Blood is pounding in my ears. At the window, I frantically scan left and right, but I can't detect any movement outside. No one. No sound. No woman being attacked. The chairs and table are where we left them. Shadows darken every corner of the garden, and there are parts I can't view clearly from here. Could the attack be happening on the other side of the fence? Has the perpetrator run off and left a woman dying? Or is his hand smothering her face?

There's a knock at the door. Sarah opens it a couple of inches, and peers round. She's wearing a towelling dressing gown, her hair up and ruffled from sleep.

'Did you hear it too?' I ask, turning round. *How could she not?*

'God, yes. Made my blood run cold.' She wraps her arms around herself and joins me at the window. We both gaze out.

'Do you think it came from over the fence?' I ask.

'Maybe. Shouldn't we call the police?'

'I don't know. Could it be an animal?'

'What's that shadow in the pool?' Sarah points at the far end shrouded in darkness.

'It's probably a branch or something fallen from the big trees at the back.' It's hard to see from where we're standing, but she's right, something darker appears to be on the surface of the water. Or under.

'You don't think that man has come back, do you?' Sarah clings to the sleeve of my pyjamas.

'I don't know. Let's find Danielle and go and have a look.' I pull on my dressing gown, my ears still pounding. I try to block my worst thoughts of it being Danielle face down in the pool.

On our way to the stairs, Sarah knocks gingerly on Danielle's bedroom door. No reply. She pops her head round to see if she's still asleep, then opens it wide for me to see that Danielle is not in her bed, or anywhere in her room. My heart rate spikes. It looks like she has thrown back the covers at some point.

'Maybe she got up as soon as she heard the first scream?' I suggest. 'She's braver than me so she probably went straight down to see what it was.'

'So where is she now?' Sarah shrugs.

We creep down to the kitchen but don't turn the lights on. If an intruder is outside, I don't want to alert them to our presence. Sarah loosely holds the back of my dressing gown and follows me through the lounge area in the darkness. A soft creek comes from a low easy chair in the corner. I jolt to a halt, my heart in my mouth. Sarah walks straight into the back of me, expelling a lungful of air.

'Who's there?' I say into the room. No answer comes and a moment of silence passes. I clench my fist by my side. Have I got it wrong assuming it's Danielle and it's someone else sitting there without the lights on, waiting for us to come down? I carry on regardless. 'What are you doing down here?'

A side light clicks on. Danielle is wearing her coat over her pyjamas and her slip-on trainers without any socks. 'I couldn't sleep,' she says in a strange voice, 'so I thought I'd come down for a glass of warm milk and listen to a podcast.'

'Oh. Are you okay?' I ask, relief overwhelming me.

'There was some sort of noise while I was sitting here, so I had a look around outside to see what it was, but there was nothing there.'

'You didn't see anyone?' Sarah asks.

'It sounded like someone was being brutally attacked,' I say and Sarah nods.

'I didn't hear it that clearly. I had my buds in.'

'Jesus, are you sure? It was loud enough to wake the dead,' Sarah says.

Danielle shrugs. 'So what was it?'

'We don't know. We came down to find out.' I go to the patio door and unlock it.

'From upstairs it looks like something's gone in the swimming pool,' Sarah tells her as she catches me up.

Outside, the closed parasol flaps in the gentle cooling breeze, rustling the leaves, making it sound like someone is moving amongst the surrounding trees and bushes. I take a few steps towards the edge of the pool and crouch down. The breeze is rippling the surface of the water. The dark shadow we saw from upstairs looms over at the far end by one set of steps. It's hard to say what it is because now the security light is on all the other shadows have gone.

'It's probably a leafy branch fallen from a tree,' I say, but the breeze has only just picked up and it's not been strong enough today to cause such damage. Curious, I move a chair aside and squeeze my way around a table to take a closer look.

'What do you think it is then?' Danielle asks, stalking behind me towards the darker corner. Sarah stares at the pool further up. Her body jolts, like mine does sometimes when I wake myself up. She backs away, terror etched on her face as though she's witnessing a zombie rising out of the depths.

'I saw an eye.' Her voice is high-pitched. She wriggles squeamishly, the same way she does when she comes across a spider. I walk closer to the edge and peer in. The water is murky in this half-light and with the beam from the sensors not reaching this far into the garden, it's hard to say what it is exactly. We glance at each other to gauge our thoughts. Danielle and Sarah are silent, gripping each other's arms as they back away, staring at the dark patch of water as though something will burst out and grab them at any moment.

As my eyes become used to the light, the shape in the water becomes clearer.

Someone or something is floating face down in the pool, and from where I'm standing, it looks the size of a small child.

24

'Quick, grab the lifesaver ring behind you,' I yell to Sarah. How has a child wandered into our garden? Unless the man Sarah saw was dumping someone in here. I swallow down the urge to be sick. I can't wait for Sarah, she's flapping her hands in panic mode. I strip off my dressing gown and dive into the water in my pyjamas and swim up to the body. It's still not moving. Sarah chucks in the inflatable ring, and I swim over to retrieve it, hook it through my arm and swim back again.

'Shall I call an ambulance?' Danielle asks, but I don't reply. I'm not sure what we're dealing with yet.

As I get closer to it, a dank musty smell catches in the back of my throat. I swat away a fly. Whatever it is, it's half-submerged, face down. It has reddish, course hair. I come to an abrupt halt, baulking at the sight before me. The body of a fox is floating on its side, bushy tail splayed out to one side, an ear raised above the surface, mouth slightly open. One glassy eye is staring straight ahead. The stench of the rotting animal hits me, and I struggle to swallow down the globule of vomit in my mouth. I try to lift its head and feel for a pulse in its neck, knowing there won't be one; it's heavy and floppy. I'm too late. Tears fill the backs of my eyes. I clench my teeth. I could slap myself for being so slow, so indecisive. What if this had been a child?

'What is it?' Sarah calls from the other side of the pool, her and Danielle too scared to come closer.

'It's a fox,' I say, then add, 'it's dead,' guessing they probably can't make it out from where they're standing. They nod, no doubt as relieved as I am that it's not a child, or any person.

'Do you think it fell in by accident, then couldn't get out?' Sarah asks.

'I should think so, poor thing.' I imagine it falling from the edge with a splash, scrabbling to grip onto the straight, slippery walls. There is nothing for it to grab onto with its claws. Its head would have sunk below the water at each attempt until it was too exhausted to try any more.

'Can you help me lift it out?' I ask and they look at each other before both coming to the far edge of the pool. I push the fox's body as high as I can, but neither of them do anything to help.

'Come on, I can't hold it much longer. It can't stay in here, it's... contaminated water.' I do my best to keep my chin up so as not to accidentally let any water near my mouth, but it's almost impossible, especially with no one helping me.

'I'm sorry, I can't do it,' Danielle whimpers, her fingers over her mouth.

'Nor me. I've never touched anything dead before.' Sarah cowers away and I have to let the fox back down into the water because I can't hold the weight of it any longer.

'I'll do it,' a bold voice says from the patio door.

We all look round. Brooke is standing there with Lauren next to her. My mouth falls open, gobsmacked that they have the nerve to come back.

'What are you two doing here?' Danielle asks.

'You've got a cheek showing your faces after what you did to Megan,' Sarah says.

I cannot deal with either of them right now when I'm shoulder-deep in a pool trying to retrieve a dead fox.

Brooke ignores what they've said and strides over to the pool, rolling up her sleeves as though she hasn't just been pretending to be someone else. She kneels by the side in front of me. 'On three, lift him as high as you can.'

I nod, ready to hold the weight of the fox's dead body. At least she's prepared to help me when the others won't.

'One, two, three,' Brooke shouts.

I push the body up with all my strength, keeping my mouth tightly shut so no drips of water go in my mouth. Brooke reaches down and takes hold of the fox's body. In one swoop she has the poor thing cradled in her arms and is gently resting it on the patio.

I swim to the side and climb the steps of the pool, water dripping from my sodden pyjamas.

'Looks like a male,' Brooke says, crouched over the body. 'Nasty wounds. Might be roadkill. How did it get here?'

Sarah tells her about the man she saw lurking around.

'Maybe he came back and dumped it here. God knows why. Anyway, I thought you lot would be in bed.'

'We got woken up by someone screaming. It sounded like a woman was being attacked or murdered,' I say.

Brooke laughs and we all stare at her, straight-faced.

'What's funny about that?' Danielle says.

'If there are foxes in the area, you probably heard a vixen.' She smiles at our blank faces. 'A female fox. They screech to let the males know they're ready to mate. It's known to sound like a woman being murdered.' She laughs, hopefully at our ignorance and not at a woman being attacked.

'Seriously?' Sarah says.

'Frightened me to death,' I say, squeezing the water out of my hair.

Lauren is standing away from everyone in the shadows. I'm not ready to deal with her right now. Neither her nor Brooke are who I thought they were. I give her a wide berth as I walk over to Danielle and whisper that I need to have another shower. She nods once and asks if I'm okay. I nod back, grab my phone, and go up the stairs before anyone can stop me.

25

As soon as I'm in my room, I dial Jamie's number. To my surprise he answers straight away.

'Megan is that you? Are you okay?' His words are slurred and there's muted dance music in the background.

'Not really. Are you still in the pub?' A note of alarm chimes in my voice.

'Nightclub. What can I say? I'm... a little tipsy.' He pauses. 'I need to apologise to you, about my behaviour tonight, with Lauren and... particularly Brooke.' His voice is high then low, like an adolescent boy not yet in control of his vocal cords.

'You've humiliated me dancing with Brooke, not telling me straight away that she was your ex.'

'I know, I'm sorry. I honestly didn't know it was her until she took off the mask. I don't know who contacted her. None of my friends are admitting to it.'

'And you let Lauren kiss you. What were you thinking?'

'I tried to tell them they should go, but I was so drunk, they wouldn't listen.'

'But in one of the photos I saw, you were drinking with them at the bar.'

'I couldn't stop them, it was a set-up. I didn't want them there. I was playing a drinking game, doing shots with the lads, and they came in and were buying me drinks, egging me on to have another. I could barely stand up after that, and I got angry when Lauren kissed me. I felt so out of it, I think they might have put something in my drink.'

'It didn't look like you tried very hard to stop her, that's all.' Tears press the backs of my eyes. I don't want to get upset about it, but he's hit a nerve.

'I did try, I promise you. I'm sorry you think it looked like I didn't. I'll make sure Brooke knows she is not welcome at our wedding. I promise.'

'Okay.' I bite my lip, trying hard not to let the tears spill over. 'Have you any idea what they did to me, tying me up and soaking me?' I ask.

'They told me. Lauren laughed about it to my face. You know they've got photos of you?' He pauses as though he wasn't going to tell me that. 'I'm so, so sorry. They've posted them up on the socials. It was too late for me to stop them.'

'Emma showed me. And now they've come back, they're downstairs, acting as if it was nothing. No apology from them for any of it.'

'You should tell them to leave, especially Brooke. You don't know what she's like.'

'Lauren's the one who instigated the whole thing. So much for repairing our friendship. Have I done something to upset her apart from being with you? Did she say anything?'

'I've no idea.' His answer comes a bit too quick. He's protecting my feelings.

'The others think it's just because we're getting married. I didn't know Lauren felt so bitter about it.'

'Does she?'

'You know she's always liked you. Wished you'd gone out with her instead of me.'

'I know, but I didn't realise it ran so deep. She's not my type at all, you know that.'

'Maybe *you* need to tell her. If it came from you, she'd have to believe you two could never have got together, and she'd realise it wasn't my fault.'

'Seems harsh, being so blunt.'

'I don't see any other way. I'm beginning to think she's a bit obsessed with you. Today she seemed to latch onto Brooke as soon as she met her, and it's brought out the worst in her. They left me handcuffed to a bloody lamppost, then drenched me in a bottle of Coke and covered me in two bags of flour.' As soon as I say it, I imagine the photos he's seen of me on social media. Liked and shared hundreds of times. It's so humiliating.

'For God's sake. What were they thinking? I mean there's having a laugh and then there's being downright nasty. I'm so sorry. I really thought it was my cousin Beth there, not *her*.'

'And you really had no inkling that your ex-girlfriend was going to gate-crash my party or be your entertainment for tonight?' I emphasise the word 'entertainment' because I can't bear saying stripper.

'I did think it was odd when you said my cousin Beth had turned up uninvited, because I haven't spoken to her or my aunt and uncle for years. But I had no clue at all that it was Brooke pretending to be her, I promise you.' His tone is so innocent. Perhaps too innocent. He's not stupid.

I don't answer. I want to believe him, but a tiny part of me senses he's not quite telling the whole truth and knows more than he's saying. I can't help dwelling on what Brooke said about her ex. How he changed towards her as soon as they got serious. What if Jamie changes like that? He's got a side to him when he's drunk. He must have recognised it was Brooke dancing in front of him, even with her face covered; her costume didn't leave much to the imagination and there's no doubt he was enjoying it.

'I'll call you back in the morning,' Jamie says. 'I'm sorry for upsetting you. I love you, Megan. You know I do. I can't wait for everyone to see you become my wife.'

'Neither can I. I love you too.' I wish I didn't sound so vulnerable and pathetic. I know how much he loves me; he's proved that over and over again, so why won't these niggling doubts go away?

We say goodbye and I check my other messages. Only one from Mum to say Freya went to bed without too much fuss. That's a relief. I look forward to seeing her tomorrow.

I run the shower in my en suite while I take off my wet pyjamas. I chuck them on the granite-tiled floor and step under the jet of hot water.

Jamie did sound sorry, so perhaps I'm reading too much into what happened. His best man or one of his other friends could have booked Brooke to get him into trouble with me. Maybe one of them doesn't like me? It wasn't Jamie's fault Lauren and Brooke gate-crashed his stag party and behaved so appallingly. I think the events of the day are catching up with me.

I should make Lauren and Brooke leave immediately, but the problem is I don't want to give them a reason to tell Jamie what I did.

One of them is trying to stop me marrying Jamie, and I need to work out if it is Lauren, my so-called friend. Because if it's her, I'm not sure how far she's willing to go to hurt me.

26

As I get out of the shower, I hear raised voices coming from the patio below. I wrap myself in a towel and switch off the bedside lamp. Peering out of the window, it looks like Danielle and Sarah are having a full-blown row with Lauren and Brooke about what they did to me. I hear Danielle telling them to do the right thing and go home. As I turn away to dry myself, the sound of smashing glass stops me dead.

I quickly put on my spare pair of pyjamas. There's a second fluffy white dressing gown on the back of the door so I pull it on and hurry downstairs.

They all go quiet when they see me appear. Sarah is backed against a wall, Lauren in front of her holding a broken wine bottle. I draw in a breath.

'What are you doing, Lauren?' I ask in a loud but steady voice, holding my hands up to show her I mean no harm.

'You should have heard what she said, accusing me of all kinds of crap.' Lauren sounds drunk, not her usual jokey self.

'I'm sure she didn't mean it,' I tell her and edge closer, my hands out in front of me so Lauren can see they are empty.

'Why don't you put the bottle down, Lauren, and we can talk about it?'

'Why should I?' She pivots towards me, the bottle in her hand, pointing it at me. 'I don't have to put up with any of this rubbish any more. None of you have ever liked me.' She swings in an arc, taking us all in. 'I know you just put up with me, let me tag along because you feel sorry for me. Well enough is enough.' She scowls at us, pointing to each of us with the broken bottle. I'm taken aback that she feels so bitter towards us. This has to be the drink talking because it's simply not the case.

'That's not true, where did you get that idea? I know we've had our ups and downs, but I've always liked you. I asked you to be my bridesmaid because you're my friend and I value our friendship.' I say this while thinking how much tonight has changed everything I thought I knew about her, and now I'm not sure we can continue to be friends if all she wants to do is hurt me.

'Are you sure it's not driven by guilt or pity?' There's more than a hint of sarcasm in her tone. It's as though someone else is in her head, changing who she is.

'What do you mean? Of course not.'

'You knew I liked Jamie. It's so unfair.' She crosses her arms and scowls at me. I don't know why she keeps bringing it up. She's completely out of order still going on about it, especially on my hen night.

'But Jamie and I have been together for years; we've had a child together. I honestly didn't know you liked him this much. I swear I've not done any of it to spite you.' I hold my hand on my heart. 'Jamie and I know we're lucky we found one another. One day you'll find the right person for you.' I reach out to touch her arm but I lose my balance and she shifts her body away as if I've cut her.

'Don't patronise me,' she growls.

I don't answer. It's kinder to stay silent.

'Oh, I get it.' She waves her finger at me. 'You've discussed it with him, haven't you? Wouldn't have been seen dead with a frump like me, is that it?'

'He didn't say that.'

Brooke laughs and I glance at her. She's sitting on a sun lounger, the security light cutting across her body every time it flicks on. Her feet are up on a cushion, and she's smoking a thin cigar, drinking from a can of beer. She looks like she's enjoying this, watching us. She's not saying anything to try to calm Lauren.

'Please put the bottle down,' I say again.

Lauren grins at me as she opens her fingers and lets the bottle smash to the ground. Sarah screams. Danielle dashes towards me.

'Why did you do that?' I cry, instinctively stepping back as the shattered glass bounces across the stone tiles. Danielle takes my hand and guides me backwards.

'Why not?' Lauren smirks like a naughty child. I'd love to kick her out, but I need to try to keep her and Brooke onside so they don't tell Jamie my secret. I shouldn't have told Brooke. It's meant to be my VIP weekend away with people I trust. It would devastate Jamie to know I'd been with someone else, even though it was a mistake.

'Don't move,' Danielle says, training her eyes on the pieces of glass scattered on the ground. She grabs a dustpan and brush from the kitchen and starts sweeping it up.

'I'm going to bed.' Lauren stomps off into the house, past all the other guests arriving back from the club.

I greet them in the kitchen. They've heard about what happened to me and want to know if I'm okay. I tell them briefly and they say sorry I couldn't return to the club. It sounds like they had a great night. I leave them to make toast and tea. Danielle finishes sweeping up the glass. Brooke is still outside, smoking. The fox's body is rolled up in a beach towel and has been left by the bins. Somehow, I need to make sure Brooke and Lauren don't get up to any more mischief.

Before I get back into bed I can't help checking my phone. There's a new text from Ryan, giving me a final ultimatum.

27

It's almost 5.30 a.m. when I pull myself out of a dream where Lauren had tied me to a lamppost and was about to pour boiling water over my head. I shudder. It still feels real. I'm thankful it wasn't, but Lauren's hatred for me felt genuine.

I reach for my dressing gown and walk downstairs barefoot. I need a milky coffee to help me deal with this thumping hangover. I sobered up pretty quickly after being sick and Lauren and Brooke tying me to a lamppost, so I didn't expect to feel this rubbish the next morning. I lost track of how much I drank with everyone buying me drinks plus all the drinks we had before we left for town. I'm not a big drinker since becoming a mum; I only have a glass of wine here and there. Bingeing like I did last night is not something I ever want to repeat.

I warm a mug of milk in the microwave then drop in a shot of coffee from the instant espresso machine. I no longer have sugar as a rule, but I can't resist a perfect little sugar cube, so I drop in one, two, three and give it a stir. It's bound to help bring my blood sugar back up, I reason to myself.

The front door clicks loudly. My back stiffens. Wasn't it

locked last night? Who was the last person up? Soft footsteps are coming this way.

'Morning, Megan,' Brooke says, entering the kitchen wearing Nike running gear, her cheeks pink, a slick of sweat across her face. She's holding a bottle of water and her phone.

'Oh, it's you. You gave me a fright.' I press a hand to my chest and let out a short breath. 'I thought we had another intruder.' I stare at her for a second. She really has some front coming back here and carrying on as normal.

'Another?' She frowns and puts her phone down, refills her bottle with tap water and has a long drink.

'You've got a cheek staying here after last night.' I pause, trying to be calm. 'You should leave. I didn't invite you, remember?' My words are sharp, but she needs telling because she doesn't seem at all that fazed by me finding out she's Jamie's ex or catching her erotic dancing for him. I'm still in shock and not sure what to make of her. She could easily have said no to Lauren roping her in to cause mischief, but she didn't, she went along with it.

'I'm truly sorry about last night, Megan. I should have been honest with you about who I was from the start. I really didn't mean any harm by turning up. I was just curious. I was going to masquerade as Jamie's cousin and then go home. That's all. I promise. And it was completely unfair of me not to mention that I'd be working at a stag party the same night.'

'Yes, you should.' I suppose if she'd told me who she was, I'd have kicked her straight out of my hen party. And it feels like she was genuinely curious. Nothing more.

She slaps her hand on top of her head. 'I got so swept up in the party games and playing tricks on you with Lauren, I didn't think how it might affect you.'

It's a thoughtful apology and reminds me why I like her,

despite everything. She's not a bad person. Perhaps none of this is as awful as it seems. There's no reason for me to feel insecure, because Jamie's with me now and we're about to get married.

'By the way, do you know there's a parcel for you on the doorstep?' she says, changing the subject.

'Is there?'

'Yeah, I didn't know if you wanted it bringing in. I kind of had my hands full.'

'I'm not expecting anything.' I can't help the bitterness in my tone. Even though she apologised, the idea of continuing the weekend so cordially feels wrong.

'Maybe it's not for you. I just assumed. Do you want me to go and get it?'

'It's okay, I'll do it in a minute.' This whole weekend has been too much to take in. I open a packet of pastries. I suddenly need more sugar.

'It's no trouble.' She puts her bottle and phone down and leaves the kitchen. I can't help having a sneaky peek at the screen. A message from 'Bros' pops up. Brothers? I thought she said she was an only child.

'It's quite heavy,' she says seconds later, and places the medium-sized brown box on the stall next to me.

'I could have got it myself, but thanks.' I peer at the label with my name and 'The Cottage' scrawled in thick black pen. We're all going home this morning so I can't think what it would be. Danielle didn't mention she was expecting a delivery. Maybe it's some homemade cakes or cookies to hand out to everyone before they go home, and she wanted it to be a surprise.

'So tell me about this intruder,' Brooke says, acting as if our last conversation didn't happen and she's just one of my hens. One of my *friends*. 'Did any of you get a good look at him?'

I sigh and explain how Sarah thinks the man might have

tried to break in the back door, then she saw him prowling around in the garden.

'She said he was wearing a black hoodie and balaclava. Made off as soon as the security light came on.'

'Probably no point checking on the CCTV then.' Brooke wipes the sweat off her forehead with her forearm. 'So, you're an early bird too? I had you down as someone who prefers a lie in. Especially on a Sunday.' She smiles.

'Not really,' I say and then elaborate. Brooke really does have a charm that makes me want to forgive her. 'I don't sleep too well so I'd rather get up, do some work. I'll probably have a nap later.'

'Same for me. I always go on an early run, sets me up for the day.' She sips from a bottle of water. I'm guessing it has electrolytes in it.

'Good for you. Better than trying to fight it, I always think. I like to make the most of these light mornings if I can. I'm usually woken up by our daughter. She's only two and has just started sleeping in her own bed. Well, for part of the night anyway.' I touch my forehead with the back of my hand and smile, thinking of Mum and Dad having Freya's smiley face to wake up to this morning. I miss her so much my chest aches.

Brooke doesn't answer but purses her lips and turns her face away. Shit. Maybe she doesn't like children, or worse, can't have any but wishes she could. Oh God. I've got to stop assuming women even *want* kids these days. And I need to remember that not everyone is interested in hearing every little detail about my daughter.

'So, what time did you get to bed?' I ask, in a poor attempt at changing the subject. Brooke seems to relax again, looking back at me, a weak smile on her lips and I'm reminded of her vulnerability and how much I like her.

'Maybe two, three o'clock? I like to follow what my body tells

me to do. It's less problematic in the long run. Excuse the pun.'
She smiles with what seems like genuine warmth. 'Are you going
to open the parcel?'

'I should leave it for Danielle,' I say. 'She's the one who would
have made the order, whatever it is.'

Brooke sips her water and shrugs. 'It's got your name on it.'

She's right. It must be for me. She passes me a sharp knife
and I stab through the tape across the top.

'Wow, strong smell. Is it a venison meat pie or something?'
Brooke says.

I wrinkle my nose. I've been eating less and less meat, so I
don't find the smell appealing. I rip off the tape and open the
flaps. There's a polystyrene food box inside. I open the lid and
scream, jumping away.

'What is it?' Brooke almost falls off her stool trying to get up
too quickly.

'It's some poor animal's guts,' I cry, backing away, cupping my
hands around my mouth. A shiver runs through my body, and I
can't stand still. I want to leap around the room until I've shaken
off the image of the pile of entrails riddled with maggots. I can't
say anything else in case I vomit.

She looks inside and covers her mouth. 'That's so disgusting.'
She glances at the underside of the lid and shows me a message
written in black capital letters.

YOU'RE NEXT IF YOU DON'T PAY UP

'What the fuck?' Brooke shoots a look at me. 'Who sent this?'

'I don't know,' I say and wrap my arms around myself.

28

'I've been getting threats demanding money on WhatsApp, but I'm not sure who they're from.'

'Not that ex of yours then?' Brooke puts the lid back on the box.

'Yeah, it could be. He sent me a final demand threatening to send that video to Jamie, if I don't pay him twenty thousand pounds, but the WhatsApps are anonymous, threatening to ruin my wedding, asking for smaller amounts of money. I was tempted to pay the first one, five thousand pounds, just to stop them, but they're already asking for more.' I tell her about the funeral flowers on my parents' lawn yesterday morning.

'Shit. Someone's really got it in for you. I mean, this is a death threat.'

'I don't know what to do.'

'Let's get this out of here,' she says, picking up the box. My hands fumble to unlock and slide open the patio door. I lift the garden waste bin lid, and she drops the box in. 'Take this,' she says, handing me the label she tore off the box. 'It might help you find out who sent it.'

'Thank you.'

'Maybe don't mention it when the others come down, see if anyone acts a bit strangely? They'll be expecting you to tell everyone about it, won't they.'

'Good idea, thanks.' I can't bear the thought of it being one of my close friends, but I have to consider all possibilities.

'Can I make you a coffee, or tea?' I fill the kettle to maximum in case any of the others come down needing a hot drink, although I doubt they'll be up this early after the night they had, unless they heard me scream.

'Yeah, coffee please. White, no sugar.'

I take a mug out of the cupboard. The silence between us balloons.

'Look, about last night...' Brooke says, and just from her sorrowful tone, I'm prepared to hear her out.

'What we did to you was... out of order. Way over the top. And I really didn't set out to ruin your night. It was only meant to be a bit of fun.'

'Thank you. I hoped you'd say that. Although I could hardly believe it when I saw it was you dancing for Jamie.' I look at her face. I'm surprised to see her cheeks redden. Maybe she's not as forthright and sure of herself as she likes to make out. I spoon the coffee into her mug and pour in boiling water.

'I didn't expect to see you there to be honest.' She shakes her head. 'It was just another job to me, pure and simple.'

'It was a shock to find out you're his ex. A shock that you thought you could come here at all.'

'Jamie and I are ancient history, but like I said before, I really wanted to meet you. Find out who Jamie had chosen to spend his life with.'

I nod, although I'm not okay with it.

'I did not expect to get caught up in Lauren's shenanigans.'

'You could have said no,' I say firmly.

She does a double take. 'Yeah, that would have been the sensible thing to do, but getting up to a bit of mischief at the bride's expense is hen night tradition, isn't it?'

'I suppose so.' I give a wry smile.

'Lauren likes to create a lot of drama around herself, doesn't she?'

'She does like the attention.' I glance at Brooke. If she's so curious about me then I guess I'm allowed to ask her more about herself. 'So are you with anyone?'

'Not right now. I'm happily single.' She looks down at her hands, at the mixture of rings on her fingers. 'Actually, I've not wanted to date anyone since Jamie and I split up.'

'Oh, did it not end well?'

'He really wasn't very nice to me.'

'He's not the ex you were telling me about yesterday?' I ask, shocked.

She nods.

I frown. 'He's nothing like that. He's lovely and kind and so good with our daughter Freya.'

'He could have changed. But when I was with him, he drank too much and would fly off the handle in a rage. It was frightening how unpredictable he could be.'

I stare at her, a pain pulsing in my forehead. 'He does drink quite a bit, but I try and keep it under control.'

Brooke tips her head. 'If you say anything to him, he'll deny it. I know he will. He'll call me all sorts, but you deserve to know about it. I wish someone had warned me. I think being in the army messed with his head.'

'He told me he was bullied by three older lads.'

'Yeah, they were relentless. Didn't like Jamie from day one apparently. When he complained, he was told to "embrace" the locker-room culture.'

'He's been having therapy. I think it's really helped him.' It's good to talk to someone who knows Jamie and can tell me more about his past, although I've not known his behaviour to be as extreme as she's saying.

'That's good. I know I'd be mad at myself if anything happened to you or your daughter, and I hadn't said anything.'

My mouth opens for a second, but I don't know what to say. I can't imagine Jamie being abusive. Is this another lie of hers?

'We all fall for the fairy tale though, don't we?' Brooke gives a tight smile as she sits down opposite me at the breakfast bar and sips her milky coffee.

'He's always been the perfect gentleman to me.' I turn my back on her and use the tongs to take the pastries out of the air fryer. I swallow down the threat of tears and take a moment to calm myself. I put the warm pastries on a plate between us. Brooke takes a pain au chocolat and proceeds to pick out all the pieces of chocolate and line them up on the side of her plate, then lick every scrap off her fingers. 'I'm sorry, but I had to warn you. It's up to you what you do.'

I nod, still processing what she's said. My stomach is a tight ball. Was he really that bad with her? I have so many questions that have been going round and round in my head since I found out she's Jamie's ex-girlfriend, but part of me doesn't want to know any more.

'So how did you two meet?' The words fall out of my mouth. She looks as surprised as I do. I didn't intend to say it out loud.

'Through a mutual friend. They introduced us.'

'You were both really young. Did you date for long?' Part of me wants to shut up but the other part is curious beyond belief.

'A couple of years. It was perfect in the beginning. I thought he was the one.'

'Oh,' I say and clench my teeth, hoping she stops right there before I hear some detail about their intimacy that I won't be able to erase from my mind.

'By the way, you never got the chance to show me those messages from your ex.'

'Oh yes. Thank you.' I tap open my phone and click on Ryan's name, relieved she's changed the subject. A list of messages comes up on the screen. I hand the phone to Brooke and she scrolls through them, reading what she needs to.

'And I take it this is the link to the video?' She points at one particular message where Ryan has said I might like to view this *before* deciding to block him.

I nod and she presses play. After a few seconds she stops it and I'm grateful she doesn't look at me. I'm so embarrassed at the noises I'm making and her seeing us naked like that. I can only imagine Jamie's horrified reaction if he ever saw it. It would send him on a downward spiral. Or could it set off the rage that Brooke talked about?

'I think I've seen enough.' She makes a note of Ryan's number on her phone and hands mine back to me. 'Now I've seen exactly what he's up to, I'll contact him and warn him off.' She takes a big bite of the pain au chocolat.

'Don't you worry, I'll make sure he never bothers you again, believe me.'

'What will you say to him?' I break off a piece of pain au raisin and put it in my mouth.

'He'll back right down if I threaten to go to the police.'

'Maybe I should just go to the police?'

'Don't waste your time. I tried that the first time Jamie flew off at me for talking to a guy at a party.'

'What happened?'

'As soon as we got home he went mad about it, pushed me so hard I fell and broke my arm.'

'Shit.' I frown, trying to imagine Jamie losing control like that. I can't. The Jamie she is describing is so different from the man I know and love.

'So if you do report Ryan, the police will log it but they'll say they don't have the resources to take it any further. Although *he* won't necessarily know that.'

'And what if he ignores you?'

'Oh I'll just threaten him with a Bobbitt,' she laughs.

'The wife who chopped off her husband's penis?'

'That's the one. He'd been abusing her.'

I blink at her. I hope for Ryan's sake that he does as Brooke says. 'Tell me more about what happened to you, if you don't mind talking about it?' I sip my tea.

'Same sort of thing. Except it was Jamie who was my abuser.'

My breath quickens. How can she use that word so easily to talk about my Jamie?

'He'd get jealous if another man even looked at me,' she continues. 'Controlled what I did, where I went, who I saw. He didn't let me leave the house without him or even go to the toilet with the door shut, in case I was on the phone to someone.'

'Seriously?' He was bad enough that she had to go to the police? A chill floods through me. I'm beginning to believe her words. Is this who my fiancé really is? Is this what he'll be like if he finds out about me and Ryan? What if he already knows? Is it possible it was him lurking in the garden last night, putting a dead fox in the pool to scare me?

'Yeah, he was such a nice guy when I met him, but he gradually became so possessive.'

'How did you get away?' I screw my eyes up at her, trying to imagine what she went through, if I'm going to face a future like this. I'm seeing her with fresh eyes. No wonder she's so ballsy and no nonsense.

'It took me weeks to work out a plan to leave him. When I finally ran away, he threatened to post private footage of me on a revenge porn site and send the link to all my family, friends and colleagues.'

I swallow hard. 'So what did you do?'

'The police were useless, so I had to deal with it myself.' She gives a wry smile and I wait for more, my mouth open. 'Put it this way, I made him regret ever thinking of doing that to me again.' She swipes her hand so hard against the bamboo fruit bowl, it makes me jump as it launches into the air and across the room, scattering apples and oranges everywhere.

I imagine her threatening him with a Bobbitt. Women are capable of anything when pushed to the edge.

'When did his behaviour towards you change? Were there any warning signs?' I'm not sure what to think. Jamie has been drinking more as our wedding day gets closer and he does lose his temper sometimes, but I thought it was down to his anxiety. Now I'm not sure.

'After he broke my arm that first time, his drinking and anger towards me gradually got worse. An old boyfriend spoke to me in the pub one day and Jamie went crazy, put the poor bloke in hospital. Jamie's drinking had escalated, and he was losing his temper more often. I found out later that a lot of the things he'd told me were lies. I'd trusted him completely, believed what he told me, because I thought we were in love.'

'God, I'm so sorry.' I wring my hands together. My head is all over the place. Should I be worried? Could he really turn against me? He was a lot younger when he was with Brooke and maybe he was lashing out because he was bullied in the army. He's had hours of therapy since then and it has helped. But the truth is he'd go ballistic if he knew I'd slept with my ex, and worse if he saw the video of me cheating on him. But any bloke would, wouldn't they?

Brooke picks up a mini croissant and cuts it open with a butter knife. Confiding in Jamie's ex-girlfriend may not have been my smartest move. I hope I can trust her to keep it to herself, because whatever happens now, she knows all about my darkest secret.

29

'You promise you won't say anything to Jamie about Ryan and the video?' I say to Brooke.

'No, of course not.' She looks offended that I'd think that. 'I wouldn't put you in danger.'

'Thanks. I had to ask.'

'Of course. You're a woman who's been treated appallingly by a bloke. I know exactly how that feels.' She frowns, her eyes creased with understanding. I'm still finding it difficult to believe Jamie was capable of being so awful to her.

'I'm ashamed of what I did with Ryan and I don't want to jeopardise my relationship with Jamie. I do love him.'

'I know you do. I'm hoping you're right about the therapy and that he's kinder than he used to be.' She pats my arm and I sigh inwardly with relief.

'Thank you for helping me,' I say, and she smiles briefly.

I don't want to mention that Jamie is going to tell her not to come to our wedding, although 'Beth's' name wasn't on the guest list in the first place, I asked her to come. She may think she's welcome as Brooke, but it's probably better if she wasn't there given how angry he was when he last saw her.

'Who will you say you are to Ryan?'

'Your lawyer.' A smug smile appears on her lips. 'Then I just need you to let me know if he dares to contact you again, okay?'

'Yes, of course. That's amazing, thank you.' I press my palms together. I'm not an overtly religious person, but despite everything that happened last night, I want to thank a higher power for sending Brooke my way.

'I don't want to have to break his bones, or anything,' she chuckles, 'but I will if I have to.' She flashes another smile.

'Thank you for doing this for me.'

'We don't know if he's going to stop yet. If he's really dumb and carries on, I'll have to move on to Plan B.'

Her expression is serious now, menacing even. Ryan's going to wish he'd left me alone if he's not careful. I don't think any of my friends would offer to do something like this for me. I slide off my stool and open my arms out to her. She leans forward and I hug her briefly.

Brooke steps back and pushes her hair behind her ears. 'The quicker we can rid ourselves of toxic men, the better.' She lifts her coffee cup, and I raise mine to hers.

She goes upstairs for a shower while I tidy up and pick up the fruit and bowl from the floor. By the time I've had a shower, dressed and come back down, most of the others are up having breakfast, in various states of recovery from the night before.

'How are you?' Danielle asks, bowl of cornflakes in one hand, spoon in the other. She's only wearing an oversized T-shirt and nothing on her feet.

'I didn't really drink that much towards the end of the night. I'd already puked up, so I don't feel *too* bad today, how about you?'

'I'm okay, thanks.' Danielle always drinks in moderation.

'Given the state of everyone, I propose we have an hour catching up on sleep or lounging around the pool until it's time to leave. Although I've warned everyone not to go in the water after the fox incident last night. I've pinged an email about it to the owners.'

'Good, thank you. Sounds like a plan to me. I could not handle any more party games.'

I sigh with relief and she grins, mouth full of cornflakes and milk. The truth is I'm desperate to get home to Freya. I've texted Mum this morning and she said they were at the shops. She told me not to rush home. I asked her to FaceTime me so I can say good morning to Freya face to face, but so far, she's not answered. I'm trying not to let it worry me, but I just wanted to say hello to my daughter, see her face, make sure she's happy. She's used to me being there, so it's bound to feel a bit strange for her. I don't want her to think I'm not coming home.

'Have you seen Lauren or Brooke this morning?' Danielle asks.

'Yeah, Brooke was up early with me. We had a chat. She's genuinely sorry. Says she didn't mean any harm by coming here. She thought, with so many hens, I wouldn't even pay attention to her. And it does sound like Lauren was the one behind all of the antics, tying me up and going to Jamie's stag. This jealous streak over Jamie is making her quite unpleasant to be around. Brooke has been so understanding and helpful.' I look up at Danielle, trying to see if she believes me. 'She said she didn't have a good relationship with Jamie,' I add in a lowered voice.

'Really?' Danielle snaps round to frown at me.

'I can't tell you any more because obviously it's personal and not my place to say. She's not nearly as full of herself as she first seemed, that's for sure,' I say in a whisper. Danielle raises her eyebrows. I can't tell her what I told Brooke about Ryan just yet either, but maybe when he leaves me alone, I'll be ready to confide in her. Much as I love Danielle, she can be a bit strait-laced, and her finding out I was unfaithful to Jamie is already making her look at me with judging eyes.

'Someone said Lauren went off for a run in the Peaks about an hour ago. I don't think Brooke went with her and she probably didn't invite anyone else because most people were still in bed.'

'I went back upstairs soon after Brooke went for a shower. Maybe she's in her room,' I say. 'She already went on a run around five o'clock this morning so I don't suppose she went again. Lauren's probably gone off trying to avoid me.'

'Lauren definitely went on her own,' Sarah says. 'I saw her out of my bedroom window, because Tilly and Bonnie had just gone for a walk in a different direction.' Danielle is only half listening, distracted by Emma who needs help working the air fryer.

I don't mention that I left a note under Lauren's door earlier to say we needed to talk. She didn't reply. Maybe she'd already gone by then, or perhaps it was her way of avoiding coming to speak to me?

Brooke must have contacted Ryan already, because I've not heard from him this morning, which is unusual. Her warning him to leave me alone seems to have worked, which feels like a miracle after weeks of him pestering me. I can hardly believe it. I check my phone again and there's nothing from him, not even one emoji. I'm ridiculously buoyed by the result of her intervention until I see a new WhatsApp message.

> PAY £10K INTO THIS BANK ACCOUNT TODAY
> OR YOU WON'T MAKE IT TO YOUR BIG DAY

30

My heart starts pounding as I scan round the kitchen at all the faces of my friends, innocently chatting to each other, serving themselves pastries and coffee, toast and rashers of bacon. Not one of them looks guilty let alone capable of blackmail. But someone has sent this to me, demanding even more money and threatening my life.

I refuse to give in to whoever is sending these demands. I need to catch the person red-handed. There's one sure way of finding out the culprit. Three of my friends are holding their phones. The others have them face up or down on the counter or table in front of them. Emma has just gone outside with a bag of rubbish. I tap open WhatsApp and type a question mark in the reply dialogue box. I scan round the room again. No one is watching me as I discreetly press send.

'What's this rotting smell?' Emma suddenly shouts from the patio. Everyone goes outside, so if there was a flash or a bleep on anyone's phone, I've completely missed it.

Emma is standing beside the bin with the lid up. 'Who dumped a box of worms in here?'

'That smell is utterly foul.' Danielle waves her hand in front of her nose. She flashes the torch from her camera into the bin. 'Oh my God, are they worms or maggots?'

Emma looks in and nods then doubles over and retches.

'They're entrails from some poor animal,' I tell them. 'I'm guessing one of you hens thought it would be funny to send them to me this morning.' I don't look at anyone in particular, but I try to gauge their reactions. No one reacts strangely or does anything out of place.

'Why would you think someone here did it?' Danielle frowns, clearly offended.

'I don't know. Because of the nail varnish on the bed and the message in lipstick on the mirror,' I say, careful not to upset her further, but taking her point.

'What message in lipstick?' Samantha asks, turning to the others, bemused. I tell them about the death threat on my ensuite mirror.

'That's evil,' she says and the others agree.

'And so is this. Does anyone know anything about it?' Sarah studies everyone's faces. 'Did you see anyone outside, a car maybe, the person who delivered it?' All the hens cast their eyes suspiciously at each other and troop back inside.

Emma's phone beeps, and for a second I can't help wondering if my message was slightly delayed in the ether.

'It's Bonnie,' she says, frowning at me staring at her. She swallows before continuing. 'They tried to contact Lauren to meet up but got no reply, so they walked along part of the Monsal Trail and have found her unconscious on the ground.'

I blink rapidly and press my hand to my chest, speechless for a second. 'What do they think happened?'

'She says it looks like Lauren slipped. They've called an ambulance and it's on its way.'

'I can't sit here waiting for news. I'm going down there. Anyone else coming?' I say to all the shocked faces gathered around me. Danielle starts to cry.

'I think I know which way they might have gone,' Emma says, taking off her dressing gown and putting on her waterproof coat and trainers. 'Lauren asked me yesterday for suggestions on an easy route she could take straight from the doorstep.' She pulls up a map of our location on her phone and pinches the screen. 'I suggested a scenic route near Monsal Head, which isn't too far from here.'

'Great. You lead the way.' I can't see my red hoodie, so I take my fleece from a hook by the front door.

'I'll come,' Sarah says and grabs her hoodie off the back of the breakfast bar stool, at the same time slipping her feet into a pair of flat ankle boots.

'I'm coming too,' Danielle says, wiping her eyes on the back of her sleeve and taking down the first aid kit from the kitchen wall.

Ten minutes later we're jogging along a hilly road in the Peak District National Park. The early morning sunshine has gone and a misty rain is hanging in the air, making it difficult to judge what's up ahead. The rough, bumpy terrain is marked out by dry-stone walls. Thistles sway along the roadside and there are no trees around for shelter, not that the sheep seem to mind. It's not the easiest or safest place to go for a run without the possibility of twisting your ankle, or worse, missing your footing completely and falling into a ditch.

The Headstone viaduct becomes visible in the distance, and the River Wye meanders snake-like through the landscape. It's been raining overnight, and the early morning sun wasn't warm enough to dry it out, so everywhere is muddy and slippery. Lauren didn't bring her walking boots as she told me she wasn't expecting to have time to go out. She'll be wearing her usual trainers, which won't have enough grip for this damp weather.

As we reach the top of a slope, I spot a dot of red in the distance.

'Is that them?' I ask the others, and wave anyway, calling Bonnie's name.

'Yes, I think it is,' Danielle says and we hurry on, trying to move faster but we're also mindful not to slip and have a second casualty on our hands.

As we get nearer, we see Lauren lying on the ground. She's wearing my red hoodie. She didn't ask to borrow it but thank goodness she did because it's a beacon in the middle of this wilderness. We head straight towards Bonnie who is standing with Lauren, waving and calling to us. In the distance is the faint sound of the ambulance siren approaching.

We manage to reach them before the paramedics do. Lauren is still unconscious and lying awkwardly, her leg at an angle, eyes shut, body completely still.

'Are you okay?' I say to Bonnie and Tilly.

'Thank God the ambulance is on its way,' Bonnie says, her hands in her hair.

'What do you think happened?' I ask then lean over to catch my breath, hands on my knees.

'See these skid marks? It looks like she lost her balance and slipped down this muddy slope. I think she's broken her leg. I didn't want to move her. I called 999 straight away and texted you. Luckily, I brought my phone with me. She must have banged her head, because she's out cold. Do you think she'll be okay?' Distress fills Bonnie's high-pitched voice.

'I hope so.' I kneel beside Lauren. My hands hover above her, not knowing what to do. I resist the need to comfort her, in case she's injured her neck or spine. There are a couple of cigarette butts near her. The brand she was smoking last night.

I feel bad all over again for chucking Lauren's phone in the swimming pool. If she'd had it with her, she would have called for help. Thank goodness Bonnie and Tilly came to find her or she could have been stranded for hours.

Danielle and Emma wave to the ambulance as it approaches. They park as near as they can and two paramedics hurry over with a stretcher. Bonnie repeats to them what she's just told us.

Tilly offers to go with Lauren to the hospital and I give them Lauren's mum's phone number. The ambulance leaves with Lauren still unconscious.

Back at the holiday cottage, I tell the others what has happened, and we hug then pack up our things in sombre silence. The owners have waived the late charge for leaving after 10 a.m. given the unforeseen circumstances. Most of my friends are ready to go and leave straight away. There's no sign of Brooke, so she must have gone home early.

Danielle drives me to my parents' house. We don't speak except about the weather.

Lauren may not have been the best friend to me lately, but I'd never wish something like this on her. What if she's been left brain damaged? I'll never forgive myself if she doesn't get better. The sad truth is, we don't know if she's going to pull through.

31

On the drive home, I call Jamie to see if he's at Mum and Dad's yet. I've not told him about the funeral flowers turning up on the lawn, and I don't know if they'll tell him themselves or wait for me to. He's not answering so I leave a message to let him know I'm on my way.

I've not had another message from Ryan. By now I'd probably have had five or more, pestering me for an answer to his demands for money, giving me another extension to his ultimatum. I assume Brooke's message to him pretending to be my lawyer has hit the right nerve, and he knows not to pursue me, or he'll suffer the consequences. At least I hope his silence means that.

Could he be quietly following through on his threat to send the sex video to Jamie? What if he goes ahead and emails it to him without warning me? My stomach curdles at the thought of not knowing and what Jamie's reaction will be. I've imagined a thousand times him opening it and realising what it is, and each time I feel a bit sicker. With the wedding only a few days away, I don't want anything to sour his feelings for me or make him jealous and angry. I made one stupid mistake. It feels wrong not to have been honest with Jamie. I feel terrible about sleeping with Ryan one last time, and I wish with all my heart it hadn't happened, but I can't let it ruin the rest of my life. I can't let Ryan hold it over me. Who's to say he won't keep on demanding I pay him £20,000, and then more? Where will it end? Ultimately, I need to break his power and tell Jamie myself. But I can only do it when I feel safe and ready.

'Are you okay?' Danielle asks.

'Yeah, just a few things on my mind. It's been a strange weekend.'

'I'm sorry it turned out like this. It was meant to be fun.' She sounds hurt. It's just like her to take it to heart. I hope she doesn't think I'm having a sideways dig at her party planning skills.

'But it's not your fault at all; you weren't to know about Brooke turning up and Lauren behaving like that.'

'I'm disappointed too,' she sniffs. 'I wanted it to be the best hen weekend for you.'

'It wasn't all bad. The meal was lovely, and it was so good to see people I've not seen in ages. I need to make more effort to stay in touch.'

My phone pings. It's a message from Bonnie. 'Lauren regained consciousness on the way to the hospital. Thank goodness.'

'Hopefully it means she's going to be okay.'

We carry on in comfortable silence.

'Do you think I should have gone with Lauren in the ambulance?' I ask.

'Absolutely not. Your daughter is your priority, and quite honestly, after the way Lauren has behaved towards you, she doesn't deserve your care and attention, even after what's happened to her.'

'I'm glad Tilly went with her. At least she wasn't alone when she woke up. She didn't deserve something like that happening to her.'

'I'm sorry Megan, but karma came for her; that's how it works in my book.'

'Really? Isn't that a bit harsh?' I'm shocked at Danielle's attitude. She's supposed to be Lauren's friend. I thought she'd have more empathy than this.

'I believe karma always catches up with people in the end.'

I'm not sure I believe in karma. There are plenty of people who do bad things in this world and get away with it. It doesn't mean they're bad people.

'If you say so,' I mutter, wondering if she's making the point so strongly because of what *I* did wrong. Is she trying to tell me I'm going to get my comeuppance for being unfaithful to Jamie?

'I do say so.' She pauses and pulls a wide smile like she's bursting to say something else controversial. 'Because, you know what I think?' She doesn't wait for my reply. 'I think Lauren and Brooke had an argument.' She presses her finger to her lips but can't help smiling.

'What do you mean?'

'Why else did Brooke leave without saying goodbye?' Danielle scoffs.

'I don't know. She mentioned to me she might leave early.'

'You don't think it's strange that Lauren went off on her own when they've been so tight all weekend?' She says it with an undertone of conspiracy as though this is the only possible explanation as far as she can see.

'I suppose it's possible they had cross words.'

Danielle shrugs but seems to have a lot more she wants to say.

'Brooke's really not as bad as you think,' I say. 'It's not fair that you're jumping to conclusions.'

Danielle scrapes through a gear change. 'Well, I don't like her. Turning up at Jamie's stag do as the stripper, and his fiancée's hen party uninvited? Please. Why didn't she do the right thing and turn it down?'

'I think you've got her all wrong. Yes, she was annoying going along with Lauren's stupid pranks, and I admit I was taken aback that she's Jamie's ex, but someone booked her to do that job. Maybe she can't afford to turn work down. If you took the time to get to know her, you'd see she has a vulnerable side like the rest of us. She's had a really hard time.'

'I'm sorry to hear that, but honestly, how can you be so nice to her when she lied to you about who she really is?'

'Because she went out of her way to help me with something. Anyway, she admitted she lied because she was curious about me. She wanted to find out who Jamie was marrying.' I'm careful not to mention that she also wanted to warn me about his behaviour.

'Is that something I couldn't help you with?'

'I hadn't told you about it.'

Danielle is silent.

'It's to do with my truth question. The secret I've been keeping from Jamie.' I pause and she glances at me then looks back at the road.

'You don't have to tell me the details,' she says in a sulky voice.

'I didn't want to worry you and you'd be like me, not knowing what to do about it.'

'Whereas Brooke has all the answers?'

'Ryan has been trying to blackmail me. He filmed us that last time. Now he's threatening to show it to Jamie. Brooke managed to put a stop to him pestering me because she's been through something similar, that's all.'

'I see. So she doesn't think you should be honest?' Danielle says it in such a disappointed voice.

'It's not that simple.'

But it's not only Danielle who doesn't trust Brooke. The words of the woman in the queue for the ladies pops into my head. *Steer well clear of that one if you value your sanity.* She didn't say how she knew Brooke or why she said that. Maybe she didn't know her at all. Maybe Brooke flirted with this woman's boyfriend, and to get her own back she decided to go round making bitchy remarks about her? I've seen people punched for less. Or maybe it's a simple case of rivalry. The woman was jealous because Brooke was chatting up the bloke she was after. She's much prettier than that woman and at least ten years younger. Similar to how she would have looked like once, I guess.

We spend the rest of the journey in near silence. It's not been the fun, joyful weekend I'd hoped for. When Danielle pulls into my parents' road, I already know that she won't come in for a cup of tea. Sure enough, she politely declines, so I grab my small suitcase and wave goodbye to her from the pavement.

Mum comes rushing out of the house to greet me. 'Thank God you're back,' she says, throwing her arms around me in a hug.

'What's wrong, Mum? Is Jamie here yet?'

'He messaged to say he's on his way.'

'What is it then? Has something happened?'

'It's nothing really, everything's fine now,' Mum says, making hand gestures as though she's smoothing out a tablecloth, but there's an edge to her voice she can't disguise, and it makes me shiver.

'Freya's okay?' I ask tentatively.

'Yes, yes, of course she is.' She delivers the words abruptly. 'She's playing in the garden with her grandad.'

'So what's wrong?'

'Please promise to stay calm.' Mum holds the top of both my arms and looks me in the eyes.

'Go on.' My stomach twists into a tight knot.

'The thing is... we lost Freya this morning in M&S.'

32

'You did what? Tell me how, Mum?' I yell, pulling my arms out of her grasp and stepping away from her. 'Why didn't you call me straight away?'

'I wanted to, of course I did, but your dad wouldn't let me.' She opens out her palms, like she had no choice in the matter.

'You should have called me. Anything could have happened to her.' I spin away from her, a tidal wave rising in my chest.

'I know, I know and I'm sorry. We're sorry.'

'So what happened? Tell me everything.'

'I was looking for a new pair of trousers for your dad and I honestly only took my eyes off Freya for a second, but you know what she's like, she's so quick now. Anyway, I told your dad to keep an eye on her too, just for a minute, but I think I distracted him asking if he liked the cotton mix material because I remember him looking at it as he felt it between his thumb and forefinger. When we looked down, Freya wasn't there. We searched around the clothes rails calling her name, but she'd disappeared. It was awful. I thought I was going to faint with anxiety. One second she was there, and the next it was like she'd vanished into thin air.' She raises her hands. I shake my head in disbelief that this could have happened.

'I can't even bear hearing about it.' I cover my ears. 'Is she really okay? What else aren't you telling me? I need to see her right now. Did she hurt herself, was she upset?' I don't wait for Mum's answers to any of my questions, but march up the path to the front door and push it open, carrying on through the house to the kitchen at the back, where I catch a glimpse of Dad out of the window, fishing hat on, bending down to help Freya climb the steps of her mini slide in their neat medium-sized garden. My heart lifts seeing her smiling and giggling and seemingly unhurt. Hopefully she's unaware that she was ever in any danger.

My arms prickle as Mum silently approaches and stands behind me. She's trying to control her breathing. I know I'm being hard on her but the thought of losing Freya is so terrifying. Imagining her lost and not knowing where we are, or someone snatching her away and never seeing her again halts my breath.

'Why didn't you take her out in her pushchair like I told you to.' The words shoot out of my mouth without me even looking round at Mum. I regret the accusing tone immediately, but I can't help it. It took all my strength and trust to leave her with them. I cannot believe my parents lost her. What if they hadn't found her?

I step outside to the edge of the lawn and as soon as Freya sees me, she squeals with delight and toddles towards me faster than ever, her gorgeous chubby little arms outstretched. I bend down and sweep her up into my arms, holding her warm body close to mine. I never want to let her go. I inhale her sweet soapy-smelling hair and my eyes fill with tears of relief and gratitude.

Dad comes over and puts an arm out to hug me, but I step back, and a puzzled frown passes over his brow.

'How could you not be more careful?' I ask him, squinting at the sun piercing my eyes.

'We're sorry, darling. She's so quick and curious. I'm sure she didn't mean it.'

'Of course she didn't mean it!' I blink in disbelief that he could think it was her fault. 'Are you suggesting Freya hid from you on purpose, to cause trouble?'

Dad opens his mouth and closes it again, looking to Mum to feed him the right answer.

'She's not capable of being naughty, if that's what you're thinking.' I hold Freya closer to me.

'He's not saying Freya's naughty, love. We took the pushchair but she just wouldn't stay in it. She was squirming around and grizzling, dragging her nice shoes along the ground. We had to let her out; people were beginning to stare at her, and us. Probably wondering why we were letting her behave like that.'

'Were they really? Does it matter what other people think?'

'Well yes, people may have been wondering if she was okay.'

'She was only gone for a few moments.' Dad's face screws up. He really seems to believe this makes it okay.

'But it felt much, much longer,' Mum sniffs and wipes her damp eyes with her fingers.

'Was it really only a few moments? Are you even sure if you were so taken up with... a pair of trousers.' I can't believe I'm talking like this to them. My anger and frustration from the weekend are catching up with me. It's not like me to take it out on my kind and helpful parents.

'We are so sorry, Megan. I can't even contemplate how we'd have coped if we hadn't found her.'

'Don't even go there, Mum.' I shake my head and tears fall from my eyes. I reach out and hug them both, whispering how sorry I am for losing my temper and silently thankful that Freya hadn't wandered too far away.

'I did suggest reins, didn't I?' Mum says in the highly strung voice she slips into when she's being challenged. I pull away from her.

'I really don't like the idea of holding my daughter on something that looks like a leash. I always keep her in the pushchair when I'm at the shops.'

Mum opens a drawer in the dresser and hands me a box. 'I took the liberty of buying these for you. I hope you don't mind.'

I turn the box over in my hand and raise my eyebrows at the picture of a happy child wearing a full harness while her parent is holding the lead.

'Please try them,' Dad says. 'We used them for you.'

I take the box with good grace and a brief smile, but I can't help thinking of a small dog being taken for a walk.

'So where *did* you find her?' I ask.

'The funny thing is, it wasn't us who spotted her in the end, was it love?' Dad says to Mum with a broad smile.

Mum nods at him which means she thinks it's okay for him to tell me more.

'It was some kind chap apparently,' Mum says.

'He found her wandering around and took her to one of the staff. They put out a call to all the customers to see if anyone had lost a child,' Dad says, 'so of course we went straight over. The manager said one of her female colleagues was looking after Freya, then she asked us a few questions about what Freya was wearing and who we were and asked her mummy's name. I suppose it was to make sure it matched up with what Freya had told them and we were who we said we were.'

'She said the man saw Freya on her own, running around the

side of a rail of summer dresses.' Mum wipes her eyes with a hanky.

I blink at Mum then Dad and shake my head. 'So you didn't get to thank the man?'

'Oh no. He'd already gone,' Mum adds.

'We were so relieved to see Freya coming towards us holding the manager's hand, weren't we Dora?'

Mum nods, unable to speak, tears welling up in her eyes as I stare into them to communicate that she let me down.

I involuntarily shiver thinking about what could have happened.

That man could so easily have walked off with my daughter.

33

'I can't get my head round what I'm hearing.'

They both blink back at me.

'What if this man had left the shop with her?' I say with dismay.

'We're so sorry. We know it's unforgiveable,' Dad says, visibly shaken by my reaction.

'I just can't believe you actually lost her and you didn't even think to call me.' I cover my mouth.

'We didn't know what to do for the best.' Mum clings to Dad's arm.

'Please tell me again exactly what happened.'

Dad runs through it again, about the trousers he was looking at and how he became distracted.

'We let go of her hand and lost sight of her. She didn't run off exactly, just toddled away. Maybe she thought hiding from us was a good game,' Mum says.

'What if this man snatched her and made it look like she wandered away?'

'Now you're being silly. I think we'd have noticed if she'd

been taken,' Dad says, exchanging another side-glance with Mum, clearly convinced I'm overreacting. I can tell neither of them are going to change their minds.

'How do you know she "just toddled away" if you didn't see her go?'

Mum and Dad look blankly at each other.

'You're right, we aren't certain,' Dad says.

'Do you know what the man looked like, what he was wearing?'

'The manager made a comment about how our generation shouldn't be so quick to judge young people who wear these black hoodies because this young man, as she called him, did the right thing handing the little girl in.'

I nod. Problem is, from that description, it could be anyone. The distinctive hum of Jamie's car pulls up on the drive.

Moments later, the doorbell rings.

'Please don't say anything to Jamie about losing her. I want to tell him myself.' It's been distressing enough for me, so it's important I pick the right moment when I can fully support him.

Mum and Dad look surprised but nod at me, tight-lipped. I can tell they're not happy keeping this from him. I pass Freya to Mum and answer the door.

Jamie is standing on the doorstep. He's wearing jeans and a T-shirt and looks like he's not slept for ten years. Despite all the questions that have been building up in me about Brooke, I throw my arms around him and let the relief flood through me that our daughter is okay.

'Are you all right? That's quite a welcome. I was expecting a bollocking after last night.'

'That can wait.' I kiss his lips.

Mum and Dad say hello.

He takes Freya from Mum.

My phone beeps. It's a text from Bonnie at the hospital.

> Lauren has a severe concussion and a broken leg but is otherwise okay. Thinks a man pushed her over.

I text a reply.

> I hope she's going to be okay! OMG, could it be the same man who was at the cottage?

> Don't know. She's gone for scans. Will try and find out what she saw.

I tell them all about Lauren's accident and the update.

'That's terrible, does she think the man pushed her on purpose?' Mum says.

'I don't know.'

'I hope she's going to be alright,' Dad chimes in.

Jamie doesn't say anything. Strange that there's no reaction from him, although I imagine he has mixed feelings after her unruly behaviour last night. He wouldn't have gone for a run and bumped into her on purpose, would he? Their hotel wasn't too far away from Monsal Head. No, that's silly. I shake the thought away. After everything Brooke said, my mind is inventing all sorts of crazy scenarios.

'Why don't you come in for a cup of tea?'

I thank her but decline, saying we need to go home.

We say our goodbyes and thank them for having Freya. I won't tell Jamie about them 'losing' her until we're alone. I don't want to embarrass them or upset him. He trusts them as much as I do.

Jamie picks up Freya's overnight bag.

'Wow, this is heavy, what have you got in here?'

'Freya and I did some baking, so I've packed a tin of fairy cakes for you,' Mum says with a smile.

'Thanks,' we both say and I instantly feel terrible for getting upset with them when they're so good with Freya. I'm hardly in a position to make a moral judgement about their behaviour.

How little they would think of me if they knew the growing number of secrets I'm keeping from my husband to be.

34

'How are you?' I ask as Jamie straps Freya into her car seat. I don't really want to talk about last night but know we're going to have to. He kisses my cheek, then Freya's, and shuts her door. We jump in the front seats, and he gazes across at me as he fastens his seatbelt.

'Rough as anything. How about you? Have you recovered from your ordeal?' He starts the car, fixing his eyes ahead.

'Which one?' I say sarcastically. 'Being tied to a lamppost or finding your ex-girlfriend stripping for you?' It hurts more than I'm letting on. I wish we'd gone out for a meal like I'd originally wanted to. It would have been much more civilised, and I could have been home the same evening. But my friends wanted to organise it for me, and I let myself be swayed. Right now, I can't imagine leaving Freya with my parents again any time soon, or with anyone else come to that. How are we going to get away on our honeymoon? I'll have to broach the idea to Jamie of taking Freya with us.

'I'm so sorry, Megs. I feel responsible for Brooke turning up.

If I'd realised she was pretending to be my cousin to get into your party, I could have warned you about her.'

'She was actually quite kind to me.'

'You can't believe a word she says.' He glances at me and scratches the stubble on his chin. Brooke warned me he'd say this.

The car pulls away. I wave at my parents standing on the doorstep. Dad holds up a hand in a final salute before they go inside and close the front door. Much as they adore Freya, they're probably relieved to have some peace and quiet again.

'I didn't realise Lauren still has such a crush on you. She thinks I stole you away from her.' I'm still trying to make sense of her behaviour towards me. I'd really hoped that asking her to be one of my bridesmaids and letting her help organise the party games might show her how much I want to mend our friendship. I picture her lying in a hospital bed and I feel bad talking about her, but there are so many things I want to understand. I'd like to know why she's still adamant that I stole Jamie away from her, and why tell Brooke about it, who she barely knew? Was she aiming to ruin my weekend? I hope we can fix our friendship after this. I want her to fully recover. I'd never wish anything bad to happen to her.

'Yeah, I thought Lauren was acting weird, wanting to put her arms around me, and kiss me.'

'Maybe she's been suppressing anger and resentment towards me all this time. I thought she was pleased for us, because she's been happily helping organise the party games.'

'So what exactly happened this morning? How did she end up in hospital?' Jamie checks the rearview mirror.

I explain everything Bonnie told me.

'Poor Lauren. I feel bad saying this, but she was beyond annoying last night. But no one would wish that on her, would they? I'm glad she's woken up, and I hope she's going to be alright,' he says and checks the rearview mirror again, frowning. 'So what lies did Brooke tell you about me?'

A spike of adrenaline stabs my chest. 'Not much really. Only that you dated years ago.' I daren't say anything else and make him angry, especially when he's already told me not to believe a word she says.

'There's no way she's coming to the wedding.' He stops at a set of traffic lights and checks all his mirrors.

I hesitate a moment, but he's going to find out. 'I told her she could come,' I say quietly, half hoping he might not hear because he's not going to like it.

'Why would you do that?' he snaps back. He seems preoccupied with the car behind him.

'She's not as bad as you're making out. Not really. Anyway, it would seem ungrateful because she turned out to be an unexpected hero for me. She helped me a lot this weekend, despite doing what she did.' I tell him about the dead fox in the pool, and how she was the only one who'd helped me fish it out, and then this morning with the animal entrails delivered in a box.

'What the hell?' He frowns at me.

'And she apologised profusely about tying me to a lamppost. Said it was meant to be a bit of fun that went too far. We talked, and she opened up to me about some things that have happened to her in the past, and then she gave me some advice about something... important.'

'She gave *you* advice?' Jamie snorts a laugh, but it's short-lived. 'About what? I hope you've not given her any private information about us, because she loves to gossip.'

I decide not to answer his question. I'm not telling him what we discussed, when she's told me in confidence. Especially as some of it is about him. I'm disappointed he hasn't got anything nice to say about Brooke. I've not seen this mean side of him before, except when he's had too much to drink. Maybe there is some truth in the things she told me about him. It's possible he was like that back then, because he'd been through a terrible time, which probably made him an angry young man for a while. But he's not like that now. Not with me or Freya.

'She didn't strike me as a gossipy sort of person,' I say. 'I think she's quite loyal and when she promises to do something, she sticks to her word.'

'Yeah well, you don't know her like I do. She's known for having a baggy mouth when it suits her. But not always, I'll give her that.' He looks again in the rearview mirror and a giggling Freya seems to distract him. He sticks his tongue out at her.

'Oh right.' I glance down at the black car mat, half expecting the space beneath my feet to open up and suck me in as realisation hits. Shit. What have I done? Brooke promised not to tell anyone anything about what Ryan did to me, but can I trust her? What if she blurts it all out to Jamie the first chance she gets? He might never forgive me. I shouldn't have said a word. I need to tell him everything myself, but as I go to speak, he does first.

'There's something else I need to tell you about Brooke.' Jamie pulls up sharp at a set of traffic lights. His focus is straight ahead, as though he's blinkered.

'No need to make it sound so ominous,' I joke, but Jamie isn't laughing. His face is serious. He glances over his shoulder at the car behind. My stomach flips. What's going on? He's not his usual jolly self, keen to share something amusing with me. What if Brooke has already told him about Ryan? Is that why she took the job at his stag do? Jamie could be biding his time, seeing if I confess or waiting to tell me it's over.

'The thing is, I didn't want to mention her deception and ruin your hen night.' His head dips a touch in my direction, as though he considers looking at me and then can't face it. The lights change to amber.

I frown. 'What do you mean?' My stomach turns to jelly.

Jamie slams his foot down the moment the light turns green, jolting me forward as we take off towards the bypass. I check the side mirror then twist round to see if Freya is okay. She's holding her teddy up to her nose and sucking her thumb. I sit back round, pressed to the seat by the centrifugal force of the car speeding, as though Jamie's a pilot about to lift off. He joins the motorway and crosses straight over into the fast lane, all the time checking behind him. I hold my breath. He's usually such a careful driver.

'Are you going to tell me what you mean?' There's a ring of alarm in my voice. He glances across at me, hands gripping the wheel tighter. A black van moves into the middle lane right next to us. From where I'm sitting, it looks far too close. The driver is wearing a black beanie and his ginger hair and beard sprouts wildly from most areas of his face. Another black Mercedes van suddenly brakes hard in front of us.

'Shit!' Jamie shouts and hits the brakes just in time to avoid hitting the back of it. We all jolt forwards and Freya starts crying.

'What the hell is going on?' I scream. Other cars are hooting and swerving into the slow lane to manoeuvre around us. The van in the middle lane won't budge. 'He needs to move; he's boxing us in.' I press my face to the window and point and shout at the driver, but either he can't see me or he's ignoring me. I wind down the window and wave my hand and shout at him but he's not looking at us. The van edges closer to the side of our car until it's only inches away. It's still moving in, closer and closer. I scream again and my hand flies up to my mouth as the van scrapes into our car, nudging us over.

'What the fuck?' Jamie glares across at the driver. I've never seen him so angry and terrified at the same time.

Now a third black van is driving up behind us at such speed, I wonder if this is the end. I press myself into the back of the seat, gripping the door handle and squeezing my eyes shut. I snake my arm behind me, reaching for Freya, bracing for the impact at any second.

Praying we all survive.

35

I open one eye, bracing myself for the full force of a van ramming into the back of us, but the impact doesn't come. Instead, from what I can see in the wing mirror, the van has slowed right down within inches of our rear bumper, remaining dangerously close. We are trapped. The van in front of us is dictating how fast we can go and the one in the middle lane to our left has moved to a more normal distance, but it's still driving parallel to us, creating a blockage so no other driver can move around us. Beeping horns sound in all directions from infuriated drivers.

'Where are the police when you need them?' My hands hurt from gripping the door handle and stretching to Freya behind me. Jamie leans forward, hyper-concentrating, his face a sheen of sweat. I check my side mirror again and relief washes over me at seeing a blue flashing light behind us, heading this way. Moments later a police siren fills the air and just as quickly as they arrived, the three black vans speed off. I have my camera ready to snap photos of their number plates, but they're too quick, so I try to memorise the one from the side of us as it zooms away. Two police motorbikes zip after them, sounding like giant killer wasps.

'Are you all right, sweetheart?' I twist round and gently stroke Freya's bare foot. Her crying has turned into a grizzle, which is sometimes a sign of thirst or hunger, but this time it must be the shock of the car jolting so hard or from our stress and shouting.

'It's all right, darling, we'll stop in a minute.' I try to speak in a soothing tone, but there's a distinct rattle of nerves in my voice I can't hide.

'I think we should pull over, get a coffee,' I say to Jamie in a low voice. 'You look like you need it too. I know I do.' My hand is trembling when I touch his leg, and he jumps so violently I think he's going to swerve right out of the lane. Without answering, he flicks the indicator and follows the signs for the services.

In the café, I sit at a table with our coffees and a small strawberry milkshake in a carton for Freya while Jamie slopes off to the bathroom. He comes back with red eyes and blotchy cheeks. I'm guessing he's washed his face, although he looks like he's been crying. I reach for his hand, but he doesn't take mine. He sits in the chair opposite me and hunches over the table, wiping his face on his sleeves.

'I can drive the last stretch home if you don't feel up to it,' I say. 'That was quite an ordeal.' I turn the pushchair so we can both see Freya.

He shakes his head, looking down at the wet smears on the freshly wiped table.

'We need to report this to the police.' I gently push his coffee towards him. 'Do you know who those men were?'

He shakes his head again and lifts the cup of coffee to his lips. His hand is trembling, but he manages to slurp a mouthful before rattling the cup back into the saucer.

'I took down part of the number plate of the van that scraped the side of our car. I want to report it, but I think as the driver, they'll want to speak to you too.'

'Leave it,' he snaps, fixing me with his puffy eyes. Maybe he *has* been crying.

'But they shouldn't be allowed to get away with that dangerous behaviour. We had a child in the car.' Tears fill my eyes at the thought of what could have happened. I'm still shaken too. They completely boxed us in and left us at their mercy. I feared for our lives. I thought at any moment the car behind was going to shunt into us, and we'd crash into the car in front.

He shakes his head as though it's non-negotiable.

'Are you saying you *know* who did this?'

He stays silent and stares down at the table.

'Is there something you're not telling me?' I ask him.

His fingers lace together. He doesn't answer so I carry on talking.

'You were going to tell me something about Brooke. Is what just happened to us to do with that?'

'I think so.' His voice sounds strange and small and broken. He rubs his forehead with the heel of his hand.

'You said something about her deception. What did you mean?'

He sighs deeply. 'Brooke has a dark side to her.'

'What are you talking about?' I blink rapidly as I try to comprehend. 'I don't understand.' I think of the easy way I opened up to her. Told her private things I'd barely told anyone else.

He doesn't answer. He's holding the tips of Freya's fingers.

'Jamie,' I snap, trying to make him look at me. 'What is it?' I push my hair behind my ear. 'Is it to do with who booked her for your stag do?' I pause. 'Was it you?'

He purses his lips.

'Come on, you need to tell me.' I am not going to confess to him about Ryan until I understand what he's been holding back from me. I believed Brooke when she introduced herself as his cousin, then I found out she used to be his girlfriend, and then she said she'd been booked by someone anonymous to dance at his stag party. She lied to me once, but I let it go because I like her and it didn't seem that important. I'd already trusted her with my secret. Perhaps that makes me stupid and gullible? I'm not usually a jealous person.

He still can't look at me.

'What is going on?' I shout at him. A couple of people on a nearby table turn their heads in our direction.

'I didn't book her to perform at my stag night. No one did, I've checked with everyone.'

'What?'

'She turned up of her own accord. Uninvited.'

36

I turn away from him as though he's slapped my face.

'How can you know for sure that she just turned up?' I narrow my eyes at him.

'Because I trust my mates. They told me they didn't book her. Believe me, if one of them had, they'd have jumped at the chance to tell me it was down to them. You don't really know her, it's just the sort of twisted thing she'd do.'

He sounds convincing but I don't know whether to believe him. Are we both lying to each other? If I tell him about Ryan now, it will shift the blame onto me but how can we begin a marriage based on lies? I'm not sure where we go from here.

'Why did she even come? What's really going on, are you seeing her behind my back, is she stalking you, or what?'

'Of course I'm not.' His head jerks back, which seems a bit of an overreaction. The image of him enjoying Brooke dancing in front of him is stuck in my head. He *must* have known it was her body, the way she moved under that costume and mask. What if they're still together and marrying me is part of their scam to get at my inheritance?

But we have Freya. He wouldn't do anything to harm his own daughter, would he?

'She was cut up when we split.' He blows a kiss to Freya, and she giggles onto her teddy.

'Which was when? You've not said.'

'A couple of years before we met.'

'A long time ago then?'

'Yeah.'

'So how long has she been back in your life?' I examine the side of his face. The muscle in his jaw is clicking, eyes focussed on his coffee. I'm trying to work out why he's being so vague. If he's lying to me.

'She's not come back into it as such, because she never properly left, not really. I blame social media for her always being around.' He sighs. 'The truth is, I've not been able to shake her off. I block her but she opens a new account under a different name and follows me again. I stupidly thought that when she saw I was getting married to you, that I was settling down, it would be enough to stop her, but it's made her worse.'

'And you never thought to tell me any of this?'

'How could I? I thought you wouldn't want to marry me if you found out. I didn't want you to think I was encouraging her and get the wrong idea. I don't like the attention. I don't *want* her hanging around and annoying me... us.'

Silence curls between us while I take in what he's said.

'Are you telling me she won't leave you alone?' My insides turn to ice-cold liquid.

'Yes! And I don't want to lose you over *her*.' He leans backwards, tipping his chair, pain creasing his face. After all his half-truths, I'm not sure if this is an act. It feels like he's conveniently latched onto my suggestion that Brooke is stalking him.

'This is all too weird.' I blink away the dark dots in my vision, making me feel cross-eyed. I'm struggling to take this in. 'Your ex-girlfriend came to my hen night.' I think of all the strange things that have happened. They must have all been down to her. The funeral flowers, red nail varnish all over the bed cover, the matching questions in the truth and dare game, the dead fox in the swimming pool, the threat on the mirror, entrails in a box and worst of all, everything I told her in confidence. What an idiot I've been. I may as well finish the job for her and cut my heart out, let it bleed.

'She sees you as a threat,' Jamie says, holding his cup so tightly his knuckles are white. 'She said she wanted to get to know you. But it's so she can get rid of you. Those men in the vans, I recognised two of them. They're her brothers. If we report it to the police, it will only make things worse for us. They won't stop coming after us and don't care about hurting anyone. When I was with Brooke, I saw them attack a guy outside a pub once, left him for dead. And she won't give up either, because she thinks I still belong to her.'

'Christ. She told us she was an only child, but there was a message on her phone from "Bros", brothers? They could have killed us. Why didn't you try and stop her? You let her come back to my party without warning me, knowing what she's like, what she's capable of.'

'I'm so sorry. I thought if I made a fuss, she'd make it worse for you.' He covers his eyes with his hand.

'If you'd told me about her from the start, that this was going on, I wouldn't have let her in.' I pull up short before I say something I can't take back. Now she knows this massive secret about me. She could tell Jamie, use it against me any time she likes. If I tell him myself, it will break her power over me, but he'd go crazy. The truth would destroy him, and I can't risk doing that.

Did Brooke manipulate Lauren too, to make her turn against

me? I have a feeling none of these bad things would have happened if Brooke hadn't turned up; my party would never have been ruined. No one else would have tied me to a lamppost or danced erotically for my future husband. Could she have had something to do with Lauren's accident? Those cigarette butts may have been hers. I don't know what to think.

'I'm so sorry.' Jamie shakes his head.

'She told me you were… a controlling boyfriend.'

'And you believed her?' He shakes his head again.

I don't know what else to say. The damage is done. Can I believe what *he* says? Brooke warned me he'd deny everything. He has to be telling me the truth, doesn't he?

We finish our drinks and get back in the car. Jamie insists on driving the short distance home. Freya is asleep, so we travel in silence, not wanting to disturb her. I mull over everything we've said. If he's telling the truth about Brooke, what do I do next?

It's not long before Jamie is turning the car into our road.

'When exactly was Brooke your girlfriend, you didn't really say?' I ask, trying not to sound jealous, but it's hard to disguise my bitterness. She is a beautiful girl. Far more attractive than me. I feel like second best next to her. Is it possible that deep down, he likes her attention? Most men would probably enjoy the ego boost of an attractive woman madly in love with them. Is he going to give in to her in the end? Maybe he's only staying with me because of Freya. I wonder why they split up. Isn't there some old-fashioned saying about men dating beautiful women but ending up marrying a plain one?

'I was nineteen, but it doesn't matter now. She means nothing to me.'

'Are you sure? Don't you think it's a bit weird?'

Jamie doesn't answer, so I carry on.

'Her coming to see me?'

'Of course it is,' he yells back.

'Does she want to break us up because she found out you're about to get married? Is she hoping you'll get back with her?'

'Like I said, she thinks she owns me. She's always been head-strong, impulsive... controlling.' Jamie shrugs as if the situation is hopeless. 'I told you it was safer not saying anything. Not putting you on the wrong side of her.'

'Safer? Have you been on the wrong side of her then, when you split up?'

'She doesn't care who she hurts. I *know* what she's like.' He parks outside our house and switches off the engine.

'Tell me what happened, why you split up.' I'm clinging onto the belief that's he's telling me the truth and it's her that's been lying to me. I have to remember that I trust him, I'm going to marry him and she's lied to my face.

'We were always arguing. She wanted everything her way, all the time.'

I take a breath. 'You need to be straight with me. Are you seeing each other again, is that why she's here?' The words leap from my lips before I can stop them.

'God no, of course not!' His face screws up, hurt. 'I wouldn't go back to her in a million years.'

I'm grateful he's not telling me I'm being childish asking such a thing, even though the thought of him being with her hurts. But I still don't understand. 'If you're so fed up with her, why allow her to remain in your life?'

'Allow her?' He laughs bitterly and drags a hand over his mouth. 'I don't have a choice. She's *always* there no matter how many times I tell her to stop.'

'Have you told the police she won't leave you alone?'

'I've tried. They don't take it seriously. They laughed at me, especially when I showed them a photo of her. *Nice problem to have*, the constable said.'

'I feel such an idiot giving her the benefit of the doubt and confiding in her.'

He nods and hangs his head. Freya wakes up and calls out, 'Mummy!'

'Don't you think it's time to stand up to her, tell her once and for all to leave you alone?'

'I've tried that, countless times.' He opens the passenger door and unstraps Freya. She squirms in her seat, impatient to get down.

'I think you need to tell the police again. I'll come with you if you think it will help.'

'But they'll say there's not enough evidence. They can't do anything. She's careful how she contacts me, makes sure she uses disappearing messages on WhatsApp.'

'But you can save them now can't you, or you can take a screenshot?'

'But anything really threatening she says over the phone, so there's no record of it. And when she follows me, she always has someone with her, so if I turn round and tell her to go away, to please stop following me, she gaslights me, says stuff like, *Leave me alone, you creep,* in a loud voice as if I'm the one who's following her. Her behaviour and gaslighting does my head in. I didn't want to drag you into all that by telling you about her and what she's like, because I knew that the more fuss I made, the worse she'd be.'

'Christ, Jamie. I told her some really private things. She's got to know my closest friends. I welcomed her and gave her the benefit of the doubt because I thought she was part of your family.'

'I know, I know. It feels like whatever I do, she's not going to let me move on with my life.'

I've never seen him look so sad and broken.

'Let's go inside. There's something I need to tell you,' I say and take Freya's hand, sweeping a quick look around the quiet street at the parked cars and mature trees dotted every hundred metres along the pavement, perfect for someone to hide behind. I can't help wondering if we're being watched right this second.

Jamie does the same, checking our surroundings as he ushers us inside and shuts the front door, throwing the deadlock across. He looks terrified.

'Is that really necessary?' A shiver runs through me.

He turns to me, face pale, and grabs my hands in his. 'I know what she's capable of, Megs, and after today, I'm worried she's going to hurt one of us.'

37

'She wouldn't go that far, would she?'

'Look what happened on the motorway. Anything's possible when Brooke's not getting her way. She can be very controlling.'

'What is it she wants?'

'She doesn't want me to get married. Still blames me for us breaking up, but it was all her doing.'

'Now her behaviour is starting to make sense to me.' I tell him about the funeral flowers on my parents' lawn, and the red nail varnish thrown on my bed at the holiday cottage and all the other threats. I hold back mentioning the Truth or Dare game and the duplicated question.

'They sound like the sorts of things she would do in a rage.'

'Is it possible she hurt Lauren too?'

'Like I said, anything's possible where Brooke is concerned.' He shakes his head solemnly.

I make us a cup of tea while I air-fry fish fingers and sliced vegetables for Freya.

'What was it you wanted to tell me?' Jamie asks, taking a small plate out of the cupboard.

I swallow and pause. I should confess right now about Ryan and the video, but I don't know where to begin. And what would he think knowing I'd told Brooke? So instead, I tell him about Freya going missing while she was out with my parents. At least I can be honest about that.

'What? Why didn't you tell me when we were at their house? Is that why you didn't want me to go in?'

'They feel really bad already, and I'd just given them a hard time. They didn't need to hear it from you too. Freya was only gone for a few minutes at most by the sound of it.'

'Even so, why weren't they keeping a closer eye on her?' He squeezes out the teabags against the sides of the cups.

'I asked that too. They said they looked away for a second. I was hard on them, but I know how easily it's done.'

'Can you imagine if they hadn't found her?' He presses his hands to the sides of his head and drags them down.

'And it wasn't actually them who found her.' I wrinkle my nose. I need to be honest about this at least.

'Oh. Who was it then?' He flicks his eyes at me.

'A young man found her and handed her in to one of the staff.'

'What man?' He frowns, his eyes widening. 'How do they know she wandered off?' He pulls out the air-fryer drawer and gives it a violent shake before shoving it back in.

'That's what I said. They don't know who he was. Someone in a black tracksuit, which means literally anyone, especially now you've told me about Brooke and her brothers.' I pour a drink of squash for Freya, avoiding his eye.

'Shit. It could be a warning. Like what's just happened to us on the motorway.'

'It does seem a bit too convenient that someone possibly

connected to you happened to be in the same shop at the very moment she went missing.'

'It's not just convenient, it's creepy. I think someone's been following your parents around.' He pulls the air-fryer drawer out again, looks inside then switches it off.

'My God. What if he enticed her away from them with sweets, then made out he was the one who found her, when all the time it was him who'd snatched her away?'

Jamie grips his hands together.

'She doesn't usually wander off on her own unless she's curious about something. It's hard to believe this man was there at the right moment.'

'Christ, he could easily have walked off with her and they wouldn't have known where she was or who'd taken her.'

'There's probably CCTV in the shop so he must have known he couldn't get away with that.' Using a spatula, I lift out the two fish fingers and veg onto a plate. I blow on them to cool them down.

I pick Freya up and sit her at the table in her highchair.

Jamie's jaw is set tight, probably mulling everything over.

Freya takes a bite of her fishfinger.

My phone vibrates in my pocket. It could be Bonnie at the hospital or another threatening message. I ignore it and wait for Jamie to leave the room.

When he goes to the bathroom, I take my phone out and swipe it open. It's another email from Ryan.

Pay the £20K before your wedding or I'm sending the video to Jamie

Whatever Brooke has said to Ryan hasn't worked for very long. Maybe she was lying to me about calling him. There's no way I'm paying him thousands of pounds because he'll keep coming back for more to feed his gambling habit. I once considered getting engaged to him, which is beyond comprehension now. It took me ages to see what he was really like. I'm a fool for feeling sorry for him and letting him anywhere near me.

Jamie's aware that Ryan was my long-term boyfriend before he and I got together, but that's all. I'd like to be honest with him about the video with Ryan, and the fact that he's blackmailing me, but I just can't bring myself to. It'll be like detonating a bomb and destroying our lives.

'We need to try and put all this aside and concentrate on looking forward to our big day. Only four days to go,' Jamie says, as he comes back into the room.

I nod, but I can't help wondering if that's going to be possible. If he finds out about my secret, I'm scared he'll call off the wedding and leave me.

38

I wake up early on our wedding day in the hotel bridal suite, excited that Thursday has finally arrived. I spring out of bed and stretch up onto my toes, reaching my hands up as high as I can. Then I sit back on the bed and check my phone to see if there's any news about Lauren. Bonnie has been keeping me updated and there's a text from her to say Lauren is doing well, but will be staying in hospital for a few more days, so Emma has offered to take her place as a bridesmaid. I text Bonnie my thanks for letting me know and Emma for offering to step in at such short notice, she'll be the perfect replacement.

No more threats so far from Ryan, and there's nothing from Brooke either, so I assume Jamie hasn't told her she's not invited. The person who's been sending me WhatsApp messages hasn't sent any more demands, which feels ominous.

After a cup of coffee I take a long luxurious shower using all my favourite products to make my skin smooth. I wrap myself in my new satin dressing gown and push open the balcony doors, inhaling the fresh scent of summer flowers from the garden below. As I turn my face up to the blue sky, the sun peeps out from behind white clouds to warm my skin. I can't wait for Jamie and me to start our married lives together.

There's a light tap, tap on the door. I check through the spy hole then open it. One of the staff hands me a large white box wrapped with a cream satin bow. I thank them and shut the door. I'm not expecting my bouquet to be delivered until a bit later and this box is far too big for that. Maybe it's a gift from Jamie or my parents.

Carefully I place it on the bed and pull one end of the ribbon until it's loose and falls away. I slowly lift the lid with both hands.

I draw in a sharp intake of breath and swiftly shut the lid again. They've delivered this to the wrong room. Wrong venue. I open the box again. The large jet-black funeral wreath is nestled on white tissue paper. My name is printed with Jamie's on the ribbon, pulled diagonally taut across the centre. I run my fingers over the densely packed flowers, but they're not real, they're hundreds of small pieces of satin sewn together, the edges delicately frayed so they look like petals. It's beautiful but it's not what I want at my wedding. Tucked on one side of the box is a small envelope addressed to me. I rip it open and take out a card. *MEMENTO MORI* is written in capital letters across the top. Underneath it reads:

Remember you must die.

I push the box with the wreath inside off the bed. It lands on the carpet with a thump. Whoever has sent this to me, must be the same person who delivered funeral flowers to my parents' house. Could it be Lauren having a final dig at me, even from hospital? I shove it under the bed with my foot.

Mum and Dad arrive with Freya, all wearing casual clothes

for now. Mum's updo is beautifully styled by Abby, who's gone for her breakfast before she comes back up to blow-dry mine.

'Did you sleep well, love?' Mum asks and gives me a hug, followed by Dad kissing my cheek.

'Good, thanks,' I lie. I couldn't stop the incessant chatter in my head until gone 2 a.m. Freya wraps her arms around my leg, and I hoist her up into my arms, kissing both sides of her face. She wrinkles her nose and giggles, pretending to bat me away.

'How are you today, sweetie?'

She sticks her tongue out and blows a raspberry. I laugh. Perhaps I should have kept the travel cot in my room. She may have been the tonic I needed for my anxieties, but Mum and Dad insisted I needed a good night's sleep and to not risk being woken up by her. Their room is only a few along the corridor from mine so I agreed it was the perfect opportunity for them to look after Freya again while I'm nearby. It only added to my worries, but she's here and she's fine.

Two waitresses arrive and wheel our breakfast in on a trolley as part of the bridal package. Out on the balcony, Mum and Dad eat a full English, while I have warmed croissants and coffee. I leave them feeding scrambled eggs and toast soldiers to Freya and go inside to get ready before Abby arrives. In the sanctuary of the bathroom, I take my time applying a light natural make-up of soft beiges and pinks. I want Jamie to see me as I am, not a painted version he doesn't recognise.

At 10 a.m., Abby arrives to blow-dry and style my hair, and Mum and Dad take Freya and her flower-girl outfit to their room so they can all change into their wedding outfits. The plan is to dress her at the last minute, to avoid any mishaps. Danielle and the other bridesmaids are coming to my room in about an hour. They're in a local salon getting their hair done.

'How are you feeling?' Abby asks over the noise of the hairdryer.

'Nervous, excited. A mixture I suppose.' I fill her in on everything that happened at the hen weekend after she left.

'I can't believe they did that to you. I'm not sure I could talk to them again after that.'

'I don't think it meant to get so out of hand.' I tell her about Lauren falling and ending up in hospital with a broken leg.

'Poor girl. I hope she's going to be okay. Did you say Brooke is Jamie's cousin?'

'That's what she told everyone, but now Jamie's admitted she's actually his ex-girlfriend.' I tell her about us going to the stag party and seeing Brooke doing a burlesque performance for Jamie.

'Blimey, that's a bit much. And you're okay with her lying to you about who she really is?'

'No, not at all, it was a real shock, but they went out a long time ago. He seems a bit scared of her. He thinks she's obsessed with him.'

'Don't all men think that?' She rolls her eyes.

'It doesn't sound good though. She won't leave him alone and it's a bit creepy turning up at my hen do.'

'You can say that again.' Abby pulls back from me, hairdryer hanging from her hand like a gun. 'Look, I know it's not my place to say this, but I'm going to anyway because I've known you since you were a little girl, and I care about you. But are you sure you want to marry someone who's lied to you about his ex-girlfriend? I mean not telling you about her or that she's bothering him. Why wouldn't he say if it's so innocent? How do you know they're not still carrying on... you know?'

'He's assured me there's nothing going on and I think I

believe him. I'm not perfect either. There are things I've kept from him too and I'd hope he'd forgive me.'

'Oh boy. None of this sounds good. Is this really how you want to begin your married lives together?'

'It's not ideal, but I do love him. I think it's unrealistic to have no secrets from each other. Maybe I'm making excuses?'

'Look, his ex-girlfriend helped to sabotage your hen night, Megan. She gate-crashed Jamie's stag party too and claims someone booked her to dance for him, but all the signs show she turned up again, uninvited. Have you stopped to think about what that means?'

'Now I know who Brooke really is, I see what she was trying to do, and I do blame her for messing up my hen night, tying me up and covering me in flour, but I blame Lauren too. She's just as bitter about me marrying Jamie. She's not even coming to my wedding now because she's in hospital and we've fallen out.'

'Be careful, Megan. A jealous woman is a dangerous woman, and it sounds like you have two on your hands.'

Just as she's finishing my hair, Danielle, Emma and Sarah arrive in their matching pale blue satin bridesmaids' dresses. It's good of Emma to step in for Lauren at the last minute. Danielle's outfit has the addition of a short cape and a diamanté tiara, as she's the maid of honour. Emma is holding a bottle of champagne, accompanied by a waiter carrying a tray of flute glasses, which he obediently puts down on the coffee table.

'You look absolutely gorgeous,' Emma says, handing the bottle to the waiter for him to open.

'Wait until you see the dress,' Danielle says. She's the only person apart from Mum who's been allowed to see it because she came with me to the shop to help choose it.

They all bend and carefully kiss my cheek, trying their best not to dislodge any of my make-up or hair, that's just been hair-sprayed. Emma hands round the filled glasses.

'You all look amazing too.' I hold my glass up.

'Here's to you and Jamie on your wedding day. Wishing you love and happiness for many years to come.'

'Love and happiness,' everyone says together. I try not to think about the funeral wreath hidden under the bed.

'And here's to you all for being my beautiful bridesmaids. Thank you for being here with me on my special day.'

Danielle picks up her phone and glances at the screen. 'It's a message from the hospital.'

We all stop drinking as we wait for more information. My stomach tightens.

'Lauren's asking for you, Megan. She's got something important to tell you about her accident. She knows who pushed her.'

39

'Is she sure?' I put my glass down.

'Sounds like it. I think you should go,' Danielle says, and all the others nod.

I check the time. 'I need to be ready to go down for the ceremony in fifty-five minutes. I'll never make it there and back in time, will I?'

'Do you want me to go instead?' Emma asks.

'No, it's okay.'

'You could call her,' Sarah says.

'She doesn't have a mobile, remember?' I say, picturing it flying through the air before it landed in the swimming pool.

'But you can phone the hospital.'

'I think I need to see her face to face, find out who did this to her.' It seems this is what Lauren would prefer too. I don't say it, but right now I'm not sure who I can trust. I have a feeling that whoever pushed Lauren over is linked to everything that's been happening to me – the wreath, the WhatsApp messages, the dead fox, all of it.

'But you'll have all your guests waiting for you,' Sarah says.

'This is important. Lauren's asked for me so I need to go.'

'Time to get that dress on,' Mum says, coming into my room without knocking. She stops still, taking in our long faces. 'Cheer up, you look like you're going to a funeral not a wedding.' She laughs and greets all the bridesmaids with half-hugs and air kisses. I've not told her about the wreath that arrived. I don't want to upset her. This is her day as much as it is ours.

I tell her about Lauren asking to see me and wanting to tell me who pushed her over. 'I have to find out who did it. I don't think I should wait until after the wedding.' It'll be harder to leave my guests after the ceremony, and what if Lauren changes her mind, gets spooked by whoever did this to her? Even though we fell out at the weekend, I wish she was here as my brides-maid, enjoying my big day.

'Okay, well, I can drop you there, but I'm not sure if I can get you back on time, unless you only stay for a few minutes.'

'I really think you should only go if you're sure you can make it back for the ceremony,' Danielle says.

'You can do it if you leave right now,' Emma adds, looking at her watch.

'I'm sure we can delay everything for a few minutes, if we have to,' Sarah says.

'Right, Mum, are you ready? I'll put my dress on when I come back.' I turn to Emma. 'Please let Jamie know where I am if I'm late. I *will* be back to marry him.'

'Of course.' Emma squeezes my hand hard. I look her in the eye, surprised, but she lets go and turns her head away.

I take my dressing gown off and grab a T-shirt and joggers from my suitcase and pull them on then push my feet into slip-on trainers and head out of the door.

* * *

The hospital corridor is quiet as Mum and I hurry along it, looking for Lauren's room. When we find it, the door is wide open and there's a nurse by her bedside. Lauren says my name as soon as she sees me, her voice croaky. The nurse nods at me and leaves. Mum stands by the door.

'How are you feeling?' My lips quiver seeing her like this. She's so pale and vulnerable. I hold her hand. I wish I could make her better.

'A bit dazed, but glad to be here.' Her smile grows as she speaks. 'It's good to see you. Thanks for coming. I didn't know if you would after... I've behaved so badly. You look lovely by the way.' She smiles weakly. I lift one of my curls and twirl it around my finger. It's a genuine compliment and I'm sad she won't be able to join in the celebrations.

'We've all been so worried about you.' I gently squeeze her fingers.

'Have I missed much?' she says in a more subdued way than usual but still with her dry humour. She even half manages to raise an eyebrow.

'Not really, but I'm getting married in about thirty-five minutes, so I can't stay long.' I pat her hand and put it down on the sheets beside her. 'You said you wanted to tell me something about your accident?'

Her smile falls away and a look I can't decipher crosses over her face.

'You can't trust Brooke,' she says, grabbing my hand, except there's no strength in it. 'She's the one who pushed me over.' Her focus darts around the room as if she's scared of who might hear her. I frown at her apparent suspicion and confusion.

'Are you sure about that?' I move my hand away an inch and then think better of it. I don't want her to worry I don't believe her. 'Wasn't it a man who did this? Bonnie said you told her he bumped into you and knocked you over.'

'I thought it was at first, because I saw someone in a black tracksuit. They came up behind me and pushed me with force. It happened so quickly.' Lauren gulps a breath, her eyes staring straight at me now. 'I've been going over and over it every day since Sunday, and when I really thought about it, I realised it wasn't a man. It was Brooke.'

'I don't understand. How can you be so sure?'

'I stumbled as I fell forward, and caught a glimpse of the person running past me. One of the last things I remember before I hit the ground, was a flash of orange. I didn't realise what that was until this morning.'

'So what was it?' I sit back in the chair.

'Remember those fancy trainers Brooke was wearing? She told Bonnie that they helped her running performance. I searched for them on my mum's phone and they're a pair of Nike Alphafly 3s. They must be rare because they cost over £250. They have a distinctive shaped heel with a rim, and an orange triangle down the outside and on the sole are two large orange circles. They're the trainers I saw this person wearing just before I hit the ground.'

'But I don't understand, why would she do that to you? I thought you two had become friends. Look what both of you did to me, for goodness' sake.' I scoff a note of mock laughter.

'It was all her idea. Tying you up, covering you with Coke and flour. I only went along with it for a bit of fun. Although I admit I didn't mind seeing you squirm a little.' She attempts a smile.

'Oh, thanks! But you were the one carrying the bag with all that stuff in it. And it was you all over Jamie. You even kissed him. So why should I believe you? You did everything she told you to, did you?' I realise I'm arguing with a woman who has concussion and a broken leg and tell myself to stop.

'Of course not. It was her bag, she asked me to carry it. She told me her plan and said I should be the one to take control. She wanted me to put those duplicate questions in the bowl for when it was your turn, and I wouldn't do it.'

'*She* did that?' I didn't imagine Brooke would do that when it was her who offered to help me, warning Ryan to stay away.

'I admit I wrote them out and chopped them up for her, put the real questions in the bin, but I told her it was a mean thing to do and I'm truly sorry for my part in it. Any of it.'

'Why that particular question, asking if I'd cheated on Jamie?' I'm beginning to think Brooke knew the answer already.

'I told her I was with you the night you met Jamie, and that your ex Ryan was still in love with you, so she kept going on about it, twisting it round, trying to make out you must still be in love with Ryan too, and I let it slip that you'd slept with him.'

'You what? How did you know?' I scan over her face as the truth sinks in. 'Don't tell me, Ryan told you.'

She nods sheepishly.

'Now I'm starting to understand.'

'She said we should get you to confess in front of everyone. Humiliate you and once Jamie found out what you'd done, he'd leave you, then I could step in and save him. I thought she was mucking about at first, saying we were doing this because *I* was angry at you taking Jamie away from me, like I was some kind of crazy bunny boiler trying to split you two up.'

I stand up. 'But you *are* upset with me being the one Jamie wanted to be with and marry, aren't you? All those little jibes you've made over the years about you missing out on your one true love.'

'I admit I was bitter that you'd found the one. Look at me, I've not even had a date in months. In a moment of madness, it seemed possible that Jamie and I could be together at last, and I stupidly went along with it. Brooke managed to stir up my resentment, made me believe that I should hate you for being the one marrying Jamie and then to top it all, you cheated on him – you deserved to be punished.' She splutters out the last words and her face turns pink. 'But Megan, I'm so, so sorry.'

I stare at her open-mouthed.

'She didn't tell me anything about her being the main event at Jamie's stag do. And when I saw her in her sparkly sexy costume, and found out she was his ex-girlfriend, I suddenly realised how calculating and poisonous she was. She'd just been using me to get at you and wanted him for herself. I told her I was going to tell you everything and she threatened me to keep my mouth shut.'

'Oh God, Lauren, if you'd hit your head harder, she could have killed you. It's bad enough that you're concussed and you've broken your leg. You need to tell everything to the police.'

Lauren touches the bandage covering the graze on her head, tears in her eyes. 'But I don't have any evidence. It'll be my word against hers.'

'Please, report it.'

She nods and reaches for my hand. 'Be careful today, Megan. I borrowed your red hoodie when I went for that jog, and now I'm wondering if she thought it was you she was pushing over, not me.'

40

I arrive back at the hotel with ten minutes to spare. I run up to my room and Mum helps me change into my wedding dress while I try to blot my face with a tissue. While she's doing up the long row of tiny pearl buttons at the back of the dress, I stand at the mirror dabbing the smudges under my eyes, then carefully dot concealer and smooth it in.

After everything Lauren's told me, I hope Brooke doesn't turn up. It's hard to accept that she was deceiving me when she went out of her way to help me put a stop to Ryan's threats. It felt like she was the only one I could confide in about him filming us together, apart from Emma, but it seems I was wrong to put my faith in her. She showed me a side of her that was vulnerable. The abuse she described at the hands of her ex sends chills through me, but I don't believe Jamie was capable of that. She must have been making that up to put me off him and gain my sympathy.

'You've officially got about five minutes, but a bride is allowed to be late to her own wedding,' Mum says with a smile to me in the mirror as she does up the last button. I rehearse in my mind how I'll stroll down the aisle, arm linked with Dad's.

Mum lifts my handtied bouquet of cornflowers and freesias out from the second box delivered this morning. The scent and mix of vibrant blue and cream, is heady and mesmerising. Only I know about the funeral wreath lurking under my bed like a curse.

Dad taps on the door and lets himself into the room, holding Freya's hand. She's wearing a pale blue dress, carrying a small posy of cornflowers and a matching headdress.

'Look at you, little lady.' I crouch down and open my arms to her. She runs into them for a hug. While Mum and Dad are chatting, I smooth down the petticoats of Freya's dress, adjusting it so it looks just right. I attach a mini tracking tag to the underside of the hem, hidden under the waistband at the back, then I kiss her on the forehead.

My phone pings on the dressing table, but I ignore it.

'Shouldn't you check that?' Mum says.

'I don't want to be disturbed today.' I switch the button on the side to silent and give it to Mum for safekeeping in her clutch bag. Then I stand up and adjust Freya's headband.

'Come on, it's time to go down,' I say, taking Freya's hand and checking the clock on the wall. 'We're over ten minutes late already.'

Downstairs, most of the bridesmaids have congregated together at the back of a small room which leads straight through to where the service is due to be held. As I approach, I sense a subdued atmosphere. They're all whispering amongst themselves, holding their cornflower posies downwards by their sides. When I walk in, their heads tip up, their faces etched with anxiety.

'What's wrong?' I hand Freya over to Emma, who is going to look after her in the procession of bridesmaids.

'Danielle and Joe are looking for Jamie,' she says.

'He must be pacing around outside somewhere, trying to calm his nerves.'

I peep into the main function room. It looks like all the seats are filled. The celebrant and her assistant are sitting behind an angled table decorated with an arrangement of cream and white flowers.

Dad takes my hand in his, squeezing it a few times to reassure me. My mouth is suddenly bone dry.

The bright sun is beating through the windows making the room stuffy and claustrophobic, despite two windows fully open. The air doesn't seem to be moving.

Danielle rushes in through the side door, her cheeks flushed. When she sees me, she pulls up short, eyes wide, almost as if she wasn't expecting me to be there yet.

'Everything okay?' I ask.

'Didn't you see my messages? I've been trying to call you.' Her voice is strained.

'No, have you found him?' I glance round at the bridesmaids' anguished expressions.

There are tears in Danielle's eyes.

'What's happened?' I grab her wrist. A steam roller pushes from my chest up to my throat.

'I'm so sorry.' Her face creases up.

'Tell me what's wrong.' Blood pumps hard through my veins, in my ears.

She swallows twice. 'We can't find Jamie. He's gone.'

41

'What are you talking about?' I sway and stagger to one side. Dad grabs my arm and steadies me.

'I'm so sorry, Megan, but Joe says Jamie had a few drinks and took off somewhere.' Danielle's pained expression is mirrored in the bridesmaids behind her.

'That can't be right.'

'I'm so sorry,' Danielle repeats.

'How long has he been gone?'

'Maybe only half an hour. He was right here dressed up and ready.' She shakes her head in disbelief.

'So why are you only telling me this now?'

'I tried calling you,' Danielle says again.

In the function room, Mum twists round from her seat in the front row. She stands up and hurries down the aisle towards us.

'What's going on, where's Jamie?' she whispers, prodding her watch.

'He's gone off somewhere,' Dad says with a sigh, his bushy eyebrows rising.

Tears brim my eyes. I can't stop the fear pressing against my throat. What if he knows my secret and has decided he can't go through with this?

'Joe says he drank quite a bit before he left,' Danielle says in a small voice. Her cheeks come up with two spots of red.

Mum frowns at her. 'Well, it's not like him at all, is it Christopher?' She says to Dad and he nods. I ask her for my phone.

I call his number, but it goes straight to answer phone. I can't help picturing his car in a mangled heap, the same black vans as before driving away from the scene.

'Why isn't Joe with him? He's the best man, his job is to look after the groom, not let him wander off.' I try not to let my frustration show, but my voice is getting louder, more urgent.

I press my fist to my nose, willing myself not to cry. My biggest fear has come true; he's changed his mind and doesn't want to marry me. Someone must have told him what I confessed on my hen night – Brooke, Ryan or someone else. I can't think of any other explanation for him going off suddenly without a word to me or anyone.

My phone pings in my hand. An email pops up from Ryan. I read the message and squeeze my mobile hard, suppressing the urge to hurl it across the room.

Video sent to Jamie 35 minutes ago. Have a nice wedding day.

42

I try calling Jamie again and leave a voice message begging him to call back so we can talk.

'Hadn't you better tell your guests the ceremony is postponed?' Mum says quietly in my ear, putting a gentle hand on my shoulder. 'Maybe offer them a free drink at the bar?' She shows me her watch. We're already running thirty minutes late. We have the place booked for the day, so all is not lost if I can speak to Jamie and explain myself to him. I just hope he can forgive me.

'Everyone is getting restless in there,' Mum continues, in case I haven't heard what she's said. 'Would you like me to tell them?'

'It's okay, thank you. I think I should do it. But it would help to have you by my side.' I slip my arm through hers. I feel a bit knocked sideways, but I need to take control of the situation.

Mum nods and we hold hands as we walk up to the celebrant. I quietly tell her we'll have to postpone the ceremony until Jamie is found. She's fine about it especially as she doesn't have to rush off yet.

I turn to address everyone else, sweeping a glance over all

their faces. I pause and my mouth drops open, not quite believing what I'm seeing right in front of me. Brooke.

She's wearing a maroon dress and matching fascinator and has clearly made a huge effort to doll herself up. I was hoping she wouldn't come, even though I stupidly invited her. After everything Lauren told me, I'm shaken to see her here.

Maybe if she can see us saying our vows, she'll realise it's time to let Jamie go.

I tell everyone to make their way to the bar for a free drink as the wedding has been unexpectedly delayed. I choose not to tell them the reason at this point, still holding out hope that I can tell Jamie how sorry I am and explain about Ryan.

I join my bridesmaids in the adjacent room who assure me Jamie will come back. Forcing a smile at them, I try not to let off a suspicious vibe, wondering if it was one of them who told Jamie. Emma comes up and gives me a hug. Apart from Brooke, she's the only one I confided in about sleeping with Ryan. Could she have been the person to tell Jamie? Maybe it was her sending me those WhatsApp threats, trying to squeeze some money out of me. She shakes a small packet of cigarettes by her side, and I nod and follow her through the foyer and out of the front door. I thought she'd stopped smoking. She told me she joined the running club when she quit. Maybe she still has the occasional one like I do. I can't help thinking of the cigarette butts near where we found Lauren unconscious. Standing facing the house, she takes out her lighter and is about to light her cigarette when her eyes flick upwards. She yanks the cigarette out of her mouth, drawing in a short breath. In one swift move she takes me by the arm and leads me straight back in before I've barely had a chance to step outside.

'Let's go out the other way to the lovely rose garden instead,' she says, walking me briskly down the hallway.

'No, I'm okay thanks, what's the matter with the front?' I wriggle out of her grip and walk back again.

'There's a no smoking sign. It's a bad look for a place, isn't it? Smokers hanging around puffing away like drug addicts.' She half laughs, presumably at herself as she trots along beside me.

'Sod that,' I say and march onto the gravel drive. I spin round, expecting her to follow me with the lighter, but she stays standing in the doorway, squinting, as though she's anticipating a loud bang.

When I see it, my body jolts. Usually, I'd be embarrassed at the involuntary movement, but I'm too stunned to care.

My mouth opens wider, trying to find the right words to express what this means, but there aren't any adequate. I can't believe what I'm seeing. Suddenly all my anxieties are distilled into this one moment.

Painted on the wall in huge red letters is one solitary, brutal word:

JILTED

43

'Who did this?' I cry and cover my mouth with my hand.

'I'm so sorry. I didn't want you to see it. I don't think Jamie is coming back any time soon, Megs.' Emma comes over and puts her arm around my shoulders.

'You think *he* did this?' I step away from her, my eyes hot with tears. Did I see a flicker of amusement on her lips?

'I don't know. But think about it, how many of us could possibly reach up that high?' She points at the wall then sticks the cigarette in her mouth.

'You're wrong. Jamie would never do this to me.'

'If you say so.'

'Joe is tall too. Maybe he did it.'

'If it is someone else, maybe they're in it together.'

'You don't know that, you don't know anything. *Why* would Jamie do this? It doesn't make any sense. He was looking forward to today, to becoming my husband.'

Emma shrugs and takes the cigarette out again between two fingers. 'Sorry Megs, tell me who else it could be.'

'I don't know but Jamie would never intentionally hurt me.'

'I know it's hard to take in, but if you think about it, the guests inside were only told five minutes ago that the wedding has been postponed, so no one's had time to come out here and do this.' She steps closer to it and looks up. 'That paint is almost dry.' She turns round to me, hand on hip. 'I've not seen anyone walking around with a tin of red paint, have you?'

I shake my head. I can't argue with what she's saying but I know in my gut that I'm right. And if I'm not, my heart will break.

'He's the only one who could have done this while everyone was waiting inside for you both to arrive. And then he left without saying a word to anyone. I'm really sorry, but I think that's what's happened.' She slips the cigarette between her lips again and finally lights it.

I stare at her but can't speak or think clearly. My mind has been crushed into a compact little square like a car at a breaker's yard.

'If you're so sure about this, perhaps you know who told him my secret? I assume someone's told him, if he really has stood me up. One of the bridesmaids must have done it.'

Emma blows out a trail of smoke but doesn't reply, so I carry on before she can speak.

'That's the only possible reason I can think of that could make him have second thoughts about marrying me. So I think someone who was at my hen party has deliberately and maliciously set out to ruin my life.'

'I've no idea who would do that, so don't look at me.' She holds up her hands and backs away.

'I am looking at you. You've never really liked Jamie, have you?' I hand back the cigarette she gave me.

'Not at first, I admit that, but I've warmed to him.'

'Why didn't you like him?'

'I don't know what it was exactly. He's a nice enough guy, but sometimes I felt like he was holding back, not being 100 per cent straight with you.'

'But I've not been straight with him either, have I?' I press my hand to my head.

'I suppose not; you did cheat on him.' She blows smoke upwards.

'And you made sure he knew about it, did you?'

'Of course I didn't. What makes you say that?'

'I had a look on Ryan's Facebook page. I trawled through his history over the last couple of months and at the time when I slept with him, he had a girlfriend called Amy. So I had a look at the photos of them together, and there you are on her birthday, her old friend from school.'

Emma looks up at the sky and inhales deeply on her cigarette.

'Was it you blackmailing me on WhatsApp?'

'Of course not!' She says it so abruptly, I'm tempted to believe her.

'Did Ryan give you the idea? I could go to the police and get you arrested.'

'I have not been blackmailing you. I swear on my life.' She prods her index finger towards me. 'You should have seen the state Amy was in when she found out about you sleeping with him. It split them up. She loved him but he's so obsessed with you, it broke her heart. But your life just carried on as normal, didn't it? It had no effect on you at all. You continued to plan for your big day, like nothing had happened. So I thought I'd join your running club to befriend you, find out who you really were, but more fool me, I actually grew to like you. I fully intended to tell you what damage you'd done. Remember how I got chatting to you about my friend's boyfriend cheating on her and you said what a scumbag he must be?' She laughs bitterly.

I clench my teeth. 'I didn't know Ryan had a girlfriend.'

'When you told me he'd filmed you, I could hardly believe it. There was no better justice for the hurt you caused Amy.' Emma stubs her half-smoked cigarette out on the wall.

I hold my hands up. 'I'm done with this conversation. You should leave.' As I march back inside, I'm hit by the sound of our guests in the adjacent room chatting around the bar. I climb the stairs with heavy feet and a heavier heart.

44

In my room I lie down on the bed and try to call Jamie again. Seven times I've tried, but it seems his mobile is still switched off. He doesn't want to be contacted, least of all by me. A twist of nausea rises in my chest. He'll have received the video and know I've lied and cheated on him. I can hardly blame him for reacting like this, but something about it doesn't feel right. He's not the sort of person to flounce off in a mood and create a scene in his wake. Sometimes he holds his emotions in and pretends he's feeling okay. We've talked about how doing that can be damaging. Bottling things up contributed to his breakdown. With the help of his therapist, he's been learning how to open up about his concerns or worries. To speak out and let me know if he's feeling down or annoyed about something.

He could be anywhere. What if he's not okay? My throat tightens. He wouldn't try to hurt himself, would he?

I call Joe and he answers straight away.

'Any luck?' I say, not bothering with hello.

'Not so far. He's not at your house or the cemetery to see his mum. Can you think of anywhere else?'

'The football club or my parents' house? Not sure why he'd go there, but worth a try. His phone is switched off. I've checked his social media, but he's not posted anything. Should I ask on there if anyone has seen him?'

'I think you'll have to, although you can guarantee some of your guests will see it.'

'I'm beyond keeping up appearances,' I sigh and tell him about Ryan's message saying he's sent Jamie a video of me in bed with my ex. Joe agrees that's likely to be the reason why Jamie's gone AWOL. But he's also surprised that he's gone off without a word to anyone.

'He probably just needed to calm down, a bit of time on his own to process finding this out.'

'Obviously let me know if you find him, and when you get back to the hotel. I'll be in my room.'

As I end the call, there's a quiet knock at the door. I don't want to see anyone, but it could be important. I sit up and carefully manoeuvre myself off the bed, trying not to tug at my wedding dress, which is already full of creases. I open the door a centimetre, squinting through the small crack and immediately wish I hadn't. Of all people, Brooke is standing there. I hardly recognise her. She looks so different every time I see her. A chameleon fitting into whatever surroundings she finds herself in.

'Can I come in?' she asks kindly.

'This isn't a good time,' I say, aware that she's the person who put Lauren in hospital.

'I heard what's happened.'

'I really need some space right now,' I say and go to close the door, but she keeps talking, her foot far enough over the threshold that I have to hold the door ajar.

'I just want to speak to you alone. *Please.* I think I can help.'

'There's nothing you can say to make this any easier for me.' My knees feel soft beneath me. She shifts and I move to shut the door again, but she shoves it hard with her fist. It opens wide and bangs on the wall.

'But this can't wait.' She steps inside and slams the door behind her. 'There's something I think you should know right now.'

My breathing quickens. She stands in front of me in her posh frock and fascinator, our eyes locked. *I don't really know you. You lied to my face about being Jamie's cousin, but you were in a relationship with him. You said he was abusive, and yet here you are, at the moment when our lives are falling apart.*

If he has jilted me, I want to know if it's anything to do with this woman.

I let out a long breath and fold my arms across my satin bodice. 'What is it you want to tell me that's *so* important you couldn't tell me before now?'

'It wasn't my place to say, it was Jamie's, and if I had told you, you wouldn't have believed me.' She coughs and looks down at her feet, which are in strappy green heels. 'Maybe you still won't, but considering Jamie's gone off and not been honest with you about the reason, I feel it's my sisterly duty to tell you the truth. Woman to woman.'

I step back. What is she really here for?

'I'm sorry to say but Jamie has been lying to you about something else, from the moment he met you.' She fixes me with her all-knowing green eyes, and I feel like smacking her smug face.

'What about?' I lift my chin and tighten my folded arms higher over my chest, silently bracing myself.

'I wasn't his girlfriend at all.' She dips her head and a sense of relief spreads through me.

'So you've come up here to tell me that?'

'No. I'm here to tell you I'm his wife.'

45

'You're what? You can't be his *wife*.' I blink at her and take a step back, my vision clouding over.

'Ex-wife,' she corrects herself.

'No, that's not possible.' I move away from her but keep blinking, trying to stop the black edges closing in on my vision. 'You're wrong. You don't mean Jamie.'

She nods. 'The framed photo I gave you was of us on our wedding day in our going-away clothes. Not that we went anywhere. His real cousin Beth took the photo.' Her eyes tear up. 'I tried to warn you about him, that's the real reason I came to your hen party.'

This is another one of her lies. He would have told me if he'd been married to her. And he is not an abusive person.

Her sad eyes look straight at me. What she told me she went through was horrendous, but it wasn't Jamie. She's trying to destroy us. I can't breathe; it's as if she's sucked the air from my lungs. The Jamie I know could not hurt anyone.

'Prove to me you were married to him,' I say. I believed we were both going into this commitment for the first time. But if he'd already made vows and broken those promises, does it mean he's capable of all the other things Brooke has told me about? I won't believe it. I've not seen one hint of Jamie being like that. But they say those sorts of people are master manipulators. They draw you in with their charming personality, put you up on a pedestal and then knock you down.

'I thought you'd ask that because you're smart, Megan, so I brought this with me to show you.' She pulls a photo out of her clutch bag and hands it to me. 'It was taken on the steps of the church.' She's standing next to Jamie outside a small village church, under a shower of multicoloured confetti. Jamie is wearing a navy suit with a white rose pinned to his lapel and Brooke is the picture of elegance in an ivory satin and lace shift dress, shimmering in the sunlight. Her veil is pushed back from her face and she's holding a modestly handtied bouquet of blush pink roses. They're both smiling at the camera. My head swims. Why has he never told me about this? What else is he capable of keeping from me? Maybe it is true that he'll become a different person once we're married. One face for the outside world and another behind closed doors.

Without asking, Brooke opens a bottle of mineral water from the mini bar and pours it into two clean glasses. She hands one to me. I sit on the bed and take a long sip.

'I'm lucky, I managed to get away before he completely destroyed me,' she says quietly, sitting next to me. 'But I'd already made the mistake of marrying him.'

I never thought Jamie would keep something as important as this from me. He should have told me he'd been married before. I finish the water and put the glass down.

'Like I said, I'm lucky. I escaped and divorced him, although I had to wait five years because he wouldn't give his consent. But I was able to start a new life. I thought it was over, but then he met you and at first I admit I tried to look the other way, but eventually I couldn't ignore it, stand by and watch him do exactly the same to you as he did to me. I knew deep down that one day he'd do it all over again, so I had to stop him.' She stares ahead, as though she's ready to go into battle.

'This can't be happening,' I say, pressing my hands to my head. I stand up and pace in a circle. 'The Jamie I know and love would never do anything to hurt me or Freya. He'd never harm anyone.'

'I know it's hard to take in. I begged him to leave you, but he wouldn't. I thought if I told you I was his cousin and caused enough trouble at your hen party, it would make you think you were marrying into a dysfunctional family and maybe put you off him. I admit I played on your insecurities about Lauren, encouraging her to kiss him so I could take a photo. I wanted you to suspect there was more to his relationship with her, so you'd change your mind about becoming his wife.'

'I love him, and he's not this abuser you've described.' But she's not listening to me.

'Once he realised it was me, he tried to keep me away from you.'

I shake my head, I won't believe it.

'Now you can see why, can't you? Because we didn't just date, we were married. Husband and wife. In sickness and in health. He's been lying to you all along.' She hands me another glass of water.

'I promised myself I wouldn't give up trying to save you.' Brooke gently touches my arm, looking directly into my eyes.

My head is starting to feel fuzzy. Perhaps I'm getting a migraine from all the stress. Although it's the same feeling I had on my hen night when I thought I'd drunk too much and I've only had one glass of champagne today.

She hands me another photo. 'My parents are on the right and the woman on his left is his mum. Was his mum, I should say. She died not many months after this was taken.'

I push the photos back into her hands and run to the toilet to be sick.

When I come back, my head is a bit clearer. Brooke hands me the topped-up glass of water. I look down at it and wonder why she's so keen to keep refilling it. I put it down and stand away from her.

'I went to see Lauren at the hospital about an hour ago,' I tell her. 'She told me that you pushed her over. Is that true?'

'Of course not! Why would you believe her?' Brooke rubs her palms together. 'Poor Lauren, she must have damaged her head and become confused. I popped in to see her just after you. She said you'd been there and she admitted to me she's muddled in her head about what happened. It was a man who bumped into her, not me.'

'You're lying. She remembers seeing your Nike trainers.' The room begins to sway. I blink in rapid succession.

'You warned her not to say anything to me about your plan, how you blamed her for everything when really it was you behind tying me up and the truth question. That's why you pushed her.' I point at her but Brooke grabs my arm and guides me to sit back down on the bed, not letting go.

'Oh dear, is that what she told you?' Brooke laughs. 'Did she also tell you why Jamie has gone?'

'No.' I try to pull my arm out of her grip, but her fingers tighten.

'When he saw I was here today in the front row, he knew I would tell you the truth and he fled. He knows what he did to me,' Brooke says.

'He's gone because of you?' I try to stand up again, but my head feels woozy. 'Was something in my water?'

'You're just too trusting, aren't you?' Brooke lets go of my arm and stands in front of me, putting her hands out to stop me tipping forward. I collapse back onto the bed. When I manage to sit up again, she's kneeling on the carpet in front of me. The room won't stop spinning.

'Why didn't you tell me you're the reason he walked out on me?' My speech is beginning to slur.

Brooke hands me the glass of water. 'Drink some more. You're probably dehydrated after being sick.'

As I tip it up to my lips, I catch a distorted glimpse of her mouth through the bottom of the glass. It's not a warm smile any more, but a grin curling her lip. Whatever she's put in this water is making me drowsy.

'What is in this?' I jerk the glass at her and the water drenches her face. 'Was it you who wrote "*Jilted*" on the hotel wall?' I snarl.

Brooke scrambles to her feet. 'Megan, please calm down. Don't make excuses for him. You've been seduced by an abuser and now you're defending him. That's exactly what he wants. I know it's hard to accept, but please don't take it out on me. I'm trying to help you.'

'He's never hurt me, not once. You're the one who's telling lies!' I shout.

'That's how he operates, he's manipulating you. Showing you his best self until you're trapped.'

'I don't believe you!' I scream and lash out at her with my nails.

'Please calm down, Megan, you're out of control.' She swings her hand at me and a slap lands hard on the side of my head in a sharp jolt.

And then in slow motion, I'm falling.

46

I wake up on the carpet, looking at the ceiling. Mum is by my side, lifting something off my chest. I touch it and it tickles my hand.

'What is that?' I screech.

'Someone's left a funeral wreath on you,' Mum shrieks. 'Do you know who did this?'

'Where's Jamie?' I ask, groaning as I try to move but my head and leg hurts. Danielle and Sarah are looking down at me with concerned faces.

'He's not been found yet, love,' Mum says gently, pushing my hair off my forehead. 'Can you remember what happened?'

'Ouch, my head stings. How long have I been lying here?'

'We're not sure. You've got a gash on your head,' Mum says, looking into my eyes then up at my friends.

'It's been a good half an hour since you were out the front of the hotel with Emma,' Sarah says and kneels on my other side, taking my hand in between both of hers. I nod once, tears welling up as I start to remember what happened after Emma and I argued.

'I came up for a rest and Brooke knocked on the door, said she had something important to tell me. She said she's Jamie's ex-wife.' I start to cry.

'That's insane.' Danielle's mouth opens wide.

'Jamie is manipulating me according to her, and now he's gone because he saw her here and knows she'll expose his deceit. I told her it was her who's lying.'

'But why didn't he tell you he's been married before?' Mum sits on the edge of the bed.

'I don't know. She kept insisting I drink lots of water. I think she put something in it, because I started to feel drowsy. I told her I didn't believe a word she was saying, but she said I was out of control and then she smacked me across the head.'

'None of us has seen her. She must have slipped out of the back door,' Mum says, taking a closer look at my head. 'I think one of her nails or ring has cut you.' Mum points to a sore patch on my forehead and Danielle nods.

I touch the place where it hurts and look at the sticky blood on my fingers. Nausea rushes at me. I swallow and try to ignore it.

'I saw her downstairs, sitting in the front row,' I say. 'I hardly recognised her with her hair down, all curled. She had loads of make-up on and a big fascinator. She didn't look much like the Brooke who was at my hen do.'

'I didn't notice which guests were here from the back room,' Danielle says.

'Same.' Sarah shrugs. 'Everyone had their backs to us.'

'Why *is* she here?' Mum asks. 'I thought you said Jamie told her she wasn't invited.'

I sigh. 'I don't know if he did and I'd already told her she was welcome, only because she'd helped me with something. I didn't think she would bother coming to be honest. How wrong

I was. I really need to speak to Jamie about all the things she said.'

'Shh now, help is on its way,' Mum hushes me and I lean back on her feeling dizzy.

'When I went to see Lauren at the hospital, she told me that it was Brooke who pushed her over. I thought she might be confused, but she says the person who was running away was wearing Nike trainers with flashes of orange on the sides and the soles.'

'They're the expensive ones Brooke wears,' Danielle says. 'So she didn't go home early. She must have followed Lauren.'

'Why did she want to hurt her?' Mum asks.

'Brooke made sure Lauren appeared to be orchestrating all the pranks, so she got the blame for everything. But Lauren worked out what she was up to and told Brooke she was going to tell me the truth, so she tried to stop her,' I say.

'That must be why Brooke didn't say goodbye, so no one knew exactly what time she left,' Sarah says next to me.

'Poor Lauren.' Danielle groans.

'She's going to be okay though, thank goodness. She was really sorry and when she realised I could be in danger, she put our differences aside and asked to see me.'

'You should never have let Brooke in. Where's she gone off to now? Causing more mayhem somewhere?' Mum says.

'I've no idea where she's gone or what's she's going to do now. Where's Freya by the way, who's looking after her?' I try to sit up. Blood rushes to my head as I struggle to remember where she was before I passed out, but my memory has gone blank. I'm glad I didn't bring her up to the room after all, otherwise she'd have witnessed Brooke hitting me.

'Freya is fine, she's downstairs in the lounge eating ice cream with her granddad.'

I try and steady my breath to control the dizziness. I think about the last time Dad was meant to be watching her. I've not seen her for over half an hour but it feels much longer. My mind is in a spin from being out of control on so many levels. I want to shut my eyes and lie quietly for a while.

The paramedics arrive and check me over and the female with curly silver hair and a kind smile sends Sarah downstairs to get an ice pack. She says I have a bump the size of a plum on the back of my head where I must have hit the carpet hard. The male paramedic patches up the scratch on my head and a gash on my leg which I must have caught on the edge of the coffee table. For a relatively small cut, it's bleeding a lot. I could cry when I see the smear of blood on my white dress.

They advise me to go to hospital because I blacked out, but first I need to find Jamie and speak to him, make sure he's okay. I want the chance to explain myself and I'm just as desperate for answers.

47

Sarah comes back with the ice pack and Joe is following behind her in his light grey morning suit. It's the first time I've seen him dressed up. One paramedic helps me sit up, putting a cushion behind my back to support me leaning against the side of the bed. The other presses the ice onto my scalp. Mum takes over holding it there for me.

'Still no luck finding Jamie, I'm afraid,' Joe says, a little out of breath. He always takes the stairs two steps at a time with his long athletic legs. He treats everything as exercise if he can. 'I've been to your parents' house, the football club and even the office, but there's no sign of him anywhere. I honestly don't know what to suggest.'

'Where else might he go?' I ask.

'I'm out of ideas.' Joe pulls a chair over from the lounge and TV area and perches on the edge facing me, legs wide, hands clasped in front of him.

'How did he seem to you this morning?'

'I thought he was... nervous, tetchy, thoughtful. Like he had a lot on his mind. I asked him if he was okay, if he wanted to talk, but he said he was fine and wouldn't share what was wrong. To be honest, he's not been the same since seeing Brooke at the stag night. His mood has been really dark.' He shakes his head.

'I thought he'd been subdued too. He wanted to make sure nothing went wrong today.'

'He couldn't wait to marry you, which is why it's not like him to go off without saying a word. If he was worried about what lies Brooke would come out with, I reckon he'd know deep down you'd stand by him, not believe he's capable of hurting anyone. He'd want to be here to prove to you he *didn't* do anything wrong, in case you had any doubts. He certainly had no intention of standing you up today, that's for sure.'

'I think it's Brooke who's told Jamie about me and my ex. Like I said on the phone, I heard from Ryan earlier saying he's sent him the video of us together. That's the reason why Jamie's jilted me.'

'What video?' Mum asks, but I don't answer.

'He has *not* jilted you. I'd put money on it.' Joe slices his hand through the air. 'I don't believe for a second he's capable of doing that to you, whatever revelation she may have told him about you and your ex. He loves you and he would not abandon you or your wedding.'

'I bet she's the one that daubed on the wall,' Sarah says crossing her arms, and Danielle agrees.

'Come on Megan, what's this about?' Mum asks, standing up.

'Mu-um!' I shake my head.

'I want to know what we're dealing with here for him to do this to you.'

I explain it to her briefly, but I don't tell any of them details about the video Ryan took of us.

'I'd like to hope he'd forgive you,' Mum says.

'Your mum's right,' Joe says. 'Jamie wouldn't chuck away

everything you have together over an ex. You have a child together who means the world to him. I don't know this Brooke woman, so I can't comment on what she might do, but from the little that Jamie told me, it sounds like she's a nightmare and is still obsessed with him.'

'Well, if she was here to try and stop the wedding, she's succeeded,' Sarah says.

'I'm sorry to interrupt, but right now, I'm more concerned about Jamie's welfare,' Joe says to me.

I fix my eyes on his. We're thinking the same thing. The two of us are the only ones Jamie's confided in about his struggle with depression after being bullied in the army. It's the reason why he had to leave before he was eighteen. Getting married is a high-stress event which is why we've been so careful with the way we've organised it. If he has found out I cheated on him, it could send him into a nose-dive of despair, back to that dark place where he can't see any hope.

Mum's phone pings. I take over holding the ice on my head while she reads the text.

Her face turns pale.

'What is it?' I ask.

'It's your dad. He's asking if we have Freya with us.' Her mouth drops open.

'Isn't she supposed to be with *him*?' A chill shoots through me.

'Exactly what I said. *I left her with you, so where is she*? But he's not replying.'

48

We stare at her screen, then at each other's worried faces.

'He says she was racing around with some older children playing hide-and-seek, but they don't know where she went.'

Blood rushes to my head, making me dizzy.

'I'll text back asking if maybe she's hiding somewhere,' Mum says.

'Sorry, I can't wait. We need to go down and find her.' I hand the ice pack to Sarah and take hold of her other hand as she helps me stand up.

Mum tuts loudly.

'My daughter is missing.' I pull open the door and hurry down the corridor.

'Hang on, he's replying...' Mum trots after me, followed by the others close behind. 'Wait,' Mum shouts before I get to the lift. 'He's calling.' She puts the phone on loud speaker. I turn and we all huddle around her phone.

'One of the kids was coming out of the hall toilets and recognised the back of Freya's dress. She was holding an adult's hand, walking towards the main door.'

'Dad,' I say quickly, 'do you know if Freya was with a man or a woman? And what were they wearing?'

'Hello, love. The child couldn't say. The person had their back to them and was wearing a thick black tracksuit and a black beanie. The sort of clothes all the youngsters seem to wear now.'

'Do they know where they were going?'

'Out of the main door. The child presumed Freya was with one of her parents.'

'So she wasn't distressed in any way?'

'Not at all. It must have been someone Freya was familiar with.'

'Shit.' Joe rubs his forehead. My eyes latch onto his for a long second.

'I'm so sorry,' Dad tuts. 'I should have kept her with me. It's all my fault again.'

'We'll find her,' I sob into the phone, then pass it to Mum while I collapse into Danielle's arms. 'I can't believe someone has snatched Freya.'

'Who would take her though?' Mum cries. It's the second time today she's looked this shaken.

'I'm not certain. But I have my suspicions.' I dab my eyes with my fingers and steal another glance at Joe. 'We need to find out where they've gone as quickly as we can.'

'What do you think they're going to do with her?' Danielle covers her mouth, tears in her eyes. Sarah puts her arm around her shoulders as we all hurry along the corridor, back to my hotel room.

'I should be able to see where they are on here.' I shut the door when everyone has come in.

'What do you mean, what's that?' Mum asks.

I swipe open my phone. 'After what happened with you

losing sight of Freya in the department store, I spoke about it to Jamie and Joe, and he suggested I buy a tag tracker.'

'A what?' Mum frowns.

'A small electronic tag; it uses GPS, a bit like security tags used on clothes in shops, to stop people stealing them,' Joe says.

'Lots of parents use them now, Mum. The man who found Freya could have easily walked off with her and we'd never have known where she was or who she was with. Jamie and I talked about it, and we thought it was a good idea given what happened.'

'Does sound like a good idea, but why would you need to tag her at your wedding?' Mum asks.

'Just in case she wandered off. The grounds here are so vast. I thought that if she went outside, she could easily get lost and neither of us would be able to keep a close eye on her throughout the day. We thought it would be the perfect opportunity to test it out. It's the first time we've used it. I attached it to the inside of Freya's dress earlier. Under the waistband to be precise. No one else will know it's there, but I should receive a signal on my phone telling me where she is.'

'That's bloody genius,' Sarah says and Danielle nods, drying her eyes.

I click open the app and it shows a small pulsing pin icon on a map. Joe and I peer closer at the location, and I zoom in.

'There she is.' I hold up my phone so they can all see.

'Oh my goodness, someone really has abducted her.' Mum sits on the arm of a chair, her eyes darting around at all our faces.

'Where is that?' I turn to Joe.

'In the older part of town. About three miles from here. Looks like a park near a residential area,' he says.

Mum holds her hand in a V shape on her chest. 'You need to call the police.'

'No. I don't want them wading in with sirens and helicopters. I need to do this. The longer the person doesn't know we're following them the more chance we have of catching up and saving Freya.'

'So you think you know who has taken her?' Danielle asks.

'I'm not sure. I have a hunch but it could be completely wrong.'

'Why would she have been taken there?' Mum asks.

I shake my head. I can't answer that.

'I need to leave right now. Will you drive?' I say to Joe.

'Yes, if you navigate,' he says.

'I'm coming too,' Danielle says.

'Thanks. Can someone undo my buttons please?' I turn my back to them and Mum and Sarah set to work.

'I'll bring my car round the front. See you down there in two minutes.' Joe gives me a thumbs up and leaves the room.

'Sarah, could you stay with Mum? Get Dad up here too please?' I dart a look at Mum who is gazing ahead, still in total shock.

Sarah nods.

I strip off my wedding dress in front of them and throw on a pair of joggers and a T-shirt. Danielle and I rush down the stairs and we jump into Joe's Audi waiting out the front.

'Left out of here, then right,' I say to him. 'The signal isn't moving so maybe they've stopped to go to the toilet, which hopefully buys us some time to catch up with them. Hang on, look. The pin marks them at a café.'

'Hopefully we can get there before they move on, because who knows where they're heading to.' Joe glances at me by his side, then his focus is back on the road, fingers gripping the wheel.

49

'Who do you think's taken Freya?' Danielle says quietly from the back seat.

'I think it could be Emma. We argued when we were outside.' I tell them she's friends with Ryan's ex-girlfriend.

'I'm gobsmacked,' Danielle says.

'Her friend Amy was dating Ryan when I slept with him. Messed up their relationship so Emma befriended me to make sure I knew how much hurt I'd caused. I told her to go, but she might have taken Freya with her as one last dig at me.'

'Have you tried calling her?' Danielle holds her phone up to her ear.

'I did but her phone is switched off or she's blocked me.'

'Yeah, her phone is off,' Danielle says, tapping her screen.

'Don't you think it could be Jamie or even Brooke?' Joe asks.

'But he left a while ago, and I think Brooke left before Freya went missing,' I say.

'Could Jamie have come back in different clothes?'

We know his fragile state of mind, but I still find it hard to believe he would do this to me, even if he knows I cheated on him. I didn't think he was a vengeful person. But right now, I'm not sure how far I've pushed him.

'Really? He'd kidnap his own daughter?' Danielle sits up straight. The possibility it could be Ryan is not far from my mind.

'I doubt *he* sees it like that. Assuming he knows about me and Ryan, he could be trying to get away from me. The first thing he's going to worry about is not being able to see Freya.'

'You wouldn't stop him seeing her though, would you?' Joe asks.

'No of course not, although if he's pulled a stunt like this, I might be inclined to rethink that.'

'Call him, and I'll talk to him,' Joe says, glancing in my direction again.

'Would be worth a try, except his mobile was switched off earlier. Won't it spook him if he's trying to run away with our daughter and knows we're after him? I don't want to panic him into doing anything... stupid.'

'Maybe you're right. We just need to get to the park asap.'

'You don't think he's going to hurt himself... or Freya... do you?' Danielle whispers. I twist round to see her sombre-looking face. There's a dark expression in her eyes and I know exactly what she's hinting at. We followed a domestic case in the news a couple of years ago, of two kids who'd been picked up from school by their estranged dad. He'd driven up to Beachy Head with them and jumped off the cliff, holding their hands.

'We don't know for sure it's Jamie. It could be Brooke. Why was she trying to stop me leaving? Could she have taken Freya and gone to meet up with Jamie?'

'I don't think so, not from the way he was talking about her,' Joe says.

'Okay. Let's focus on getting to the park.' I point to the road ahead.

The traffic lights change as we approach and I'm grateful Joe doesn't try and run the red light, although part of me wishes he could have driven a bit faster because the couple of minutes' wait for the light to turn green feels like hours. When we finally get going again, I let out a breath, but the relief is short-lived. There's a long queue of traffic up ahead, all taking the turning towards the park.

'Looks like there's some sort of local event going on,' I say, frantically tapping my phone to find out what it is. 'Great. The annual summer fayre.'

'That's all we need,' Danielle says.

I look down at my phone again. 'Shit, the tag on Freya is moving again.'

'We're never going to get there at this slow pace. Who knows how far away she'll be,' Danielle says.

'It's okay, it's stopped again,' I say. 'She's still within the parameters of the park, thank goodness. Second right up here on the left.' The queue starts moving. 'There should be a car park near the entrance, then we'll have to walk across to the café.' If it is Jamie who's taken Freya, my guess is he's brought her here to spend some time with his little girl. But if it's Emma, Brooke or even Ryan, I've no idea what their agenda might be, except to punish me, and I dread to think what that means for my daughter.

Joe flicks on the indicator as it's finally our turn to enter the car park. I half expect to see Emma or Jamie's car parked up, but I can't spot either of them. It's packed and we end up parking in the overflow area in the adjacent field.

If Jamie would just switch his phone back on so I can speak to him. Would he really have come back for Freya? Isn't it more likely to be Emma or Brooke? How far are they willing to go with this? Freya will be scared, crying for me. Brooke is a stranger to her.

I'm the first to jump out of the car and start running towards the fayre, swiftly followed by Joe and Danielle.

'The signal has shifted, so let's get moving,' I say to them, as they jog along behind me. The painkillers have kicked in, but I can still feel the skin around the wound on my leg pulsing.

The funfair is on the far side of the park, with a Big Wheel, Carousel and Helter Skelter. I stop and groan inwardly. How are we going to find her in there? I touch my forehead as I wait for the others to catch up.

'It's a huge space and it's heaving,' I sigh.

'So many places for a child to hide or not be seen,' Danielle says, hands on hips, trying to catch her breath.

'But we need to keep looking; we can't give up,' I tell them, setting off again across the grass.

'Shall we stick together or split up?' Joe asks.

'We need to find her fast. Have you both got your phones on with a strong signal?'

They both check their screens and nod.

'Then let's search separately but keep in close touch, because we don't know for sure who's with her. Whoever has taken her, could have dumped her here, left her standing on her own.'

A shiver runs through me as we go our separate ways, not knowing what we're going to find.

50

We space out as we sweep forward, making sure we're in a line, concentrating on moving towards the exact spot where the signal is showing on the map. I sidestep parents holding hands with their children, who are carrying big teddy bears or pink and blue candy floss on long sticks, obscuring my view of their faces. I get some strange looks as I peer at children being carried and children in pushchairs. I can't help checking the face of every child I see, but there's no sign of Freya.

A few minutes later, we congregate near the perimeter of the funfair, scanning around us, clueless. There's no sign of any child wearing a pale blue flower-girl dress. I throw my hands up in defeat.

'Where can she be?' I say to the others as we gather. 'The signal is still telling me she's right here, look.' I hold out the map on my phone and show the flashing icon from the tag. 'Something must be glaring me in the face but for whatever reason, I can't see it.'

'Some trackers aren't as accurate as you'd expect them to be. They can mark the spot in the middle of a field, but it could be indicating a nearby farm within that post code,' Joe says. 'Let's split up again and look more closely in this small area.' He opens his arms out wide.

'Good idea and this time we should call her name. Let's ask around, look inside the control cabins of these rides, even places like under the Carousel, anywhere a small child might hide or get lost without anyone noticing.'

Again, we go our separate ways. I find a man with a megaphone calling, 'Roll up, roll up, for the greatest fayre in town,' to the crowd and he lets me use it to call Freya's name. My voice sounds strange and I'm not sure anyone takes much notice of me. My eyes strain looking at every face which passes my way, hoping my little girl will work her way out of the knotted crowd towards me, but there's no sign of her. Next, I go into the St John Ambulance tent to see if she's been found and taken there, but she isn't and when I show the staff a photo of her on my phone, none of them recognise her.

I check my phone again and the marker is still flashing. I spin in a circle. She's here somewhere, but where? I want to scream. How can the pin on the map still be flashing when she's clearly not here? It must be faulty.

I trudge back to our meeting point and stop by a stand of candy floss and marshmallows in clear bags flapping gently in the breeze. The warm sweet smell carries in the air. As I glance at the ground, something catches my eye. I crouch down and pick up a single blue flower head, trodden into the grass.

'What have you got there?' Danielle asks, looking over my shoulder.

'A cornflower.' I look up at her and blink tears from my eyes. 'Freya's been here, but where is she now?' I wonder if she dropped it on purpose to help me find her. But what if someone attacked her and this fell from her headdress? I try to think clearly but my mind is a mush of jelly.

Danielle holds out a small silver sandal from behind her back. 'I found this.'

'Shit, that's definitely Freya's.' I press my hand over my mouth, hot tears refilling my eyes. I take it from her, stroking the soft leather in my palm. 'Where did you find it?'

'On the ground over there by the ice-cream van. I searched around for the other one, but I couldn't find it.'

'Megan,' Joe calls out, waving an arm at us near where we were standing at the perimeter of the park.

Danielle links her arm through mine as we march over.

'Any sign of Freya?' I ask. 'Danielle has found one of her sandals.' I hold it out to show him. 'And I've found a cornflower.'

'Not exactly, but there's something important you should see,' he says, turning away.

'What is it?' I look around to anticipate what he's about to show us. The tag is still flashing on my phone. We follow him to a large refuse bin with a plastic moulded top and access gaps on all sides to the almost full liner inside. I press the sandal to my chest. The tag has merged with the red spot right where I'm standing.

Joe dips his hand into the bin. He rolls up his sleeve and reaches down almost to his elbow and tugs the edge of something. A corner pops out. It's pale blue satin. I gasp.

'Is this Freya's?' he asks and pulls out a handful of the material. I nod, unable to speak. Using his other hand, he brings the whole dress out, almost as gently as if there was a child inside it. It's creased, with dirt and dust smeared on it. I lift the hem and there's the tag on the waistband, right where I fastened it a few hours ago.

'How will we find her now?' I cry.

51

I hold Freya's dress to my face but instead of breathing in her sweet candy aroma, it smells of used cigarettes. I groan and chuck it back at Joe. I need to believe she's going to be okay; we're going to find her.

'How did you know the dress was in the bin? Strange place to look, isn't it?' Danielle tilts her head as she quizzes Joe.

'I noticed the bag was open as I walked past the bin and saw something blue poking out. I've been looking for some tiny clue as to where she might be, even if it seemed to be an impossible place.'

Danielle's eyelashes flutter and she side-eyes me with the slightest frown.

I shake my head at her. 'The only person who knew about that tag apart from Joe, was Jamie. I hadn't told anyone else until I attached it to her dress.'

'So it has to be him who's taken Freya.' Danielle throws her hands up.

'Exactly,' I say. 'I told him I'd be tracking her today, so I think he's taken her and got rid of her dress to make sure I can't find them.'

'That's insane. It's not like him to be underhand. You know that, right?' Joe implores me. 'I can imagine him going off in a huff if someone told him something bad about you, and maybe taking Freya with him, but not *kidnapping* her, which is what this feels like. I mean deliberately removing her dress so you don't know where your daughter is? That's insane and cruel. No, he'd have called one of us. And he'd have come back by now with his tail between his legs.'

'Would he though? In his state of mind? You said yourself, something has been bothering him these last few days. And I think you know more than you're saying.' I point a finger at him, wishing he would be honest with me so we can find Jamie and Freya. I don't think Jamie would do anything to harm her, but as for hurting himself, I'm not so sure.

Joe steps back, holding his palms up. 'I don't know any more than you do. I wish I did, believe me.'

'Convenient you brought us here on this wild goose chase though, isn't it?' Danielle says, crossing her arms.

'How is it a wild goose chase?' Joe emphasises every word. 'We were following a tracker on Freya's clothing.'

'So you weren't in on this plan? Jamie collects Freya from the hotel, changes her clothes, plants her dress in the bin and you come here with us to keep us distracted, while he takes Freya further and further away from me.' I press my fist on my hip.

'No, it's not like that. I told you, I've not seen or spoken to him since we arrived at the hotel, and then he went off. I don't know where he went or if he even came back for Freya. I've not heard from him. In fact, I'm the one who's been searching for him the whole time.'

'But Freya clearly knew the person she left the hotel with, because the witness didn't mention her kicking and screaming. So, it's most likely to have been him.'

'No. I don't believe that.' Joe shakes his head. 'What about Brooke? What was all that about, her even being here? She drugged and hit you don't forget.'

'But there's no reason for her to take Freya, is there?'

Joe's shoulders slump.

'Freya doesn't know Brooke. She wouldn't have walked out of there with her without a fuss,' I say.

'Back to square one,' Danielle says.

'I just think if Jamie did take Freya, wouldn't he have removed the tag straight away?' Joe says.

He's got a point. But none of it makes any sense, and in the meantime, Jamie and Freya are still missing.

'The only other possibilities are Emma or Ryan. But I would have expected them to have contacted me by now, to demand money or taunt me.'

On the way back to the car, I call Mum to update her. I tell her I think Jamie may have Freya, but there's nothing concrete she can report to the police.

'What are you going to do then?' Mum asks.

'I need to keep looking, make sure it *is* Jamie that's with her, and work out why he took her without telling me. I have to make sure they are safe.' This is my fault. I should have told him what happened with Ryan at the time instead of putting it off. It's a secret that ballooned into something out of control and it's became harder and harder to be honest with him. And now someone, possibly Brooke, or maybe Emma, has told him about it and ruined our special day.

I climb into the front seat next to Joe and pull on my seatbelt.

As the car pulls away, my phone pings in my lap. I stare at it for a long second.

'Who is it?' Joe asks.

'It's a text from Jamie. Thank God.' I pick the phone up and tap to open it.

'Talk of the devil,' Danielle laughs.

But when I read the message, I'm not laughing.

52

'What does he say then?' Danielle asks.

I read the message aloud.

> I know what you did with Ryan and if you want to see Freya again, you need to do as I say

'What? Jamie said that?' Joe looks at me, shell-shocked. Like him, I've never known Jamie to threaten me or anyone.

I swallow the lump in my throat. I've not seen this darker side of Jamie before. I can't believe that the man I've known for years would be capable of turning on me so easily. Now I'm sure he knows my secret, and I've probably lost him forever. Part of me hoped he'd be more understanding. Why can't he at least try and forgive me? We have built our lives together, had Freya. Surely that's more important? Tears drop from my eyes. He's not the person I thought he was.

Joe frowns and I guess we're both thinking of our original theory, that Jamie may have gone off with the intention of harming himself, except now he has Freya with him. I shudder. He's told me about his time in the army, but not exactly what triggered his depression. I didn't want to push him to tell me, because it was clearly too painful, but maybe I should have asked more questions.

There have been a few times when I've woken in the night, and he's not been in bed. Once I found him curled up on the bathroom floor crying, and another time he was in the back garden in Freya's Wendy house, hiding under a blanket in the corner. What is he keeping from me? Would he really harm himself and his own daughter?

I text back.

> Prove you have her with you.

It takes a few seconds for the reply to arrive. I read it out.

> You've just found her dress in the park bin with the tag on it

'Shit. Only he could know about that,' Danielle says.

'Did he come back to the hotel for her, or was he there all the time, hidden away somewhere, waiting for the opportunity to take her?' Joe jabs the steering wheel with the heel of his hand.

'So he was the person that child saw in the black tracksuit,' Danielle groans.

'How did he manage to take her without an adult noticing?' I spread my hand over my face.

'What's he going to do if you don't follow his instructions?' Danielle sounds as worried as I feel.

I try to weigh up the possibilities in my mind. I shiver. He's suddenly like a stranger to me. The Jamie I know isn't capable of this.

'Why would he punish me by taking Freya?' I shake my head, bewildered. He's normally so reasonable. I thought he'd come and talk to me about it. 'He's lied to me too, told me Brooke was his ex-girlfriend when she's his ex-wife. That is not a small lie.'

I text again.

> Tell me where she is, and I'll be there

It's an agonising five minutes before he texts me an address. I tap it into the car's sat nav.

'Fifteen-minute drive. He said to come alone.'

'You can't go on your own.' Danielle's voice rises.

'She's right, you don't know what his state of mind will be,' Joe says.

'But I can't risk putting Freya in danger.'

'You don't seriously think he's going to hurt his own daughter, do you?' Joe winces.

'I'm not sure any more. I don't know what he's capable of, but I can't take any chances, not where Freya is concerned.'

Joe shakes his head and does a U-turn. 'Okay, we'll park out of sight and wait in the car for you.'

'What do you think he wants?' There's a tremor in Danielle's voice. She sits on the edge of the back seat, peering at the address on the sat nav.

'I'm not sure.' I take in a breath and slowly let it out.

'I think we should tell the police he's threatening you,' Danielle says.

'I can't, not yet. He probably just wants to talk. The police will say he's with his daughter meeting his fiancé, and no crime has been committed.'

No crime yet, says a voice in my head.

'Remind him Freya's welfare is your joint priority,' Joe says.

'I will. I'm going to do whatever it takes to bring my daughter home safely.'

53

Joe drives to the address Jamie gave me, on the outskirts of town. There are fields of long grass all around and through an open gate is a track leading up to a red-brick farmhouse, surrounded by stables and outbuildings. The sat nav points to somewhere in the middle of a field but there's only this property here, so it must be the right place. Joe parks in the lane behind a hedge, out of sight.

'I'll come with you,' he says.

'Best to stay here. I don't think Jamie will appreciate me bringing anyone with me. I need to stick to what he asked to make sure I get Freya back without a fuss.'

'As if *he* hasn't broken any rules by snatching his own child,' Joe tuts.

'I don't suppose he's thinking straight. Please stay with Danielle and let Mum know where we are in case we lose signal.'

'Keep your phone close to you, okay?' He plants a reassuring hand on my shoulder. 'Be careful.' Danielle reaches for my fingers and gives them a gentle squeeze.

'Will do.'

'If you're not out in about ten minutes, we're coming in,' he adds.

'Don't be a hero, Joe. It's probably going to take longer than that to negotiate with him.'

'Okay, I'll give it a bit longer. All I'm saying is, I don't think he's well, and he's clearly in shock or something and acting out of character. What bastard has told him on his wedding day? He won't have had time to process it. He'll be feeling betrayed and maybe desperate; who knows what he might do. So, I'm not taking any chances, okay? Your parents would never forgive me if something happened to you or Freya.'

'Okay, okay. Thank you for looking out for us, for being here. And thank you too, Danielle.' I take a deep breath and climb out of the car, closing the door as quietly as I can. I start walking down the dusty lane to the path leading up to the house.

The front wall is cloaked in wisteria. The lilac blooms drape heavily over the leaded windows. There's no sign of life in or around the cottage and I wonder if we've got the right place. Everywhere is eerily quiet except a bulldog jumping and barking behind a reinforced wire gate on the right side of the house. I love dogs, but it doesn't look like the sort that would lick my hand in a friendly hello. More likely to snap it off given half a chance.

Parked out the front is a black van next to a souped-up Mustang with flames painted down the sides. Could that be one of the vans that boxed us in on the motorway? The number plate doesn't mean anything to me, so I'm not sure. What is this place? Jamie's never visited here with me. He owns a BMW, but I can't see one. Why has he brought Freya here? Maybe this isn't the right place.

I turn to go then glance over my shoulder at the side window of the house. Was that a shadow of someone standing there watching me? Goosebumps rise all the way down my neck. I walk up to the solid wood front door which has a big brass handle in the middle of it. I'm about to lift the lion's head knocker when I step on something. I daren't look down. The sensation of a soft crunch under my shoe makes me cringe. Closing my eyes for a long moment, I try to block out the thought of a slug or snail being flattened. Or perhaps it's some other poor unsuspecting creature? I step back gingerly and whatever it was is now stuck to the sole of my shoe. I curl my toes up to see, and the colour of it startles me. A single blue cornflower head is crushed there. I peel it away and examine it. It's a fresh flower, and looking around I can't see any growing nearby, so it must have come from Freya's headdress.

I knock once on the front door and wait. I sneak a look through the window again and wonder if I imagined someone there before, because there's no one there now.

The barn door is slightly ajar, and I'm drawn to peer inside. No one is coming to answer so I'm guessing no one is in, or maybe there's a garden behind the house and they're sitting out there and can't hear me. But surely they can hear the dog jumping and barking and rattling his chain?

I can't see far into the barn in the murky light. There's no one around, so I slip inside.

The concrete floor is scattered with hay and there are bales of it stacked high to the ceiling on both sides, creating a dark corridor. I creep further on, past a stack of cardboard boxes of what look like toys from China, maybe knock-off goods. The natural farmyard aroma of manure changes as I walk on, to the thick unmistakable metallic smell of blood. My stomach flips over. Dread climbs my throat at what I might find. I pivot on my heel, not sure I can face this without Joe and Danielle, but a pain-filled moan makes me freeze. The hair on my head prickles. I strain to hear it again, but it's so faint it's hard to make out *what* it is. I shiver. My gut tells me it's human.

'Freya?' I tentatively call into the darkness, a tremble in my voice.

I listen hard for a reply but there's only silence followed by a faint shuffling sound.

'Megan?' says a weak voice. It sounds like Jamie. *Is* it him?

'Where's Freya?' I creep cautiously towards the voice. 'What have you done to her?'

54

In the darkness I make out the shape of a man sitting hunched on the ground, arms behind his back. There's a tiny window to the side of him, with newspaper taped to the glass letting in enough light to show me it *is* Jamie. I gasp at the state of him. His wedding shirt is hanging out of his trousers, his silver-grey jacket has dirty finger marks on it and blood is smeared across his face.

'What's happened to you? Where's Freya?' I ask, but his head lolls forward. There's a gag in his mouth, tied around the back of his head. His hands have been secured with thin rope to one of the barn's structural posts.

'Who did this to you?' I crouch by his side and try to untie the gag but can't loosen the knot. The cut on his face is deep. Blood is dripping off his face onto the ground. 'I thought you'd deserted me and taken Freya.'

He shakes his head with enormous effort. I try to release his hands, but they are tied too tightly. With trembling fingers, I carefully pull down the gag. He winces, then looks right at me for a second. His eyes are dark, hollow looking and creased with pain.

'Get yourself out of here.' His voice is rasping and hoarse, as though he's been shouting or screaming. 'Call the police, they'll find Freya, don't worry about me.' His words are rushed and desperate.

'But I have to help you, I can't leave you like this,' I cry.

'You can't let him catch you.' His words are barely audible.

'Let who?' I glance round but no one is there. 'I need to find Freya and get you out of here.' I search around for something to help me cut away the rope binding his hands.

'Just go!' he strains to say, his voice almost lost.

'Who did this to you? Someone sent me messages from your phone telling me to come here and I assumed it was you.'

Jamie is about to answer but his eyes widen with fright at something behind me.

'You're here at last,' a familiar voice announces. I freeze. Jamie shoots me a look as if to say he tried to warn me.

'We've been waiting for you, haven't we?'

I recognise that voice. I stand up and swivel round.

'You?' I spit the word from my mouth.

Ryan swaggers towards us in a black suit, waving Jamie's mobile in his hand with the Manchester United football logo on the back cover.

'Good to see you too, Megan.'

'What have you done to Jamie?'

'We had a little chat. Didn't go too badly, for me anyway.' He laughs. 'I wanted to meet the man himself. The chosen one.'

'Why have you brought him here? He hasn't done anything to you.'

'He's got you though, hasn't he?'

'Where's my daughter? Did you abduct her as well?'

'I might have done.' He grins. 'Abduct is harsh though. She was very willing.'

I frown. But he's a stranger to her. We've spoken about not talking to people we don't know, but perhaps she's too young to really understand what that means.

'Did you get my message on the hotel wall?'

'That was you?'

The barn door opens and Ryan half turns. 'Here she is.' He claps his hands.

'Mummy!' Freya runs up behind him, arms up, heading towards me. She's wearing a plain cream dress. The headdress of cornflowers has gone.

'Thank goodness you're safe. Come here, angel. Are you okay?' I lift her up and hug her tightly in my arms. 'Ryan hasn't hurt you, has he?' I say in her ear. I pull back a touch to check for any signs she's been badly treated.

'He gave me a strawberry ice cream and I ate it all up.' She giggles, looking as bright and fresh as when I last saw her at the hotel.

'She's been such a sweetheart,' Ryan says, putting his hand on her back.

I stand and fix my eyes on him. 'Get your hands off my daughter,' I say in a low steady voice. He lifts both his hands up in surrender and I pull Freya closer to me.

'Hurting me, Mummy,' she says, frowning up at me. She rubs her wrist with her other hand. Perhaps I was a bit rough, but I'm desperate to protect her. I kiss the silky hair on her head.

'I'm sorry, darling. I just want you to stay with Mummy so I can keep you safe.'

'Daddy,' she cries, spotting Jamie slumped on the ground. She wriggles away from me and runs to him, wrapping her little arms around his neck and holding her cheek close to his face. 'Why don't you get up, Daddy?' She tries to pull his arm but it's too heavy and immobile, tied behind him.

I turn to Ryan, my arms crossed. 'So it was you who texted me on Jamie's phone.'

'I knew you'd come running if you thought it was from *him*.' He indicates to Jamie like he's a piece of trash he's dumped on the ground.

'It was you who took her when she was out shopping with my parents, wasn't it?'

'I might have encouraged her to come and say hello to me.'

'How dare you. You need to leave us alone.'

'Come along Freya, it's time to go and get ready,' Ryan calls to her and an old woman appears behind him. And just like that, my daughter runs towards this stranger and holds her hand and walks away as if she knows her.

'Freya, stay with me,' I call, my tone sharp, but she looks over her shoulder at me with a silly grin and waves. 'Get ready for what? Where are you taking her?' I try to go after them, but Ryan stands in my way.

'What I want to know is, why didn't you want to marry me?' Ryan says. 'I'm better than him by miles. You and I were amazing together.'

'You're only remembering the good times. What about all the debts you ran up from gambling and drugs? It was always just one more spliff, one more bet. Never being able to hold down a job.'

'I would have changed if you'd wanted to marry me, wanted to have children with me.'

I shake my head. 'I don't think you were ever going to clean yourself up. You enjoyed the risk of losing every last penny to the slot machines. But what about me? What about what I wanted?'

'You loved it really, the thrill of it all.' He winks.

'Maybe in the beginning I was easily impressed when you

won, but not once you started losing. You never changed. You never grew up. I couldn't bring a child into such an unstable home.'

'You always were a bit of a prude. But I still love you, no matter what.'

'Tell me why you took Freya.'

'Isn't that obvious?'

'Not really. Tell me before I call the police.' I reach for my phone in my back pocket.

'I wouldn't do that if I were you.'

'Don't threaten me. Why is Jamie tied up here when we are supposed to be getting married?' I ask, irritation seeping into my voice.

'He turned up in a van and bundled me in,' Jamie mumbles and nods in Ryan's direction.

'And no one saw a thing? Where was Joe?' I ask.

'He'd gone to make sure everyone was in their seats ready for your grand entrance. I suppose when he came out to get me, I'd gone.'

'I thought I should make sure Jamie knew what he was getting into.' Ryan smirks and folds his arms.

'What do you mean?'

'I told him all about our evening together. How much you enjoyed it.'

'No!' I cry.

'Let them go, Ryan. This is between you and me,' Jamie half croaks, half whispers, his voice almost gone.

'Oh, but I haven't shown you the whole video yet. I only sent you a short clip. You need proof of what your beloved did to you, don't you?'

'Not really,' he mumbles.

'Ryan, please don't show it to him.' My tone is more begging than I intend it to be, but I really can't bear Jamie to see any of it.

'So it's true, is it?' Jamie's voice is a low whisper. He sighs deeply.

'I'm so sorry. Ryan tricked me, plied me with drink on his birthday. I didn't know he was filming... us.' Now I'm overexplaining and it probably makes it sound worse.

Jamie nods but he's staring at the ground.

'So now we're all here, I think we should watch it together.' Ryan puts Jamie's phone down and rubs his hands. He lifts the gag back into Jamie's mouth then plucks his phone out of his back pocket and presses play, holding it close to Jamie's face.

'Switch it off,' I shout, then clench my teeth at hearing the sounds of me in bed with Ryan. 'Enough!' I scream when he doesn't stop it. I shove his arm and he staggers to one side, loses his balance and falls to the ground. I go to make a run for it, but Ryan is up on his feet in seconds.

'You're not going anywhere.' He herds me backwards towards Jamie. I couldn't have left Jamie tied up, but if I could just get out of here, find Freya and go and get help, I'd come back for him.

'Why are you doing this to me, Ryan?'

'I thought that was obvious.' He pauses but I say nothing. 'Because you're not meant to marry *him*.' He scowls.

'But we finished years ago, why can't you accept that?' I look beyond him to the way we came in, trying to work out how far it is. I should have brought Joe with me after all.

'You think *I'm* jealous?' Ryan snorts with laughter. 'I'm not the one who's been messing with your head.'

'What do you mean?' I fold my arms. The barn door creaks and opens wide. I'm praying it's Danielle or Joe, coming to save us.

'This is the one you should be worried about.' Ryan points, grinning.

Someone is standing in the doorway, a silhouette against the bright light flooding in from outside.

As they stride towards me, I think I must be seeing things.

Brooke halts a few steps away from me, wearing what horrifying looks like a wedding dress. Its ivory satin and lace is verging on sallow yellow in the dim light of the barn.

'What are you doing here with Ryan?' I step back. I think of when she first turned up as Beth, and how she helped me, but then she came to my hotel room when I was about to marry Jamie and attacked me, claiming she was saving me from her abuser.

'I've been waiting for you, Megan.' Brooke's voice is soft and dream-like, as though she's beginning a meditation.

'What are you talking about?'

'You've been fighting it, but you and Ryan are meant to be together.' She smiles and tips up her chin.

'No, we're not.' I squint at her and take another step back. 'You helped to stop Ryan threatening me, remember?'

'But you told me yourself, you and Ryan still have that special spark, something that you admitted has been sadly lacking with Jamie.'

I feel my face heat up at her saying something so personal in front of everyone. 'I confided in you when I said that,' I snap and glance at Jamie. He's staring into space. 'I trusted you not to tell anyone about any of this.'

She laughs as though she's enjoying my discomfort. I'm transported back to my hen night, remembering the joy in her eyes when she threw a bag of flour over me.

'What you mean is, you didn't want Jamie to see the video of you reunited in bed with Ryan.' She says it with a sharp edge of sarcasm.

'It was a mistake,' I shout. She's so determined to hurt me.

'The video I asked Ryan to take of you both, so there was proof you'd cheated on Jamie?'

'You did what?' I turn to Ryan. 'How could you?' I spit the words at him, and he cowers away from me.

'I needed something to use against you, so I could make Jamie see what you were like and leave you, and at the same time win him back for myself. And when you asked me to help you stop Ryan contacting you, all I had to do was call him and say it was time to stop texting and phoning you until we were ready for the next phase of our plan.'

My mouth drops open. Lauren's warning about Brooke crashes into me head on.

'It was easy really. I already knew you'd had his baby, but as you weren't married, I didn't believe he was genuinely committed to you, and he'd eventually move on. The Jamie I knew was never interested in having brats. But when you got engaged to him, what was it, a year ago? I needed to know who you were and put an end to it. I followed you on social media and contacted Ryan through your Facebook page. He was posting about how heartbroken he still was. There were photos on your page of you with Jamie, *my* Jamie, showing off your engagement ring. I could not allow the wedding to go ahead. So I got in touch with Ryan and we hatched a plan for him to get you back and for Jamie to be mine again. I asked him to seduce you, sleep with you and film it. He was hardly going to say no. I promised him that if we managed to split you two up, you would go back to him and Jamie would come back to me. It could almost be like we'd never been apart.'

'That's insane.' I touch my throat and back away, looking from one to the other.

'Ryan's been following your every move.'

My body stiffens, stomach rigid. 'I always had a feeling you were never far away but I thought I was being paranoid. How could you do that to me, Ryan?'

'I enjoyed being near you. It was almost like we were together again. I was looking out for you, keeping you safe, wherever you went.'

I shudder. All those quiet moments when I thought I was alone, he was watching me, violating my space just by being there.

'It *was* you who wrote "*Jilted*" on the hotel wall, wasn't it?' I say to Brooke. 'Or at least you got Ryan to do it for you. And the funeral flowers, the wreath to my hotel room, you even demanded money over WhatsApp. All of it was you.'

Brooke nods, grinning. 'They were little warnings from me. But the nail varnish and lipstick on the mirror were too tame, so I got Ryan to find some roadkill and chuck it in the swimming pool. I tried everything to try and put you off going ahead with the wedding. But not even the fox's entrails worked. You're a stubborn one, aren't you?'

'Because I *love* Jamie.'

Jamie moans and tries to speak with the gag in his mouth, but none of us can understand what he's saying.

'The truth is, Megan, Jamie has never stopped loving me. He's found that hard to admit to you and himself. But we're meant for each other. I know that's difficult for you to hear, but it's the reason why I had to put a stop to your wedding. For all our sakes.'

Jamie groans.

'What do you mean? I don't believe you.' I mustn't let myself be taken in by what she's saying. Jamie loves *me*. I glance at him, hoping for a sign that I'm right. He groans again, louder this time. I run over and pull the gag out of his mouth. Ryan makes a move to stop me, but Brooke waves her hand at him to leave it.

'I've never loved Brooke, you have to believe me, Megan.' The words come out of Jamie in a splutter. He coughs and clears his throat. 'She fled Australia after attacking her ex,' Jamie says.

'What?' I cast my eyes over Brooke's smug grin.

'I didn't find out until after our wedding.' Jamie flicks sweat off his face.

'But if you didn't love her, why did you marry her?'

'Go on, admit to Megan the real reason why I married you,' Jamie blurts out in a hoarse voice.

'You can tell her. She probably won't believe you.' Brooke rattles out a laugh.

Jamie's head points to the ground as though it's too heavy to hold up any longer. He swallows hard, then lifts his face and looks me directly in the eye.

'She paid me to marry her.'

56

'What do you mean? No one does that.' I frown. 'This is a joke, isn't it?'

Jamie shakes his head and strains to speak. 'It's true.' He coughs then swallows a couple of times. 'She said she needed to stay in the UK to get away from her abusive ex in Australia, and the only way of doing that was by having a sham wedding. Getting a fool like me to legally marry her as quickly as possible.'

'What? But why you?' I ask, still hoping he's going to tell me this is a cruel prank.

'A mutual friend suggested me to her, because I'd just come out of the army and desperately needed some cash.'

'How much did she pay you?' It's crazy that I'm even asking this.

'Three grand. That was a lot back then, especially in my situation.' He coughs and winces with pain.

'Back when, what year was this?'

'Thirteen years ago, in 2011. I was nineteen.'

'Bless him, he had trouble pronouncing my middle name. The celebrant gave us some funny looks. I thought we were going to be found out.' Brooke strokes the hair on his head with her long nails.

'How did you get away with it? I thought sham weddings were against the law.'

'A lot of the extra checks that had been brought in were dropped that year, something to do with discrimination issues, so she managed to slip it through undetected by getting married in a church. Even my mum was fooled. I couldn't bring myself to tell her. But of course she found out, and that's why she stopped speaking to me.'

'That's so sad.'

'It was meant to be a short-term thing so Brooke could stay in the country legally, and once all the paperwork was in order, we were going to file for divorce a few weeks later, cite irreconcilable differences. I thought I'd get Mum back on side once it went through. But I didn't realise Brooke had other ideas. She never intended to end the marriage.' Jamie starts coughing then choking. He spits phlegm on the floor. When he looks up at me, his eyes are small and red.

'But why?'

'He's exaggerating.' Brooke flicks her hand in the air as though he's an irritating fly.

'Tell me exactly what she did, Jamie.' I fix my eyes on her as I speak to him. His head lolls to one side, eyes half shut as if he's given up on life. I raise my voice and continue. 'Because she told me *you* abused her. She confided in me about it and said she wanted to save me from the same fate.'

He shakes his head like a mangy dog and glances up briefly with hollow eyes. 'It was the complete opposite. She tied me up and beat me. Locked me in the house for hours and barely left me any food.'

'You don't believe any of this, do you?' Brooke laughs.

Jamie ignores her and carries on. 'I had to sleep on the floor while she had the whole bed to herself. Then she'd make me shower in steaming hot water and lie on the bed naked. She tied my hands and feet to the posts and bit me, hit me and forced herself on me... raped me.' His voice cracks and he breaks down crying.

'What the hell? That's disgusting. You're disgusting!' I scream, charging into her sideways with my shoulder. She staggers backwards.

'Don't listen to that rubbish. He enjoyed every minute of it. Loved me being in charge. You know men like dominant women.' She laughs.

Jamie sniffs and slowly shakes his head. 'No, it wasn't like that at all. I didn't want to have sex with you. You made me swallow a little blue pill. I had no control over my body. You abused me,' he shouts, spit coming out of his mouth with the words, and he carries on crying.

'You were my husband, you had a duty to satisfy me, so no one believes you, Jamie. It's okay to admit to liking a bit of kinky sex.'

'You disgust me! I married you for the money and to do you a favour, help you get away from an abusive ex, or so I thought. That's it. Purely a business transaction. I didn't love you. Never have. I wasn't even attracted to you. You belittled me and made me a prisoner in my own home.' He sobs. I make a move to go to him, but Ryan holds my wrists. I've never seen Jamie so utterly broken.

'That's just not true, you had your own key. You could come and go as you pleased. I didn't stop you. Why are you making out I kept you locked up? Are you embarrassed Megan will find out how wild our sex life really was?'

'You're lying! I never had my own key and I never agreed to

have sex with you,' he shouts until his voice is so hoarse we can hardly hear him. 'You repulse me,' he growls from deep in his throat.

Brooke marches over and whacks him hard across the head. Blood and spit fly from his mouth and nose.

'Leave him alone,' I scream, but Ryan restrains me harder.

'Now you're just being nasty and cruel and spiteful, because you want to show off in front of Megan. You forget, I know the *real* you. And I know how much you really love me.' She turns to me again, her voice softer once more. 'And just to prove it, Jamie and I are going to get remarried and then we're going to live together again.'

'What? You can't, he's marrying me. He doesn't want you; he divorced you.'

'That was Jamie having a tantrum, trying to upset me. He regrets it now, don't you darling?' She ruffles his hair, and he flicks his head away from her.

'No,' he bellows, thrashing from side to side like a tormented bear on a chain.

Ryan ties my hands behind my back with a piece of rope then brings Freya back in. She skips towards us, holding a bouquet of pink rose buds. Has she been kept in the house next to the barn? She's now wearing a pale pink dress.

'Why have you dressed my daughter like that?' I shout.

'I told you. Jamie and I are getting remarried today, and we need a bridesmaid. I want you to be a witness.'

'You can't do that. He doesn't want to marry you,' I shout and try to pull away from Ryan who's still holding onto my bound hands.

'But I promised Jamie I'd never let him go.' Brooke raises her eyebrows at my dissent. Ryan grins at me and pulls me to him so I'm close enough to feel his body heat through his thin shirt. I draw away from the sour smell of his hot breath, willing Joe and Danielle to come and find us, to call the police.

A man I recognise from one of the black vans on the motorway comes in wearing a smart morning suit. His distinctive mop of white hair has been gelled back on his head like a helmet. He grunts as he drags Jamie up from the floor. The woman who took Freya away before appears from the darkness and scrubs Jamie's face clean with a dirty-looking flannel. The man unties him and walks him further into the barn.

'Where are you taking him?' I shout.

The doors at the far end are opened by another man in a suit, revealing a small brand-new wooden building decorated with strings of twinkling white fairy lights.

Ryan hooks his arm through mine in a firm grip. I tug down, trying to pull away but he won't let go. He jolts me to walk forwards with him and I have no choice but to move or be dragged. He's hurting my arm. Freya is in front of us, tightly holding a posy of flowers and I don't want to lose sight of her.

Through the back of the barn, we are led to the Moroccan-style doors carved from soft wood and painted with orange and yellow swirls.

'What is this?' I ask, just as I notice a man holding a black book in his hands, which I assume is the bible, except there's no Jesus on the cross above the altar behind him, only a symbol I don't recognise.

'It's a chapel,' Ryan says.

'For what god? I don't recognise that sign.'

'You don't need to,' he whispers to me and licks my ear. I stamp on his toes and he yelps and squeezes my arm tighter.

In the corner, the man with white hair presses play on an old CD player and Handel's 'Arrival of the Queen of Sheba' starts to play. I groan inwardly. It's one of the tunes we'd considered for our wedding. We all turn to see Brooke walking towards us, wearing what I realise from the photo she showed me, is her original wedding dress and veil, holding a bouquet of fresh flowers. Before she even reaches Jamie's side, he turns to face her, with a look of hatred I never knew he was capable of. I reach out for Freya's hand and she moves closer to me.

'I am not marrying you again, Brooke, so you need to stop this ridiculous farce right now.' Jamie's shoulders rise and fall with the effort of speaking. His voice is deep again, loud and clear.

'There's nothing stopping us, we're meant to be together. You know that,' Brooke says, indicating for the celebrant to begin.

'No!' Jamie kicks out at the man guarding him, and swings his arm, jabbing his elbow into the man's groin. Ryan lets go of me and pulls out a knife, holding it against Jamie's arm, forcing him to face the altar. Jamie's body stiffens.

'You're not listening,' he says over his shoulder. 'I'd rather die than remarry Brooke.' He spits blood on the ground. 'She's the reason I had a breakdown. After everything she did to me.' He heaves in a deep breath. 'Besides, it's not legally possible, because I'm already married to Megan.'

57

'No, you're not,' Brooke bellows. 'You can't get out of it that easily. I was sitting right there at the front to make sure you didn't go through with the ceremony.' She smirks and tries to kiss Jamie's cheek, but he ducks away. I try to wriggle my hands out of the rope, but it's too tightly bound. Ryan side-eyes me, turning the blade so it catches the light. Freya is on my right, away from him. I will her with my eyes to stay back.

'Actually, you're wrong,' Jamie scoffs, his chin up. 'Megan and I had a civil ceremony in private two weeks ago, long before the hen party and stag do. So we're legally husband and wife already and there's nothing you can do about it.'

'You're lying,' Brooke screams in Jamie's face.

Jamie slowly shakes his head, beaming, nostrils flaring. 'The service at the hotel was just for show and to celebrate with family and friends.'

'This can't be happening. You're making this up. Who else knew about this? Did you?' Brooke prods the celebrant in the chest. The man swallows and shakes his head. Freya buries her head in my dress, whimpering.

'It's true,' I say. 'Why would he lie? You're the one who lied to me about who you were, getting me to confide in you when you're the one who set me up with Ryan. You told me Jamie abused *you* when it was the other way round. How could you lie about such a thing?'

In a flash of white lace, Brooke spins round and punches me in the face. I stagger backwards, my nose and head throbbing.

'It's all your fault,' Brooke screams. Blood is dripping from my nose. I taste it on my lips and wipe it as best I can with the back of my hand. When I steady myself and look up, Ryan is holding his arm around Jamie's neck, the knife poised above it.

'Daddy,' Freya cries out and I keep her with me.

'Please, Ryan, this is not the way to end this,' I say. 'You're not a bad person and it's not Jamie's fault. Brooke deceived you, led you on and used you to manipulate me and Jamie.'

'Get away from him,' Brooke booms at Ryan, holding her hands out ready to lunge at him.

Ryan bares his teeth at Brooke and tightens his grip around Jamie's neck. 'You've lied to me. Used me to get what you want.'

'I swear if you hurt one hair on Jamie's head,' Brooke yells, moving towards him.

'Look what you've made me do.' Ryan touches Jamie's throat with the blade. 'All because you made me believe I could get Megan back.'

'I'm warning you, Ryan.' Brooke's voice deepens and she takes a stride closer to him, the flat of her hand out for him to hand her the knife.

'She thinks she's got it all worked out,' he says to me.

'What do you mean, Ryan?' I ask in a quiet voice, my legs trembling.

'Making sure Jamie never left her again.'

'Shut up,' Brooke shouts.

'Yep. Right underneath the house. The whole cellar decked out just for him to live in, be there ready for her whenever she wants. A bed, toilet, and a bowl of water to wash in.'

He takes the blade away from Jamie's neck and holds it out in front of him, pointing it at Brooke. I hold my breath.

'Put that down, Ryan.' Brooke holds her hands up as though it's a gun.

'You said Megan missed me, thought the sex was amazing. You even made me believe their relationship was on the rocks and the wedding would never go ahead. But you lied to me. They're already married!' he bellows, his face reddening. She rushes at him, hand outstretched to grab the knife, but there's a sudden look of surprise on her face and a trickle of blood runs down her white dress.

Brooke collapses onto the floor. Ryan drops the knife and runs. Freya screams and I move her away, shielding her eyes from the blood. Jamie goes after Ryan and leaps at him from behind, his arms loop around Ryan's neck. They fall to the ground and Jamie holds him there.

'Call an ambulance,' I shout at the celebrant who's trying to leave. The other man and woman run out of the barn. I go after them calling for them to get help, but they get in the black van and drive away.

Danielle and Joe are running up the lane towards me. When they're close enough, I tell them what just happened. Joe goes straight over to Jamie and joins him in holding Ryan down. I unclip the veil from Brooke's head and Danielle helps me press it to Brooke's chest to stem the blood flow.

It feels like an age, but the police and paramedics finally arrive, and they take over attending to Brooke who's lying on the floor unconscious, then blue light her to hospital.

A policewoman arrests Ryan for attempted murder while a

policeman unties the rope around my hands. Two more para-medics arrive and sit with me and Jamie, cleaning up our cuts and bruises while Danielle comforts Freya.

As soon as they've finished, Jamie and I hug each other tightly. We kiss despite the pain, then we take a moment to examine each other's faces as though for the first time in years. Without having to say a word, we nod at the state of each other, and how lucky we are that Ryan turned on Brooke and saved us. His description of her plans for Jamie sends shivers through me. She came too close to getting what she wanted. It's a miracle that we're all okay despite the blood, the cuts, and the things we've found out about each other, although hard to take in, are in the past. Even honest people have secrets they're ashamed of.

Now we have the chance of a new life with each other and our daughter, we're determined to rebuild the trust.

EPILOGUE
TWELVE MONTHS LATER

It's taken us longer than we expected to feel ready to go through with the wedding celebrations again. This time we're renewing our vows of love, honesty and communication on a beach in Guadeloupe. We've scaled it down, but we'll still have a party when we get home. Right now, it's just us and Freya, my parents, Joe and Danielle.

The sun is scorching, and the palm trees are gently swaying in the breeze. I'm barefoot in a new loose-fitting wedding dress and Freya is wearing a pale blue dress, similar to her last one because she liked it so much, but of course she's grown since then.

Lauren is fully recovered and our friendship is growing again. She told me how sorry she was to have let Brooke manipulate her like she did.

Brooke's recovered well considering how deep the stab wound was. Lucky to survive, they said. She's in custody awaiting sentencing. Jamie's solicitor doesn't think her injuries will mean she'll receive a lighter sentence for kidnapping or the abuse she inflicted on him. Ryan's been charged with attempted murder and abducting a child.

'Are we all ready?' the celebrant calls us over. Jamie and I walk barefoot through warm golden sand beside waves gently crashing on the shore. We stop in front of her, next to an arrangement of white orchids on a stand. Mum, Dad, Joe and Danielle watch on as the ceremony begins.

I take Jamie's hand on one side, and as I reach for Freya's on the other, my fingertips brush my stomach, and the new life growing there.

* * *

MORE FROM RUBY SPEECHLEY

Another chilling and addictive psychological thriller from Ruby Speechley, *Guilty,* is available to order now here:

https://mybook.to/Guilty_BackAd

ACKNOWLEDGEMENTS

I hope you enjoyed reading my latest novel, *The Uninvited Guest*.

The idea for it started to develop after I heard a radio phone-in about hen parties. One caller described how a bride to be was stripped to her underwear, covered in flour and tied to a lamp-post by her friends! I wondered what sort of friends would do something so cruel. Maybe one or more of them were jealous of her in some way, or didn't really like her. It led me to wonder another question: What if a wedding wasn't based on love, but was purely an 'arrangement'? It reminded me that I attended a 'scam' wedding over thirty years ago. The groom struggled to pronounce the bride's middle name, which was a dead giveaway that they didn't know each other. Thankfully wedding rules have been tightened now, but for the purposes of this novel, I took advantage of the time a few years ago when the rules were relaxed, and such ceremonies could go ahead in churches unchecked.

Other issues that have stirred my interest and are touched on in this novel are, bullying of young men in the armed forces, and a lesser discussed area of domestic violence – against men.

As with all my novels, it takes a small army of people to bring it to you polished and shiny, and I'm deeply grateful for everyone's hard work on this one too. Any errors are wholly my own.

Thank you to my editor, Emily Yau, for her expert eye and wise suggestions, and for being so easy to work with. Thanks to my agent, Jo Bell, for her enthusiasm, encouragement and support, and to everyone at Bell, Lomax Moreton. And a special thank you to the whole brilliant team at Boldwood Books.

Many thanks to the cover designer, Aaron Munday, copy editor, Candida Bradford and proof reader, Rachel Sargeant. I appreciate all your hard work in helping to make my novel the best it can be.

Special thanks go to all my writing friends, most notably Susan Elliot Wright and Rose McGinty, particularly for their restoring writer chats and continued belief in me.

Thanks to all the writers online who continue to support me, and to the bloggers, the readers and not forgetting the Facebook group, **Crime Fiction Addict**, run by Susan Hunter, Sean Campbell, Tara Lyons and Anita Waller. Thank you all for allowing me to share my books. Thanks to a new group I've joined, **Psychological Thriller Readers**, also on Facebook. Another excellent place to meet avid readers.

It's been a funny old summer (2024), with barely any sunshine here in the UK, and the sad loss of many friends, including ex-Harrow Land Registry colleague, Doreen (Jackie) Hatton, a keen reader, all-round lovely human and supporter of my books. Also, Kevin Gooch and Ross Parsons from my year at school, family friend Graham Clarke and David Anthony, who I met at a Paul McVeigh workshop nine years ago.

Finally, deepest gratitude to my family for their constant belief and support, and special thanks to my wonderful daughter-in-law, Becky Heapy, to whom this novel is dedicated.

ABOUT THE AUTHOR

Ruby Speechley is a bestselling psychological thriller writer, whose titles include *Someone Else's Baby*. Previously published by Hera, she has been a journalist and worked in PR and lives in Cheshire.

Sign up to the Ruby Speechley mailing list for news, competitions and updates on future books

Visit Ruby's website: www.rubyspeechley.com

Follow Ruby on social media:

facebook.com/Ruby-Speechley-Author-100063999185095

x.com/rubyspeechley

instagram.com/rubyjtspeechley

ALSO BY RUBY SPEECHLEY

Gone

Missing

Guilty

The Uninvited Guest

THE

Murder

LIST

THE MURDER LIST IS A NEWSLETTER DEDICATED TO SPINE-CHILLING FICTION AND GRIPPING PAGE-TURNERS!

SIGN UP TO MAKE SURE YOU'RE ON OUR HIT LIST FOR EXCLUSIVE DEALS, AUTHOR CONTENT, AND COMPETITIONS.

SIGN UP TO OUR NEWSLETTER

BIT.LY/THEMURDERLISTNEWS

Boldw**oo**d

Boldwood Books is an award-winning fiction publishing company seeking out the best stories from around the world.

Find out more at www.boldwoodbooks.com

Join our reader community for brilliant books, competitions and offers!

Follow us
@BoldwoodBooks
@TheBoldBookClub

Sign up to our weekly deals newsletter

https://bit.ly/BoldwoodBNewsletter